Cougar Undercover

Heart of the Cougar

Book 5

TERRY SPEAR

ISBN-10: 1633110257
ISBN-13: 978-1-63311-025-0

DEDICATION

Kathryn Royce Martin—thanks to a lovely lady from Down Under, who loves getting into character, and loving the cougars in a much more personal way. You breathe life into them. Thanks, Kat! For being a wonderful friend.

ACKNOWLEDGMENTS

Thanks so much to Donna Fournier for all the time she takes to keep me straight on my worlds. And to Dottie Jones and Donna Fournier who did a wonderful job critiquing. And thanks to all my cougar fans who keep me writing in the cougar world!

PROLOGUE

Near Ft. Benning, Georgia

FBI Special Agent Addison Davidson needed a husband. Not just any guy, but someone highly skilled in weapons' training who had served in combat, Special Forces; a hard-charging, unattached male who could handle crises situations under pressure and was preferably a cougar-shifter like her. The last skill was something she knew she wouldn't be lucky enough to find, but it was the reason she had turned down a dozen men for the job, and was still looking for the right man.

When Captain Dan Steinacker appeared at the Hamburger Spot, a fast-food hamburger joint located right off post from where he was assigned at Fort Benning, Georgia, she watched him step in line to order a meal. He was dark haired and blue eyed, tall, well-muscled, just the way she liked her men, only this one would be her pseudo husband, if he was up for the task. His training was just what she needed, if she could let go of her requisite to have a cougar to serve as her husband and he went along with the plan. He was number thirteen on her list, maybe lucky for her, maybe not so lucky for him, if he agreed to it.

She moved into the line, three people behind him, to order her lunch. As soon as he took a seat, she had every intention of sitting down with him and having a talk. She knew just what he'd order—a triple cheeseburger, large order of fries, and a cup of coffee, loads of creamer and sugar.

The fans overhead swirled air-conditioned air around the small hamburger joint on this hot summer day.

She was wearing a flowery strapless dress, going for summer-time sweet, except that the dress was red with giant sunflowers, setting off her dark hair and eyes. She was wearing strappy sandals, not good for anything but showing off her ankles and legs. Running? Chasing down bad guys? She'd be better off tossing them.

Suddenly, Dan turned and she knew the moment he took a deep breath, he'd smelled she was a cougar. And that had to mean only one thing. He was one too. He nearly forgot to pay for his meal, and smiled broadly at her as the clerk tried to get his attention. She smiled back at him. She was hooked. He was hooked. Dan would be her one and only husband for this mission and beyond. If they didn't end up getting killed while doing missions together. If he agreed to the plan.

***

"Addison Davidson, but you can call me Addie," she

offered, holding out her hand to Dan, and he was in lust.

He smiled warmly back, shook her hand, and said, "Dan Steinacker. Do you want to join me at a table?"

"Sure. I'm not here with anyone. Just find a booth for us and I'll join you after I order my meal."

"Why don't I pay for it?"

She smiled so disarmingly at him, he thought he might even be in love.

After she ordered her meal, and he paid for it, they found a window booth. Dan sat down with the beautiful she-cat, not believing his luck at running into one here, just outside of Fort Benning.

Dark brown, long, silky hair, dark brown eyes, dark red lips—a seductive she-cat if there ever was one. "Let me just text a couple of guys who were meeting me for lunch to say I have to cancel."

She smiled at him, and he felt his heart trip.

Dan pulled out his phone and called Chase. "Hey, Chase, tell Stryker and Hal that something's come up, and I've got some other plans for lunch." Dan was eyeing the minx while she was smiling at him, appearing amused that he'd cancel on his friends.

"Seriously? You're standing us up?" Chase asked, humor lacing his words and he chuckled. "Who is she?"

"Uh, yeah, well, we'll get together later."

Chase laughed. "Hell, man, you can't tell us that and then expect us not to check her out."

"Just don't make a nuisance of yourself." Dan could imagine the guys all telling Addie they were best friends of his, shaking her hand, and giving him a hard time.

"We'll be on our best behavior."

Dan didn't want to ruin his first date with the she-cat, especially if she lived locally, and he could see more of her. "Yeah, sure. Talk later. Thanks for understanding." When he hung up, their meals were ready and he stood. "Let's go somewhere else."

"A park by a pond? Or your place?"

He smiled broadly. "It's awfully hot out. Why don't we go to my place?"

"It won't be too hot there, will it?"

He laughed and picked up their meals, asking the server to make it to go. They carried their sacked meals out to his Jeep, and he was glad she didn't want to follow him in her car. He wasn't into one-night stands, but it had been too damn long since he'd met a she-cat while he'd been stationed here, and never one who appealed as much as she did anywhere that he'd been assigned. He really thought it would be a nice change of pace to date her, if she and he enjoyed the same kind of things.

"Do you live here? Work here? I've never seen you at the Hamburger Spot before." Dan drove to his housing development that was located off post.

"I'm here on a mission. To recruit you to be my husband. *Faux* husband."

Surprised at the comment, he laughed. "Don't tell me Chase, Hal, or Stryker had something to do with this? Did they put you up to this? My birthday is too far away." He thought about it for a moment more. "Nah, Chase was genuinely surprised I was standing them up. And they wouldn't have wanted you to meet me before they had a chance to see you." He considered a different scenario. "Ahh, you need me to pose as your husband because you're going to your best friend's wedding and a former boyfriend is attending. You don't want him, of all people, seeing you alone, because he's hooked up with some new she-cat."

She smiled. "That's cute. And nope. I'm a Special Agent for the FBI and I need a husband."

He couldn't believe it. She sounded serious. Unless she was a nutcase. "I'm in the military." Unless the FBI contacted him and his commander, officially, he wasn't going anywhere, if this was all on the up and up.

"Which is why you're the perfect candidate. I've already rejected a dozen possible candidates, but none of them were cougars. I'm hoping we can work out a deal. We're prepared to pay you a substantial amount of money, just to be my undercover husband."

"Benefits included?" he asked, still not believing any of this.

She smiled and sat back against the seat. "That's what's so perfect about it. You don't have to do anything for the pay, unless I call on you to make an appearance. Then it's just a show."

"How dangerous is this?"

"Dangerous. That's why we had to ensure the candidate had weapons and hand-to-hand combat training. You've been vetted, and I've seen your war record. You're an honorable guy. You're leaving the service and returning to Yuma Town in two months, right?"

Dan pulled into his driveway and parked. "Correct."

"Your life is your own unless I need your help. And we'll

only continue this if I need you and you are willing."

"No benefits though? Are you sure?"

She chuckled and grabbed her sack of food and left the Jeep.

He unlocked the house and wished he'd picked the place up a little more before he went into work this morning. He'd never in a million years expected to bring a she-cat to his house when he had taken off just to have lunch, or any other time, for that matter.

"You should see my place when I have unexpected company," she said, as if trying to make him feel less guilty about it, as he set his sack of food on the kitchen table and moved into the living room to grab up clean clothes from the laundry that he'd left on the sofa to sort and put away.

"Okay, so tell me what I have to do. Exactly." He joined her at the kitchen table and sat down.

"You can't tell anyone you know that you've married someone."

"If I'm your cover..."

"You are, when you go with me on a mission, if it happens. We have to play things by ear, but we had to set this up, just in case. You also can't be married, or about to be married. If you fall in love with someone, you must terminate the contract. We can't endanger your loved ones."

"All right. No issue there for now." And he hadn't met anyone he'd been interested in, so he didn't see that as a problem, short-term anyway. "How long is this going to be for?"

"A hundred and fifty-thousand dollars for every year you're my husband. You can divorce me at any time. Though none of this is real."

"A hundred and fifty thousand dollars for doing nothing? What's the catch?"

"If I need you, you'll have to drop whatever you're doing, join me wherever I'm at, and be my lawfully-wedded husband."

He unwrapped his burger and she sat across from him and brought out her chicken burger and fries.

"What do you know about me?" He wondered how long they'd been watching him. Though he didn't really vary his routine much, which must be why she had so easily intercepted him at the Hamburger Stop, and way before his friends had arrived. They were always running late because of job commitments. He suspected they'd rush over to the Hamburger Stop to see the woman and have a good laugh to find he'd disappeared with her. He knew he would have, had the roles been reversed.

"Everything."

He raised a brow.

"Your financial records, your personal lifestyle, your history, family. Everything. The Bureau is thorough. I told you that you were thoroughly vetted."

"Except for one thing. You didn't know I was a cougar."

"I got lucky."

"If I don't agree to this, then what? Do I vanish because I know too much?"

"You don't know anything. Not what I do, who I am—"

"Addie Davidson."

She smiled and took a bite of a french fry.

He sure wished she'd go along with benefits. "That's not

really your name."

"Addison Steinacker, if you agree."

"Middle name?"

"Ann."

"And I won't know anything about you."

"I was born in Boston, no parents, no siblings." She pulled a piece of paper out of her pocket and handed it to him. "This is all about me. If you decide you want to do this, you'll sign an agreement and the money will be forwarded to your bank account."

"Direct deposit? Won't that look suspicious to the IRS? Or some agency that goes after bank fraud when large deposits are made that are unaccounted for?"

"It's all tax deductible and we have you covered."

"Unless I want a divorce so I can get on with my private life."

"Yes."

"Even if I get this money up front and don't do anything for it?"

"Yes."

He knew the government wasted money. "Let me read over the contract." He perused the paper she gave him that had personal information about her, or at least the cover for her.

Then she handed him her phone and he began reading the contract. He glanced up at her as she finished her sandwich and licked her fingers. He wished she'd let him do the honors. "Are you sure there can't be benefits?"

She smiled. "Sign the contract and we can...seal the deal."

"I'm only doing this because you're one of our kind, and I'd hate to think you'd have to find a guy who isn't, to take part in this business."

"Or are you worried that I might check out your friends?"

"Stryker? Chase? Hal? Don't tell me they're on your list of candidates." He was damn glad he was always early to the Hamburger Stop.

"We vetted your closest friends, and yes, they are."

Dan gave an exaggerated sigh and signed on the bottom line. "I can't let them endanger themselves if you were to approach them with this deal next. Why come to me first?"

"You are always early to the Hamburger Stop."

"Hell, you could have lied."

She laughed, took her phone from him and signed the contract, then sent it off. A few minutes later, his phone dinged. Frowning, he pulled it out and saw he'd received a payment in his bank account in the amount of a hundred and fifty-thousand dollars.

"Ready to seal the deal?" she asked, a dark brow raised, her luscious lips curved up a smidgeon.

"I was only kidding." Not that he didn't want to, but he didn't want her believing that's the only reason he was willing to do this job. He was serious about also helping out a fellow cougar.

"I wasn't kidding." She rose from the table and snagged his hand, lightly squeezing, as if to say this was all right between them.

"Do you work with for-hire operatives like this often?" Dan asked, wondering if she did this all the time. He realized just how much that would bother him if he was just another notch on her belt.

"Never."

Marginally relieved, he hauled her toward the bedroom, cognizant that he had to return to work soon. He wasn't sure he believed her though. After all, this was all make-believe. Her identity. The marriage. Still, even if she was just saying it to appease him, he'd go along with it.

"I've never done this before," she said again, frowning at him as they reached the bedroom, and she began unbuttoning his shirt, as if she were really serious. And he believed her. "I've never had a husband, never one who works undercover with me, either." She stripped off his shirt and then yanked his T-shirt out of his pants, sliding her soft, warm hands up underneath it, caressing his bare chest. "And, if I'd chosen some other candidate, it wouldn't mean I'd go this far with him."

Hell, the she-cat was red-hot, making him even hotter. He wanted this to be special between them—mostly because he hadn't been with a she-cat in eons, and that was even before he joined the military. He hadn't met any after that. Plenty of human females over the years, but this wasn't the same. And he didn't think she'd be the same as any other she-cats he'd known either. She was unbelievably sexy, a total spitfire, and hell, after signing the dotted line, his wife.

"I don't have a boyfriend, don't date. While we have this arrangement"—she pulled his T-shirt over his head—"I won't be seeing anyone. I'm married to you until death do us part, or you divorce me."

She licked his nipple, making it tingle and pebble, and he

swept his hands down her sides, grabbing her silky sundress and sliding it up her svelte body. He was guessing she'd be wearing red hot underwear, but her bra and panties were black lace. Just as seductive.

Had she known he wouldn't be able to resist her, if he had accepted the proposal? If so, she'd been right. Or if she hadn't convinced him to do this, she would have been with Chase, Hal, or Stryker. He didn't know if his lucky stars had shone down upon him, or if he was in for real trouble.

She probably knew he hadn't been seeing anyone for the year he'd been assigned here, since they'd thoroughly vetted him. He dropped her sundress on the chest at the foot of the bed.

"I want you because you're one hot cat," she said, whispering the words against his ear, her soft, warm breath making his cock stand at attention. "No emotional attachments. I don't want to let my guard down, or for you to do so either. Strictly sex. Physical pleasure. Between two willing cats."

He should have pounced at the idea that there'd be no true commitment, just hot sex on a hot day with a hot she-cat. He suspected he wouldn't want to do this with her just once. Not the way their pheromones were running rampant, signaling there was a hell of a lot more going on between them than just pure and simple, lustful sex.

They were telling each other they were right for each other—as far as having cougar kittens together, the biological needs coming to the forefront. His cougar half claimed she was in his territory, his to keep. The human component was feeling the same kind of compelling draw—

their signing the contract that said she was his wife, his mate—as he ran his fingers through her luscious dark, satiny hair, and pulled her in for a kiss.

He knew he had to be satisfied with just this one lovefest with her until maybe the next time when he had to work a mission with her. He hoped.

And then she worked on his belt, teasing him as she slid her hand down the front of his trousers, making his cock jump. He quickly sat on the bed, and untied one of his boots, but she was suddenly crouching before him, her knees spread to keep her balance, the dark curly hairs between her legs catching his eye.

She untied his boot, and then tugged it off, falling backward against the plush carpet. The pink lips of her sex beckoned him to get on with the business of pleasuring her. He quickly removed his other boot while she pulled off his sock, and he removed the remaining one. He stood and helped her up. She moved her body against his, sliding her naked breasts against his bare chest, her nipples peaked, her hands slipping down to unzip his zipper. She slowly slid it down, the seductive minx.

And then she pulled his pants down his hips, lower, her mouth pressing tender kisses down his chest, his waist, his boxer briefs-covered cock, straining for release. He ran his hands over her silky hair. His breath hitched when she licked his arousal still covered in fabric, before she pulled his pants off the rest of the way.

"Hell, woman..." He was going to come before he even got her to the bed!

She chuckled and rubbed her body against his again, in

a feline way that said she was claiming the he-cat as her own. He cupped her face and kissed her mouth, her tongue slipping out to lick his lips. He pressed his tongue between her lips and explored her mouth. His body was on fire. She was gripping his arms so hard, he smiled, knowing he was having the same effect on her.

He yanked down his boxer briefs and pulled her to the bed where he jerked the covers aside. She climbed onto the bed and turned around, lying on her back, looking like the kind of sexy she-cat he would love to have babies with, and him, someone who never thought of having kids, ever. Not that he wasn't good with them, he was. He just hadn't considered what it would be like to have some of his own.

He moved in next to her, and began kissing her, realizing again he had to be into work soon, and began moving things along, kissing her breasts, licking her nipples, and stroking the center of her. Judging by the way she was moving against his fingers and the musky smell of her arousal, he knew she was ready for him. He kept stroking her until she gasped out his name and he reached for a drawer. He'd nearly forgotten to grab a condom, but she seized his wrist and shook her head.

"We're safe."

Glad he didn't have to bother with the condom, he pressed his cock into her velvety, tight sheath, and began to thrust.

She clawed gently at his back, lifting her pelvis to meet his thrusts, until he came and he growled. He continued to rub against her until she climaxed again, her muscles clenching him deep.

"We sealed it," she said breathlessly, smiling up at him. She looked like one satisfied cat. Not like a woman who had to play a role. And he was damn glad for it, because she'd turned his world on end. "You make one hot mate."

"Would it sound too desperate of me to ask when we have our first assignment together, if this will be part of the assignment?"

She smiled. "If we have time and can work it in."

He glanced at the clock and groaned. She might not be a "real" person, as far as who she truly was, but she couldn't fake this, not when their pheromones were kicking each other's into high-speed action. "I've got to get back to work."

"I need to catch a flight, but it's not until midnight." Addie stroked his chest with the pads of her soft fingers.

He never called in sick, ever. He wasn't giving up whatever this was between them if he could help it. It had to last until the next time he saw her and he hoped that was soon. He didn't have anything urgent this afternoon to take care of, no briefings to give. Though this was completely uncharacteristic of him, he pulled his phone off the side-table and called his boss. "Sir, I need to take the rest of the afternoon off. Something came up."

Addie moved her hand lower and caressed his cock, and he smiled and shook his head at her. He knew what he was going to do the rest of the afternoon with the she-cat.

"See you tomorrow, Dan," the colonel said.

"Thanks, sir." Dan had to admit he felt a little guilty, but he was doing this for God and country, right? Getting to know his "wife" so he wouldn't make any mistakes when he was on assignment, pretending to be her husband. Especially if it was dangerous. He was all about minimizing risk when out in the field.

After that, Dan got several texts from Chase, Hal, and Stryker, asking about the woman he'd met at the Hamburger Stop, especially when he'd left with her before they'd arrived and since he'd called in to take off from work. They must have dropped by the office and learned from the sergeant that he wasn't returning for the day. He turned off his phone.

After Dan and Addie made love again, they had pepperoni and mushroom pizza delivered for dinner, and she asked if he wanted to play a video game with her. He had his laptop and his PC and he started his favorite game so they could play either as allies or against each other. He hoped she could pick up on the game quickly. If she didn't care for it, they'd just do something else. She was eager to play. They could have fought evil together, but she wanted to fight him, to see just how skilled he was.

"Are you sure? I'm pretty good at this." Dan didn't want to ruin what had been a beautiful day and night so far with the she-cat, if he should beat her and she was upset with him.

"I'm sure." And the way Addie smiled at him, he swore she must have played it before.

When they began playing, he knew he'd met an opponent who could really test his wits and skill.

As good as she was at the game, he thought she must do this often. By sheer coincidence, or because she knew he played it? "How long have you been playing this? You're good."

"For a couple of years. And yeah, I knew you loved it too. No, I didn't scope out your house, but I know what you've purchased for the last couple of years. I hoped you'd want to play and weren't too rusty."

He laughed. "Rusty? Me? Never. Chase, Hal, and Stryker and I play this every chance we get."

Hating to do it, Dan was forced to kill her character off once, though rejuvenating potions or portals would bring them back to life, if they could reach them at barely any strength. She only smiled as she reached a portal, and returned and wiped him out.

"I don't get mad, I get even," she said, as he tried his darnedest to reach a portal in his weakened condition before she clobbered him again.

Once he was healed, he came back to settle the score. He barely managed to take her out again, his own strength weakened, and once she healed up, she retaliated and took him out again.

He loved it.

"Two for two. I'd say we make a good match," she said smiling.

"Yeah, that was fun. I haven't played it with the guys in a few days, but we always team up to fight the bad guys together. Do you want to go running? It's dark enough out now. And the woods are safe."

"As cougars? Absolutely."

They rode in Dan's Jeep to the place he always parked when he went for a run. They removed their clothes, then got out and she shifted into a stunning golden puma, her eyes a beautiful amber, her tail twitching back and forth. She was ready to play. He locked his car door and shifted. He knew then he was truly in love.

They chased each other through the woods, first him after her and then she chased him, but only because he wanted to show her the place. He wished he could take her to Yuma Town, Colorado, where he grew up and take her climbing up into the rocks, to see the waterfalls, creeks, and rivers. That's where he was returning when he got out of the service. Maybe she would meet him there sometime.

They explored the woods for a couple of hours, and he realized his friends would smell her scent and his here, when they went running together, and question him further about the mystery woman. He was glad they hadn't come out to run as cougars tonight, just in case he was out here with her. They would have smelled her scent at the Hamburger Spot too, and known she was a she-cat—and that's why he was keeping her to himself.

He wanted to get her home so he could make love to her one last time before she had to leave for the airport.

That night, they made love again, not quite so frantically, as if they might really have something. And then he had to take her to her rental car at the Hamburger Stop, but he didn't want to see her go. He'd had more fun with his faux mate than he'd had with any woman he'd ever been with. He realized then, he could really consider settling down, if he had a woman like her in his life.

He kissed her and hugged her as if he was losing his best friend, which was just the way he was feeling, and he hated to see her go.

Addie kissed him back, looking a little sad, and he wondered if she would ever want to leave her job and make a go of a relationship with a male cat. Not any male cat, but him.

"I'll be in touch," she said, kissing his cheek afterward. Then she climbed into her rental car and drove off, slipping away into the night, like a cougar would vanish in the dark woods. He couldn't stop watching the car's taillights until they disappeared.

Hell, now everything would remind him of her—the Hamburger Stop, the woods, his car, the house, playing the game, she would be in his thoughts always.

***

Two weeks later, Dan got an email—a first-class plane ticket for a four-a.m. flight to Boston, and a note to take emergency leave. He couldn't tell his friends what was going on, just that he had to leave town for some important business.

Chase ran over to see him at his house when he said he had to take emergency leave and cancel on the movie he and the guys were going to see the next night. He wouldn't tell him what was going on.

Chase folded his arms and said, "You're not going for a job interview somewhere other than Yuma Town, when we all plan to return there after our obligations are up in a month and a half, are you?"

"No. We're doing this." Dan finished packing his bag.

"Did you need me to drive you to the airport?"

"At four in the morning?"

"Yeah, I'll be here, at what? Two?"

"Yeah, sure, thanks, Chase."

"This doesn't have anything to do with the she-cat you met at the Hamburger Stop, does it?"

Dan tried damn hard to school his expression when he shook his head, but Chase smiled. "Well, hell, why didn't you say so before. When do we get to meet this remarkable woman? First, you ditched work to spend more time with her, and now you're taking emergency leave to be with her?"

"It's not what you think," Dan said, and his firm tone meant the discussion was done.

"All right. I'm sure you'll tell us when you can." Chase looked like it was killing him not to know. "Have a great time for us."

"Thanks, Chase." What if the assignment got him killed? He hated not being able to tell his friends what he was up to.

After Chase dropped Dan off at the airport curbside at two-thirty in the morning, Dan rushed to get checked in, and soon was climbing aboard the plane bound for Boston, glad he got a first-class ticket.

As soon as the hulking guy in front of him moved beyond where Dan's seat was, he couldn't believe his eyes when he saw a breath of fresh air sitting in the first-class seat next to his, Addie in the flesh, wearing a blue dress suit, looking like a billion bucks. "Hell, honey, you don't know how much I missed you." And was shocked to see her. And thrilled. "And I can't believe you're here." He hurried into his seat and pulled Addie into a hug, and then kissed her like he really meant it. He didn't care what was going to happen next, but for him, this wasn't acting. He'd missed her, and he hadn't thought of anything but getting back together with her and protecting her, if she needed protecting. And wishing something more could come of this.

For two weeks, his friends had grilled him mercilessly

about the woman he'd met at the Hamburger Stop, and ribbed him the same amount when they'd learned he'd taken off the rest of the day from work. That was the hardest part of this business. He didn't keep secrets from his friends. And they knew it. Which made them all the more curious to learn who she was. No, the hardest part was not seeing her again.

She kissed him back as if they were newlyweds and she had been separated way too long from him. Then she rested her head against his shoulder as the flight took off.

"How have you been?" He'd worried about her too, afraid she might have gotten into some trouble on an assignment. He hadn't realized how much of an emotional impact this could have on him. He just assumed it would be a job. Pretend husband. No real investment. He couldn't separate business from the way he was feeling about the she-cat, especially since she seemed to be just as interested in him.

"I missed you," Addie said.

That was the problem with this assignment. Did she really miss him? Or was this part of the role she was supposed to play?

He squeezed her hand. "I've thought about nothing else other than seeing you again."

She smiled up at him. "The feeling's mutual."

And that's when he thought maybe she was being honest, and he felt hope that maybe something could come of "them" in due time. He just had to be patient, not something he was really good at.

***

Addie knew she was playing with fire with regard to the

way she felt about Dan. She'd never felt this way toward another male cat ever. He was impossible to resist, even though she had to keep her mind on the business at hand or she could get them both killed. All she kept thinking about was running with him as a cougar, challenging him in video games, and making love to him. While she'd waited for him to board the plane, she had hoped he would be the same way with her—passionate, excited to see her, wanting more. As much as she knew that was a bad idea and encouraging it was even a worse plan, the feline shifter part of her wasn't cooperating. She couldn't help herself when he hugged her and kissed her. She had wanted this as much as he did, and she wasn't about to hold back. She told herself it was just part of the job. But it wasn't.

"You'll be doing some training for the mission," she whispered in his ear.

He began kissing her again. She had to chuckle. "I really missed you too, honey." She'd worked too hard to get this job, and she wasn't giving it up for anything. Her parents had divorced after a twelve-year marriage when she was eight, and she knew relationships could easily dissolve, and then where would she be? She'd have left her job to be with a hot cougar who would tire of her and move on. And getting her job back wouldn't be easy, if she could even manage it at all.

She loved being with him like this, cuddling, kissing. If all went as planned, she hoped she'd have time to spend with Dan before he had to fly home. He seemed to be of a like mind.

***

When they arrived at the location where Dan would be

briefed and then go through rigorous training, she participated too, to see how well they'd work together. They did great and everyone seemed to think as she did. They made an outstanding team.

A lot of it was they cued each other in as cougars, both had enhanced sight that could see movement more quickly than humans, they could spring into action faster, and best of all, they could see at night and hear things better than anyone there. They knew what was coming even before the enemy made his appearance.

After taking a lunch break, they left the training ground to carry out the mission.

"We have the advantage," Addie said to Dan as they waited in a park for the perp to show up.

"He always runs on this path," Dan said.

"And the breeze is blowing in our direction. I know his scent. I can smell him coming." She squeezed Dan's hand and pulled him in for an embrace. "Kiss me."

***

Feeling good about the extra training, and amazed they worked so well together, Dan didn't hesitate to kiss her, though he was worried he'd forget the mission. The guy paused nearby to tie his shoelace. Dan wanted to look away from Addie so he could handle the perp if he tried anything, but Addie wouldn't let him, making him concentrate on the kiss, one hell of a nice way to reunite with his pretend wife. This was an enjoyable way to carry out a mission, though from what the agent briefing them said, the perp was highly armed and dangerous, so Dan was on alert if the subject suddenly targeted them.

The guy began running again, but Addie didn't indicate she wanted to go after him, keeping her hold on Dan in a warm embrace. Suddenly, three men and a woman in suits broke out of the woods and took the runner down. Dan hadn't expected that.

"You signaled to the others that he was passing us." She was really good at this, Dan had to admit.

"Yes. We couldn't get close to him in the months we've been trying to nab him. He was so wary, we'd lost him a number of times. We didn't know if this would work, but we thought if we really looked like lovers in a park, and you don't look like one of our people, it might work, I could signal to take him down, and it would be a done deal. If the agents had scared him off, you and I would have had to run him down."

"I was your last resort?"

"Yeah, believe me, I didn't want to put you in harm's way, if we could handle it without you."

"I'm being paid for it. Besides, seeing you makes it all worthwhile." Dan slipped his arm around her shoulders and took her for a walk in the park as the other agents hauled him off. "You'd think he'd stop coming to the park." He recognized them as part of her team—a young man, prematurely gray that made him look older, a blond-haired, blue-eyed woman, who looked too sweet and petite to be able to take down an armed killer, but that's the way Addie appeared to Dan also, and an Asian agent who looked like he could beat him in ju-jitsu. The man didn't like that Dan was called in to play husband to Addie, and had voiced his opinion more than once, saying Dan would get her killed.

Addie had told him to do his job, but Dan worried the

guy might be right.

"This is only the second time we've seen him here," Addie said as they watched the man being hauled away, as if they were spectators in the crowd of hikers and runners gathered to watch the excitement. "We've been having the path watched until we could get here. And we were lucky. We might have had to wait for hours, but the perp had to get back to work in an hour, so this was our best guestimate."

"And the danger?"

"The man is a deadly assassin. He's armed, even if he doesn't look like it, but he also makes the most of anything he has available."

"Now what?"

"Mission complete. Your flight leaves at midnight."

"Can you call in sick? I think this calls for a lot of loving, some cougar running, and a lot more loving."

She smiled up at him. "Want to go to my place?"

CHAPTER 1

Ten and a half years later, Forest Park, Portland, Oregon

Special Agent Addison Davidson reported to the pickup point at a bench in Forest Park, surrounded by Douglas firs, western hemlock, Oregon grape, and western red cedar, breathing in the scents. After she'd been shot on her last mission in Seattle, Washington, doing the same kind of job, picking up information from a courier six months ago, she knew they had a mole on her team. Who, of the six people working with her, was the traitor who had told the assassin where the pickup was to be made?

As much as she didn't want to admit it, she knew she had post-traumatic stress syndrome. She couldn't let on to the psychologist, who okayed her for duty, that she felt jittery on the job, like at any moment someone would gun her down again. She hated feeling this way. She normally felt completely confident in her abilities, certain that good would win out. On the last mission, she'd taken several bullets, and the only thing saving her was that she'd been wearing a heavier bulletproof vest with the metal insert. Not even those would stop some projectiles, but at least she'd survived the attack. It had taken her six months to recover, not so much physically, because with her cougar shifter abilities, she healed faster than humans. Mentally, she'd had a hard time coping, waking with night terrors and reliving the nightmare whenever she heard popping sounds from cars backfiring, or just any loud bangs.

She hadn't seen Dan for two years for any missions and she thought she might never see him again, until she was nearly killed. Then once she could vanish, not letting her team or her boss, Clinton Briggs, know where she was going, she'd had to crash with Dan for a couple of nights. He'd been so upset with her that she'd nearly been killed, and that he hadn't had any word from her. She'd been a jumble of emotions—wanting in the worse way to leave again, to keep him safe, and to keep out of reach of whoever had wanted her dead.

That time, Dr. Kate Parker-Hill had patched her up and then Addie had stayed only as long as she felt it was safe. Dan had taken care of her the whole time, wanting to know what had happened, and why she hadn't called him for any more missions.

She couldn't even tell him she suspected a mole in her organization. He hadn't been happy with her, and after ten and a half years of being her pretend husband, he seemed to be thinking of "divorcing" her. She couldn't blame him. She couldn't give up her job, not now that she had to learn who had it in for her, and she didn't know if she could work at anything else. Could she settle down in a friendly cougar town like Yuma? She was afraid she would miss the bullets flying.

Dan was a different story. She couldn't deny she missed him, and wanted desperately to see him. She'd tried to pretend he was important only for missions, but she hadn't had one with him in two years—her boss's decision—until she needed to drop into Dan's life again, this time to get patched up. She still remembered how angry he was—at the man who had shot her, at the Bureau for not protecting her better, at her for not keeping in touch. He was, after all, her husband.

Trying to focus on the current mission again, she now watched hikers and runners making their way on Wildwood Trail in Forest Park, not paying any attention to her. Her skin crawled with trepidation. The first day back to duty, and she prayed she could keep it together.

Where was he? The man who was supposed to pass her some information about a group of bank robbers, who were targeting banks in the bigger cities, moving from state to state. It wasn't the same case that she'd been working on when she'd been shot six months earlier. That one involved stolen military weapons from a National Guard unit, and two of her team members had managed to call for help, but they hadn't captured the shooter, and she'd been pissed off about it.

Not that she hadn't been just as mad at herself for not taking him down before he had shot her so many times. She hadn't even had a chance to pull out her 9mm.

She kept thinking back to Dr. Kate, checking her over, frowning, giving Dan looks, but he wouldn't tell her who Addie was. No one in Yuma Town could know the circumstances of their marriage, nor that Dan Steinacker had been recruited to serve as her husband as a deep undercover operative. He was called on to do work with her when she needed her husband by her side as the perfect undercover couple. And they'd had fifteen successful missions in the first few years, but once they were done, they'd had to go their separate ways, no questions asked. That had been the hardest part, for both of them.

She'd thought of him seeing Dottie, his dispatcher at the time, and how Dan might have been better off just mating her and terminating his contract with Addie.

And yet, she hadn't wanted that to happen either. Which was why she put a bug in Jack Barrington's ear that he needed to return home and see what Dottie's Aunt Emily had to say about her. Of course, Addie hadn't talked to Jack directly. She'd spoken with an army buddy of Jack's, who told him he'd forever regret not trying to see Dottie again. Addie hadn't been wrong in doing so. He was the father of Dottie's twins, though he hadn't known it. And he loved her, like she loved him, if only Dottie hadn't been afraid to leave her town and lose him in some battle he might have to fight while he served in the military. At least, Addie was glad it had worked out between them. She never thought she would be an undercover FBI matchmaker for a pair of cougars.

Getting her mind back on the current mission, she glanced at the fall foliage, the trees in yellows and oranges, reds and greens, the grass still green. So pretty, yet the scene could change in a heartbeat if this went sideways. She buttoned her jacket to keep the chilly air out. Where was the blasted courier?

She was feeling tense, unsettled, wary that something wasn't right. Sure, a courier could be late, but she didn't like how this was already going down.

Then someone cried out in the woods, well away from her view from where she was standing, and she knew she shouldn't leave her position, but what if the guy was the courier and in real trouble? What if he wasn't and she missed meeting the courier?

She had to help whoever the person was and raced toward the sounds of a struggle. When she reached the man, he was lying dead on the ground. And it was the man she was supposed to meet. The courier. She called for backup and pulled her gun out and saw a man run out of the woods and away from her.

"Stop!" she ordered, ready to chase after him, but she couldn't leave the courier here, if he had the information on him still.

Paris Pepion and Dirk Carter came to her aid and assured her they would handle this. Paris was calling in the murder, while Dirk was looking through the courier's clothes for the information. Addie took off running after the murderer, having to catch him. What if he had the information? Though he could have just been a mugger.

"Wait for backup!" Dirk called after her.

She couldn't. As important as this was, *he* should have come with her.

She couldn't see the suspect. With her speed and agility

and her scent abilities as a cougar, she had the guy's scent and she was gaining on him. Then she saw the guy wearing a gray hoody, blue jeans, and running shoes. Tucked under his arm, he had a manila envelope, and she was certain it was the courier's package of the information they needed. Running after him, intent on taking him down, she knew this could be a way to help overcome her PTSD—face another assailant, only come out the winner this time. She had to do it, had to prove to herself she could.

At least that's what she thought when she suddenly realized the man's scent had stopped. Damn! He had doubled back and he had to have hidden in the brush near her. When she ran back to where she'd discovered the last scent of him, he leapt out of the brush at her. Her cat-like actions made her quick, but he was taller and heavier than her, and he took her down in the brush opposite where he'd been hiding across the path. She dropped her revolver and he slammed her head against the ground, though the fallen leaves cushioned the impact. Still, she saw stars and she knew if she didn't recover her gun, or reach her dagger, she could be as dead as the courier.

She saw the red-stained blood of the dagger he was holding before he cut her. She reached her gun in the leaves and shot him, but not before he managed to stab her.

If she didn't get out of this business, she was certain she was going to die. She'd had enough adventure for a lifetime. She wanted a cougar to love. To come home to nights. To have his babies. A cougar like Dan. After all this time, could they really connect?

That was the last thought she had as she lost

consciousness.

CHAPTER 2

While sorting through paperwork at his desk at the sheriff's office, Dan received a nearly incoherent call from Addie, his faux wife, her voice weak and strained. Instantly, he knew she was in real trouble. He'd thought of terminating the contract between them so many times, mainly because she wouldn't leave her job, and he didn't want to see her get herself killed. He'd wanted more from her, but she couldn't seem to give it.

Every time she called, needing him, he couldn't help but drop everything, wanting to be there for her. She was under his skin, in his blood, and he couldn't let her go.

Now he was sick with worry, trying to learn where she was. She'd called from a cell phone, and the line was still open. Even though he called to her, she didn't respond. He had to use cell tower triangulation to locate her at a hospital and called to speak with the hospital receptionist before he was put in touch with one of the floor nurses, who was caring for Addie. He explained he was the sheriff of Yuma Town, and her husband.

"Ms. Davidson is in stable condition," the nurse told Dan.

"Where is she in the hospital?"

The nurse told him the room and floor she was staying on.

"When she wakes, tell her I'm coming." Dan noticed his new dispatcher, Amy Mayflower, staring at him from the other room. He was in his office, but he hadn't shut the door. Not to mention he was being very vocal and their cat's hearing precluded him keeping this quiet anyway. To everyone in town, he wasn't supposed to be married.

"Yes...sir." The nurse probably thought Addie wasn't using her husband's name, just her maiden name.

As soon as he hung up, his dispatcher asked, "Sheriff, do you want me to call Stryker to come in to take care of things?"

"He's sick. Damn flu. He needs to rest. He'll beat it in no time. Call Hal and Chase. Surely someone can take over for a day or so." Dan was on his computer, making reservations for the next flight out that he could get to in time.

"Or longer? Did you need me to make airline reservations for you?" Amy was a blue-eyed blond, married to Deacon Mayflower, who worked as a reporter for the newspaper, and they had a ten-year old son named Bobby. Dan was glad when Amy said she could take over the job, having worked as a police dispatcher in Sacramento, California before this.

Dottie, his former dispatcher, had left to have fun with

other pursuits, especially since she had brand new triplets, and twins still at home now that their father was home with them too. He was glad for them that everything had worked out, but Jack Barrington, one of the newest agents on the CSF on Leyton's team, had been as much as a surprise to everyone as Dan's faux wife would be.

"I've got it." Dan grabbed his Stetson and headed out the door.

"Good luck. Let us know how things are going," Amy said, holding her hand over the phone as she was already talking to Chase.

"Yeah. Thanks." Dan was trying to think of everything he had to do before he went to the airport to fly to Portland, Oregon. He managed to have enough presence of mind to grab a bag, shove some clothes and toiletries into it, and headed for the airport.

Chase called him when he was on his way. "Hey, do you need me to drive you to the airport?"

"Already on my way."

"Amy said this was about your wife. She had to be mistaken. What the hell's going on?"

"I'll tell you and everyone all about it later. As soon as I return home. For now, I've got to keep trying to get hold of her."

"Is she all right?"

"She's in the hospital. I'll get back with you, Chase. I promise. I'm…I'm going to bring her home, if I can convince her to come home with me and stay for good."

"We'll all be there for you both. You know we'll always have your back. Let us know if there's anything we can do to help, to make her feel welcome."

"I know you will. Thanks. Just take care of things there until I return home, will you?"

"Will do. We'll make arrangements to cover for you while you're gone, Dan."

Dan was glad for having such good friends, wishing he could have told them before this about his wife. Pseudo-wife. Even if she didn't want to make it real between them, he wanted her in Yuma Town while she recovered. And maybe he could prove to her he was the only cougar for her once and for all.

Before he reached the airport, he got a call from Leyton. He was the sole person who had known he had a wife, and Dan had only spilled the beans accidentally to him. Leyton had been good about not sharing what he'd learned with anyone.

"Hey, I guess the news is about to break to the rest of Yuma Town. What can I do to help?" Leyton asked.

"I'm bringing her home, Leyton. I want to make a go of it, but I'm not sure she'll want to." He explained to him how he'd been recruited to play this role with her.

"You have something real with her?"

"Hell, yeah. It's not just a job. The thing is, can we make it on a day-to-day basis?"

"If there's enough commonality between the two of you to make a go of it, beyond the thrill of the assignment and the rest, I'd say so. You know how it was with Kate and me."

"Right, but the last time Addie was injured, I couldn't keep her here. I tried. She was hell-bent on leaving town, afraid whoever had wanted her dead would find her in Yuma

Town and kill me too. If I can help it, she's not leaving this time. I want to take care of her."

"We all will. You've got a whole community of cougars who will watch out for her."

"Thanks, man."

"You've been there for all of us. It's the least we can do. And tell her she can always come to work for me, if she needs the excitement in her life." Leyton took down rogue cougars, and others who were involved in coming after their kind, heading up the Cougar Shifter Force, CSF, in their town.

"Thanks. If she wants to be my deputy, I'll hire her in a heartbeat. I'm at the airport. I'll let you all know how it's going when I know something more." The quickest flight he could find was six and a half hours. Add the driving time of half an hour to the airport, more time to get a rental car and reach the hospital, and it was more like eight hours by the time he would arrive at the hospital to see her. He hated that it would take this long.

The whole time he worried she'd check herself out of the hospital and disappear, just like she had the last time she'd been injured and had ended up at his place. He still couldn't believe it when he returned to have lunch at his place to find she'd slipped into his house, mostly unseen. She was his only contact, he didn't have the phone numbers of anyone else who knew her at the Bureau, so he wouldn't be able to learn where she'd vanished to if she left.

He had problems he hadn't considered when he arrived on her floor of the hospital and approached the room. An FBI agent at her door warily watched his approach. Even though Dan was wearing his sheriff's uniform, the man shook his head. "You can't see her. No one can without strict authorization."

Dan wasn't going to let anyone deter him from seeing his wife, not when he was afraid she'd try to slip out of there and disappear and he'd lose her again.

"I'm Addie's husband, Dan Steinacker, sheriff of Yuma Town," Dan growled.

"No visitors unless the boss okays it." The guy in the dark gray suit didn't make a move to allow Dan entry.

Dan was surprised the agent didn't know that he was not her real husband. Maybe he wasn't on the same team as her, just someone to serve as a bodyguard for the time-being while she was in the hospital. They probably wouldn't realize he'd be coming either. "Then get the boss on the line. I work with Addie, and only Addie. And I'm not leaving here until I see her."

Looking annoyed, the man pulled out his phone and called someone. "Yeah, I've got a guy here, who says he's Sheriff Dan Steinacker from Yuma Town." He raised his brows and smiled a little.

Dan wanted to knock the smug smile off his face.

"All right. Out here." He pocketed his phone.

"Well?"

"He said no visitors."

"Get him on the line and let me talk to him."

The agent didn't move a muscle. Dan was about to pull his gun out he was so mad. He'd only end up in jail and his job as her husband would be terminated. She'd probably be so mad at him, that would be the end of any kind of relationship they might have had. "Let me talk to him. Now,"

Dan reiterated. "I flew six and half hours to get here. I'm not leaving until I see her and get to talk to her."

The man shook his head, but he pulled out his phone and punched in a number. "Sir, the sheriff wants to talk to you. All right. Here he is."

"What the hell are you doing there?" the man said.

"What the hell do you think I'm doing here? My wife is in there, injured, could be dying for all I know."

"You're not supposed to be there. We have protocols and no one, but who I say, is getting in to see her."

"I'm her husband, goddamnit. And the protocol is that she calls me when she needs me. How the hell do you think I learned she was here? She called me. I'm here. Tell your agent to let me in to see her." Dan glanced at the agent to see him smiling, but he quickly lost the smile. "Now."

"Hand the phone to Leipheimer."

Dan handed the phone to the agent. "Yes, sir. Will do, sir. Yes, sir." He pocketed his phone. "You have five minutes."

Dan opened the door to the room, stepped in, and closed the door. His heart sank as he saw Addie with tubes running to her arms, blood dripping into one of them, a saline solution in the other, her face pale as death. He closed the door and crossed the floor to join her, and leaned down to kiss her pale forehead.

"Addie, it's me, your husband, Dan. I'm here to take care of you. As soon as I can, I'm taking you home with me. No arguing." He didn't even know if she could hear him, but he wasn't leaving her side, if he could help it, until she could speak with him. He pulled a chair next to the bed and reached out and ran his hand over her arm in a gentle caress. "I don't know if we have what it would take to make it together, but I want you to move in with me. You could work with me, if you'd like, as my deputy sheriff. Or we have a"—he leaned over and whispered next to her ear—"cougar shifter organization that would hire you in a heartbeat to take down rogue cougars. I want you in my life. Not just for missions, but for always. Of course, we would get to know each other better, and we could work it out from there."

An hour later, he was still talking to her, telling her all the fun they could have in Yuma Town—swimming at Lake Buchanan, even renting a cabin there, rock and mountain climbing, hiking. "And in winter, skiing. Cross-country skiing." He told her about some of the happenings in Yuma Town, then glanced back at the door, wondering why the agent hadn't told him to leave already. Maybe his boss told him it might be good for Dan to talk to her, since they'd become close in their teamwork.

Addie hadn't stirred once, and he knew she had to rest, but he wanted to know exactly how she'd been injured. She'd heal quicker than humans, but if the wound or wounds were severe, it could still take time.

The door opened and a nurse came in. Expecting the intruder to be the agent, Dan frowned at her. "Is the agent still out there?"

"What agent?"

"Let me see some credentials," he said to the nurse, making her move back to the door so he could check outside the door for the agent. Leipheimer was gone. He wouldn't have been. Not if he was supposed to be providing protection for Addie. And not when the boss said no one could enter the room without permission. And then for only five minutes. What the hell was going on? "Let me see some ID."

"What?"

"ID to match your nametag." One good thing about being a sheriff, he was still armed and prepared to protect Addie at all costs, and he had a sixth sense when something wasn't right, not to mention the woman smelled of fear. If she was just doing her job, she shouldn't be giving off the scent.

"It's in my purse, locked in a drawer at the nurse's station." She motioned down the hall.

"Call security."

"What?"

"Call them. Addie's supposed to have round-the-clock protection. The agent should never have left."

"You're a sheriff," the nurse said as if that should have counted for something.

"There's supposed to be an FBI agent outside the door for her protection. Call. Security. Now."

She pulled her phone out of her pocket, and eyeing Dan, she said, "Call security. We've got trouble."

She was sweating and he was certain the woman wasn't a nurse, or at least not one who was taking care of Addie. She didn't call security herself. He was certain she was letting someone else know Dan was the trouble.

He grabbed her arm and pulled it behind her back, then shoved her against the wall and handcuffed her wrists behind her back.

"You're making a mistake." She wasn't screaming for security. Dan suspected the pretty blond was in on whatever the plot was to hurt Addie. He checked her pockets and found a hypodermic needle.

"If I inject you with whatever this serum is, what will happen?"

"It's just pain medication," she quickly said. "She's due her next dose."

"Then you'll be feeling no pain if I use it on you, right?"

Her eyes widened and she tried frantically to jerk away from him.

"Tell me the truth then."

"It's just like I said."

Two men burst into the room—not security, both armed with guns and silencers. Before the nurse could say a word, Dan jabbed the first of the men, who rushed through the door, in the neck with the hypodermic needle. He grabbed his neck, cried out, and sank to the floor. And that was after only using half of the stuff in the syringe. Dan wrestled the second man to the floor, and in the ensuing struggle to use his gun on Dan, it went off, the round hitting the man in the head, instead.

The nurse was trying to get around them and make her escape, but Dan grabbed her and shoved her down to sit on the floor. "Now tell me who you are and what you did with the agent."

She just stared at him mutely.

Dan pulled out his phone and called the hospital security, hoping to God he'd get the real hospital security. "I'm in room 405, two men down, a woman pretending to be a nurse in custody. The federal agent protecting his fellow injured agent has gone missing. I'm Sheriff Dan Steinacker of

Yuma Town. The injured patient is a federal agent and my wife." Then he called the FBI headquarters and explained the situation. He wasn't getting anywhere with anybody. No one knew what office he needed, and no one knew who Addie was.

"Dan," Addie said, her voice weak.

Dan whipped around and hurried back to the bed. "Addie, your protection has gone missing. These thugs came in here to kill you, the nurse intended to also. Do you have a number to call so that we can get backup? Hospital security is on its way, but what if they're not legit either?"

"You're not supposed to be here," she said, holding onto his hand with a weak grip.

"Good thing I was though, huh?"

She smiled a little, and he saw the same devilish look he'd grown to love. "Help me get out of bed and get dressed."

Dan frowned at her. She needed to be at the hospital. Maybe in another room, with another agent serving as her guard, but he didn't want to risk losing her if he tried to move her, depending on the severity of her injuries.

She frowned back at him. "Do it, Dan. That's an order."

If the situation wasn't so serious, he would have smiled at her for giving him orders like she was in charge, when she was so badly injured. He was still frowning as he searched for her clothes, and then finding them in a locker, he paused to stare at her cut up shirt, blood stains all over it.

"Don't worry about it," she said. "I can change later."

"Hell." Seeing her bloody clothes made her life-threatening situation so much more real. If they'd had more time, he would have pulled off his uniform shirt, and dressed her in his T-shirt, but time was of the essence.

He pulled out her tubes and helped her to dress, her jacket cut and bloodied too. The security officers were taking one hell of a long time to reach her room.

"Are you sure you're going to make it, honey?" he said.

"Yes, just hurry. If I thought it would help, I'd run as a cougar."

She wasn't helping and he was hurrying as fast as he could to dress her. No way could she run as a cougar through the hospital.

"Knock her out, permanently, or she'll send people after us," Addie said to Dan, motioning with her head to the nurse.

"No," the woman said. "I was forced to do this."

"So am I." Dan grabbed the hypodermic needle. He used the remaining serum on the nurse, and she collapsed to the floor. She had fully intended to use it on Addie, and so he had no regrets. They were still in dire straits and he had to get Addie out of here as quickly as he could.

He lifted Addie in his arms and hurried her out of the room and down the hallway to a fire escape.

Addie was like a ragdoll and he hated to see her so weak. "You can't carry me all the way down the stairs," she said.

It reminded him of the last time he'd seen her when she'd sneaked into his house to take refuge for a couple of days.

"I don't want to take any chances using the elevator, or the stairs closest to your room. Besides, isn't this why you selected me to be your husband? For my brawn and good looks?" Dan asked.

She smiled weakly and rested her head against his chest.

"I hope I'm not doing you further injury by moving you," he said, worried sick about her.

"If you hadn't moved me, I'd be dead."

"True. I'm taking you home. Somehow, I'm getting you home. I need to call the Bureau and—"

"No."

He frowned down at her as he entered the stairwell and took the stairs as fast as he could without dropping her or missing a step.

"Someone's a mole on my team. That's why I was injured so badly the last time. I only returned to work after six months of hiding, to try and learn who it is. I can't do this on my own. And I can't let anyone know I realize it."

"Two of the people who live in our town are former FBI agents. The Muellers. He's the bank president now and she's a loan officer. Between that and the sheriff's office, and the cougar organization, the Cougar Special Forces Agency, that deals with rogue cougars, we have two U.S Department of Fish and Wildlife Service agents who track down animal traffickers, all well-trained in combat, have licenses to carry, and investigative skills. Let us work together to find out who's behind this."

"You can't. I have to be on the team to learn who is responsible."

"Like that worked out so well for you this last time." He couldn't help how angry he was about her going back to work with someone who could be a traitor, and she never told him what was going on.

He finally reached the lobby of the hospital. "I've got a

rental car. I'm thinking we should just drive home. It's a long drive, but we might not be able to get a flight for the two of us right away. I was lucky and got a seat on the trip out here. Some of the flights home can take as long as fourteen hours. With driving, we can stop at another hospital on the way if you need more blood or pain medication." He carried her outside and was glad it was already getting dark.

"We'll drive. You'll have to make arrangements to change your rental car destination though."

"Agreed." As soon as he set her on her feet beside the car, he unlocked the car and helped her into the back seat. "I wish I had a blanket and pillow for you." He sure as hell had never expected rescuing her from a hospital and using the rental car as a getaway.

"Just get us out of here before anyone sees us."

"Yeah, working on it." He shut the back door and hurried to get into the driver's seat, then backed out of the parking lot and drove off. He checked his phone for directions to Yuma Town from Portland. "Eighteen hours." He made a quick check on flights. "No flights tonight or tomorrow straight to our destination. And the day after that they only have one that has an available fourteen-hour flight for two of us."

"You can't drive eighteen hours straight."

"True."

"It will take us longer."

"We'll have to stop at a hotel for a few hours. We'll still get home sooner than if we stayed at some place until we could get a flight out the day after tomorrow."

"Despite that I feel like shit, I'm healing. Just keep

driving until you can't any longer. Maybe I can take over the driving for a while."

No way in hell.

"I'm going to sleep."

"Was it a gunshot wound?"

"Knife. I managed to throw him off balance before he could make it a fatal stab wound."

"Is he still alive?"

"No. I shot him. In the forehead."

"Good. Sleep." Then Dan called Chase. "Hey, buddy, we need your help. ASAP!"

CHAPTER 3

Addie couldn't believe that she'd called Dan to come to her rescue. Her subconscious must have known he was the only one she could trust. And he'd come through for her. She hadn't remembered doing so. And then to hear his beautiful, but gruff and worried voice next to her hospital bedside? If she'd been conscious enough to respond at the time, she would have given him a heartfelt hug. She'd only vaguely heard him talking about making her a deputy sheriff. Despite the pain medication she was on, she had immediately thought: what if she wanted to be sheriff?

She used his bag for a pillow, after pulling out a soft, blue hoody of Dan's to wrap around herself as a makeshift blanket, and one of his soft black T-shirts so she could ditch her bloody shirt, loving his masculine and wild cat smell. Even though she knew they were not out of danger and could be in the thick of it at any time, she luxuriated in the smell of him wrapped around her, thankful to God that he'd come for her in her hour of need.

She heard him talking to his friend Chase, telling him all about the trouble they were in. And Chase telling him he'd make arrangements to send reinforcements at once. In that instant, she wished they hadn't kept their agreement secret from his friends. And she knew they could be trusted, though she still felt the only way to learn the truth about this dirty business was for her to return to work.

Sometime during the drive, she stirred and found herself wrapped in a real blanket, a soft pillow for her head, Dan's hoody tucked under her chin and spread out over her chest and waist, and she wondered when and where he'd picked up the blanket and pillow. And how she'd never been conscious enough to notice. The pain medication had to have really knocked her out. Any little sound or movement usually woke her. She took a deep breath of Dan's scent on the hoody, listened to the SUV's motor running, the tires rolling along the road, the wind whipping past the vehicle, feeling tired, sore, and soothed, and drifted off again.

When Addie woke the next time, the car was still rumbling along the highway, the windows dark. She wondered how long they'd been driving. Dan was probably dead tired. And she was feeling better.

"How long have we been driving?"

"Six hours. How are you feeling?"

"Much better." She tried to sit up, but her muscles, where she'd been cut, screamed in agony. "If I don't move. Are you stopping for the night?" She had planned to drive, but that wasn't happening.

"In Twin Falls, Idaho. That's about nine hours from Yuma

Town. We've got reinforcements coming. They'll get there about the time we do."

"Reinforcements?" Then she vaguely remembered Chase and Dan talking before she had drifted off.

"Hell, yeah. Cougars, who will have our back, no questions asked."

"After everything that's happened, they can ask away." She thought he'd already told Chase all about them. Then she recalled he'd only mentioned about the hospital—the nurse, the two guys who burst into her room, and the missing agent. "I can't trust the people I work for. If it helps with your people to learn the truth, I'm an open book."

"Are you from Boston?"

"Yes. And my name is Addie Ann Davidson Steinacker."

He chuckled. "Damn right. We have a contract that says so. And the hobbies you listed? Cross-country skiing, hiking, running, your favorite color is blue, and you love romantic suspense stories? All true?"

"Yep."

"It wasn't part of the cover?"

"Nope."

"And the physical connection you and I have?"

She chuckled. "I think you know our pheromones wouldn't be reacting to one another's if it wasn't real."

"Yeah. That's what I was thinking. I want you to move in with me."

"And be your deputy sheriff?"

"You heard me telling you that in the hospital room?"

"Vaguely. And thinking I might want to be sheriff."

He chuckled. "We really don't have elections, but you

can get one going. I won't oppose you, just anything to ensure you stay there with me. Or you can work for Leyton Hill. Or even work with Hal and Tracey as agents who take down animal traffickers. You name it, we have several different kinds of law enforcement types in Yuma Town. And the best part? We're all cougars and best of friends."

"Until I get them killed," Addie said wearily. She would like to settle down, but not until she found the mole and exposed him or her.

"Any of us know, with the kind of work we do, we deal with dangerous suspects a fair amount of the time. It's always a likelihood. No way are we going to let one of our own do this by herself."

"I'm not—"

"You're my wife."

"Pseudo." She sighed. "I don't want to quit my job, not until I learn the truth."

"Or it gets you killed?" Dan sounded annoyed with her.

"How would you feel if someone was trying to kill you and nearly succeeded a couple of times? Would you just leave it alone, or would you track the culprit down?"

"I'd go after him."

"I rest my case." She wrapped his hoody tighter around her. "You still have three more hours to drive?"

"Two and a half now. It won't be long. We'll either get a hotel, or one of the agents coming to help out will take the driving over for me. They'll swap off with each other."

"Who's coming?" While trying to keep her identity secret from the residents of Yuma Town, she'd never learned who they were, except for the few times Dan had mentioned them, pride in his voice for knowing them.

"Bridget and her husband, Travis, with the Cougar Special Forces Agency. Dr. Kate Parker-Hill will check you out. My part-time deputy, Chase Buchanan, and Kate's husband with the Cougar Special Forces, Leyton Hill, will be coming too. Hal Haverton, the one who takes down animal traffickers, is going to take one of their ranch hands, Kolby Jones, with him into town and help my full-time deputy, Stryker Hill, to run things in case we have any trouble. They know to be on the lookout for anyone who's new in town, searching for where I live, or your whereabouts."

"Which would be at your place. Unless you're planning to set a trap for anyone coming there, we can't stay there."

"We could stay at Hal's ranch. Between Hal and Tracey, their ranch foreman, Ted Weekum, and Kolby Jones, and his brother, Ricky, we should be secure. If we think we need more firepower, we'll get it. In the meantime, the Muellers will contact friends they still have in the FBI. You can tell them what you know and suspect, and they can take it from there."

"Thank you, for coming for me, Dan. I can't thank you enough for coming to my rescue."

"Hell, I nearly had a heart attack when I heard your weak voice on the phone and I knew you were in serious trouble like the last time, and then you vanished. I was shouting forever, trying to get your attention again. Once I used cell tower triangulation, I located where you were. Then I spoke with your floor nurse."

"And she was a real nurse."

"Yeah. She had to have been. I had a hell of a time getting into the room to see you, and then the agent outside your room told me I only had five minutes with you. I assumed after an hour, and he hadn't made me leave, that he felt I was good for you."

"You are."

"I wasn't sure you could hear anything I said."

"Bits and pieces. I kept drifting in and out, but I was so glad to feel your hand on mine."

"I didn't think I'd have to steal you away from the hospital. I didn't know who to—"

Hearing the abrupt end of Dan's comment, Addie feared the worse. "What's the matter?"

"I've had a tail for the last half hour. Could be nothing, just someone headed in the same direction as us." Dan got on his Blue Tooth. "Hey, Bridget, I might have a tail. I'm an hour from Mountain Home."

"Do you want us to keep going then and meet you there?"

"We don't have any way of really protecting ourselves out here. We'll just keep driving and if we get into trouble, you know what to do."

"Can you see the make and model?"

"It's too far back, and it's too dark. All I see are the headlights. It's a car, not a truck."

"Are you in a compact or mid-sized vehicle?"

"I could only get an SUV rental, so we have a little more weight behind us, riding a little higher."

"Good. We're making good time and are an hour south of Twin Falls. Keep in touch about the car that's following you."

"*If* it's following us. Have you heard any news about the

hospital, the missing patient, the missing sheriff, and the three dead bodies?"

"No. Travis has been monitoring the news, but it appears a cleanup crew took care of it. No warrant out for either of your arrests for leaving a bunch of dead bodies in your wake. Though I'm sure if anyone had reported it, they would have blamed it all on you. Addie was too injured to have done any of it. No word on the missing federal agent either. We found one transmission about hospital security getting a false alarm. When they investigated, they found nothing suspicious. Just a prank call."

"Hell."

"Yeah, whoever orchestrated this is good. But so are we."

"I see a vehicle in the dark, half-hidden in the trees and brush on the side of the road, and the car behind me is speeding up. I'm forty-five minutes from Mountain Home. I'm speeding up. Hope, it's not a cop sitting in the bushes."

"We'll call ahead to verify. We're coming your way, unless you learn it's no problem."

"Keeping the line open." Dan sped up and was going ninety on the sixty-five-mile per hour road, hoping it wasn't a cop sitting on the side of the road. He didn't want to have to explain what was going on, or his version of it. If it wasn't a cop, it was possibly someone who wanted Addie dead. Not to mention they'd want him dead too now for interfering and knowing something about what was going on.

The vehicle shot out of the bushes, intending to hit him and knock him off the road, and he swerved to miss it, gunning the gas. "It's not a cop," Dan warned, cursing under his breath as the SUV began to rock, and he had to get it back under control before it rolled. He turned the SUV hard and smacked the other car's front bumper, shoving their assailants back into the brush. The pursuing car crashed with a loud bang.

Car doors opened and two men ran after them, pausing only long enough to aim at them. Addie struggled to sit up. "Stay down," Dan shouted, his heart racing.

Three rounds hit the back window, and Addie ducked down. "Give me your gun."

Dan sped out of range. The car behind him stopped briefly to pick up the other men. He handed her one of his revolvers.

"Two vehicles, one dead on the side of the road, the other in hot pursuit, at least a driver and two shooters that exited the stranded car." He glanced back at Addie, buried in her blanket. "Are you all right?"

"Yes, just keep driving. And keep the sharp turns and crashes to a minimum."

He smiled. "I'm on it."

"Next time though, I'm shooting back."

Chase had been listening in on the conversation and said, "These guys sound like professionals."

"Hell, yeah, they are," Dan said, hoping they had a chance to take them out.

Chase swore. "I'd call the local police, but I'd be afraid we'd have some real trouble trying to explain all of this. I should be at your location in thirty-five minutes."

"Chase is driving just a little over the speed limit," Bridget said.

"You better believe it. We finally learn Dan's got a wife, and we aim to keep it that way."

Addie groaned.

"You hear that, Addie? Everyone knows it. We just have to make it official," Dan said.

She let her breath out on a tired sigh. "I'm likely to get you killed."

"The other car's coming in for the kill," Dan warned.

"Hell, I wish I could fly," Chase said.

"They're shooting, damn it," Dan gritted out.

"I'll take them out," Addie said.

"You're in no shape to be shooting at anyone. You can barely sit up. I only gave you the gun in case they wrecked our vehicle and you could defend yourself."

"If they take us out, we'll be dead. I'm doing this."

He hated that she had to in the condition she was in, but she was right. The men behind them fired at the back windshield, finally knocking out a section of it, and she leaned over the back seat, using it to steady her aim, and fired.

"One down," she said, her voice weak and breathy, the guy leaning out of the window in the car behind them, the gun dropped on the asphalt.

"Hell, good shooting."

"I can see better than they can, if I can just keep my eyes open long enough." Then she shot the driver, and he twisted the steering wheel hard and the car drove off into the trees on the side of the road with a loud bang.

Then she laid back down, placing the gun next to her on the floor, pulling the blanket and hoody over her, and closed her eyes.

"Are you okay, Addie?"

"Your gun is next to me in case we have any more trouble. Tell me when we get there, will you, if we don't have any more problems before then?"

"Yeah, honey, just sleep. We'll be with the rest of the gang shortly."

"You okay, Dan?" Chase asked.

"Yeah, I've got Addie riding shotgun. What an amazing shot. They're down for the count. We'll be there soon now."

When they finally rendezvoused with everyone at a service station, Addie was sound asleep. He was glad Kate had come along to check her out, though with her being pregnant, he hoped the hell they didn't get into any more trouble that might put her in the crossfire. At least Leyton would also help to protect Kate.

"Her blood pressure is low. She needs blood. We need to take her to the hospital and watch over her there. Just for a few hours," Kate warned.

"They won't like it that you're not a doctor there," Dan said, worried about anyone getting word where they were headed next.

"I did a rotation there. I still know a lot of the doctors there. In this small town, there's barely any turn over."

"Okay, I hope the hell this works," Dan said, feeling like, at any moment, someone could pull what they did at the last hospital.

When they arrived at the hospital, Kate had already called ahead and made arrangements for Addie's care for a few hours. Dan and his friends helped Addie onto a gurney, and she was rolled through the hospital and into a room. A dark-haired doctor met with Kate, saying, "It's been a long time."

What Dan was even more shocked about, the doctor friend of hers was a cougar too. He checked Addie over, while Dan stayed in the room with her and the others guarded the room. Dan felt much better knowing they had protection, and Kate and another doctor were checking Addie over.

A nurse started an IV.

"I want to get her home soon," Kate told Dr. William Rugel.

"I understand, but you have nine more hours to travel to reach Yuma Town. What's with all the uniformed officers? And the undercover cops?"

"She's a federal agent. Someone tried to kill her at the hospital in Portland. The whole thing's been covered up, hush-hush. No word concerning it on the news or anything."

Dan hadn't really wanted Kate to tell any of this to anyone, but he understood she wanted the doctor to know if these people caught up with them here, they could have a similar fight.

"Dan met up with trouble on the road, so they knew they were headed this way. The only thing they hadn't expected was for a contingent of law officers to meet up with Dan to help get them home safely."

"The cougar cavalry," William said.

"Right. By the way, since I'm expecting, we sure could use an excellent family physician to take my place for a few months."

"The town's completely cougar run," Dan said.

William nodded. "I'd like that. What if, after I'm there

for a few months, I don't want to leave?"

"We can always use some extra help. I never have a chance to get away."

"I'll check out your place in about a week. I have some time off then."

"Okay, good. Thanks, William. We could really use your expertise out there."

"Is Addie going to be all right?" Dan asked, coming close to take her hand and squeeze it.

"Yeah," William said. "If she gets plenty of rest and fluids, she'll be fine. A few more days and she'll be almost as good as new. The rest of tonight and tomorrow, she needs complete rest. You're welcome to take the bed next to her and get some rest too."

"Thanks, Doc. We still have a long drive ahead of us tomorrow." Dan stripped down to his boxer briefs and climbed under the sheet.

Kate was going to take a seat near Addie, but William said, "Why don't you lie down in the physician's breakroom. You can get some quality sleep before you have to take care of your patient on the next phase of your journey, especially in your condition."

"Thanks, I'd like that."

William walked out with Kate. "Tell me, who's the lucky guy?"

She motioned to Leyton, serving guard duty already. "Leyton Hill. You would never believe how we met, but if you come to work with us, I'll tell you all about it."

Leyton joined her and gave her a hug and a kiss. "Camping out has never been such an adventure." He offered his hand to William. "Good to meet you, William."

They shook hands and Dan was glad Kate had worked at the hospital and had an in so that they could take care of Addie right away. It would be great too, if the doctor decided to come work with them for a few months, while Kate took off to have her baby. He might even decide to stay once he worked with so many cougars. They'd make it their business to ensure he felt welcome.

Dan slept for a few hours, woke, then left the room so Bridget could lie down on the bed he'd used for a while. Chase was pulling guard duty in front of Addie's room now. Travis had found a couch in the nearby waiting area to curl up on. Leyton was downstairs in the lobby, watching for any signs of trouble. "No problems at all?" Dan asked Chase.

"None. They probably don't know you have reinforcements who met up with you to watch your backs. It'll probably take them some time to regroup and discover where you've escaped to after you wrecked their other vehicle and two of their men are dead."

"Good thing for that."

"So, what's going on?"

"She's an FBI agent, working on a task force to take down certain kinds of criminals, but she believes one of the people on the taskforce is a mole who is leaking their plans, and Addie seems to be the target."

"And your involvement with Addie?"

"Uh, yeah, sorry, buddy. I couldn't tell you or any of the others. I was sworn to secrecy, concerned that telling anyone could get her killed. I signed a contract with the FBI to work with Addie as her husband when they needed me. Strictly undercover. Six months earlier, she dropped into Yuma Town, wounded, but she wouldn't stay for fear those who wanted her dead would come there and take some of our people out. Me, especially, being that I was her husband. She left the house shortly after she'd arrived, when I came into work, not telling me that she was going to leave again, and I had no way to find her. Truthfully, I believe she was desperate to find a safe haven for even a couple of days before she took off again."

"Then Kate came to see her at your place, to take a look at her injuries."

"Yeah, and she said she'd be fine in a few days. That's all Addie had to hear. She didn't say anything, but I knew the look she cast me said if she would live, there was no reason to put me in danger. It's been hell for me, really having feelings for the woman, not being able to keep in touch, worrying she's going to get herself killed, and I'll never hear from her again, or know what had become of her."

"I completely understand your reasoning for keeping it secret, though I wouldn't have breathed a word of it to anyone. On the other hand, I know how by-the-book you are. And I get it. In your shoes, I would have done the same thing. I'm all for helping you to keep her there in Yuma Town, and helping you to protect her."

"That would be my plan. No way would whoever's after her be able to win against us. It's the keeping her there that's the difficulty. Once she's feeling better, I'm afraid she'll vanish, just like she did before."

"We'll do what we can to keep her there. Doc said we could get on the road around noon. Addie's vital signs are looking good. She still needs plenty of rest, but she's doing well. Mostly because she's a cougar and is healing faster than a human would, or she'd be down for a lot longer than that. Of course, this is your call because she's your wife"—Chase smiled at Dan and shook his head—"and you know her better than any of the rest of us, not to mention you're the sheriff, but if you want to try this—you stay at home with Addie. Protect her, and keep her under lock and key so she doesn't run off again. These guys are bound to come there looking for her, don't you think?"

"Yeah, I do. It wouldn't be hard for them to learn where I live. The options we have are for us to stay at my place and wait them out, or stay with someone else, but that could mean endangering someone else too."

"You know that's not an issue. We will all work together to get this done. All of us have dangerous jobs. It's just what we do." Chase stretched out his legs, leaned back on the chair, and folded his arms. "If you don't stay at your place, I was thinking Hal's ranch might work because they have two ranch hands, a foreman, Hal, and Tracey, all firearms qualified. All trained in hand-to-hand combat."

"And they've got the babies."

"True, but for the time-being, maybe Tracey could take them home to her parents. Maybe even stay there with them until we resolve this."

"Okay, that's a possibility. Or we could stay with Stryker. He's got extra room, serves as my deputy sheriff, and would be a good protector."

"Right. Also, you could stay at my place—at one of the cabins on the lake. Or with Rick and Yvonne Mueller. They are still trying to track down some information from their FBI friends to see if they can learn anything."

Chase glanced down the hall as a nurse moved about. "Good. I hope they learn something soon. Or we could stay at the Cougar Special Forces Agency safe house with Travis and Bridget helping to watch out."

"Yeah, any of those would work and wherever you decide to go, all of us will back you up with additional firepower. Did you get some sleep?"

"Yeah. Thanks for coming to our rescue as fast you did."

"Are you kidding? We couldn't get here fast enough. I sure hope she wants to be a deputy sheriff and stay put."

"Yeah, me too. She's a crack shot. Exhausted, she was still able to hit two of the men in the car pursuing us." Dan stretched his legs out.

"Leyton's going to want to recruit her, you know. Bridget would love to have another woman to work with on the cougar force as an agent."

"Don't I know it. I just hope I can convince her to stay in Yuma Town with us. With me."

"We'll all help in whatever way we can." Chase smiled then. "Stryker was grumbling about missing all the action, and he swears the mystery woman you've hooked up with is the mystery woman who intrigued him when he was playing Santa for charity last Christmas."

"Not *this* woman. She only wanted *me*." Then Dan frowned, realizing that she said she'd checked out Chase, Hal, and Stryker also when looking into Dan's background. That was way before he began working with her and before Chase and Hal had mates even. She definitely had not been the woman who'd been checking Stryker out last winter when he was playing Santa Claus for a charity event.

"I can't believe you slipped out of the Hamburger Spot with her before we could see her, and hassle you a bit."

Dan smiled. "I knew that was coming. I'm getting some coffee. Want some?"

"Sure. We thought we'd take shifts getting breakfast, and then pick up lunch on the return home."

"Sounds good to me." Dan went to the breakroom, fixed a couple of coffees, one with extra milk and sugar for Chase, and returned to where he was sitting.

"The two of you must have some real chemistry between you. You'd never take off work for pleasure. Ever. What did the colonel say when you returned to work the next day?"

Dan took a seat next to him. "He only smiled at me and said he hoped I had a nice break. You know me, I never took breaks. I wanted to tell you guys about her in the worst way. Once I signed a contract, that was part of the agreement, to keep all this secret from family and friends."

"I understand. She's beautiful. I guess the business where someone's trying to kill her negated the contract."

"Hell, yeah. If I have to ask my friends to help me to protect her when the FBI can't be trusted, the deal is off. And she's mine, if I can swing it with her."

CHAPTER 4

As soon as Addie woke that morning, she saw Dan sitting beside her bed, sipping coffee. She was glad they were alone in the room for the moment.

"Did you get some sleep?" She was afraid he'd sat up all night, watching over her.

"Hey, honey," Dan said, reaching over to hold her hand. "Yeah, I did. We've been taking turns. How are you feeling?"

"Better. I still feel like I could sleep some more."

"We have a nine-hour drive still after you're released at noon. Everyone's taking turns to get breakfast and pulling guard duty. The cat's out of the bag, by the way. Everyone knows you're my wife. I hope you're not mad about it."

She cast him an elusive smile. She was certain he wanted to make it happen for real, but she had a job to do. Maybe not the one the Bureau would assign her, but the one she had to do if she was ever to feel safe. Learn who, on the team, wanted her dead, and why.

"I assumed it was inevitable. But I also told you, because of the circumstances, I'm an open book. Thanks to everyone who came out to help us. No one's had any trouble yet?"

"No. The people after you might have lost us. We wonder if they might know we've got reinforcements. It's hard to say. They may assume we're going to my home."

"They wouldn't have expected half the town to come to my aid."

"No, they won't. We have the advantage there."

"So, your place wouldn't be safe."

"We've been discussing that. Staying at my place, having reinforcements protecting you, or staying with another family or couple who could help with keeping you protected."

"Family? No. Way too dangerous."

"Children would be removed from the premises. If we go to one of the other homes, they wouldn't know where we ended up, most likely. If we stay at home, we might be able to set a trap."

"They would suspect that."

"You think we should make them work for it? If they think they had to work really hard to learn where we are, they won't believe it's a trap?" Dan asked. "Then again, they'd probably know Stryker, Hal, and Chase are my good friends. I'd be afraid they'd go after them to learn where we are, if we're not home."

"Okay, so we go to your house and tough it out. Set up a trap. Hope to draw them in." Her stomach grumbled. She might be tired, but she was hungry too. "I'm hungry. Can we have breakfast?"

"Do you want me to have someone bring you some?"

"Yeah, not the hospital food."

"Get right on it. What would you like?"

"Whatever you want to eat. I'll have the same as you."

He smiled and squeezed her hand. "You got it."

When he left the room, Bridget came in to speak with her. "Hi, I don't know if you remember who I am from last night—"

"Bridget McKay, married to Travis, and you both work for the same Cougar Special Forces Agency."

"Right. I want to mention something I haven't told very many people because not everyone can deal with it. I'm telepathic."

"As in...?"

"I can read minds. Not everyone's. I couldn't read Travis's and I think that was some of the appeal for me."

"Omigod, that's wonderful. That could be so useful in your line of work."

"It can be, when I can do it. I try to stay out of everyone's thoughts as much as possible. And like I said, I can't always read everyone's thoughts. Do you know how muddled people think sometimes? About all kinds of things. What they had to do, what they were doing, what they wanted to do, all mixed up into a jumble of thoughts. It's when a thought is intensified—a feeling toward another, for instance, like lust, or love, then the thoughts are clearer."

"Or if someone is targeting someone to take them down."

"Right, because then the thought is completely focused. Some people are easier to read—simple thoughts, direct.

Others are really complicated, disjointed. If I think someone's in trouble, I might eavesdrop."

Addie thought Bridget was trying to tell her something personally about Dan and her, not just anything random. "You mean about Dan and the woman, me, who went to his house, after being injured six months ago."

"He was visibly upset, not caring about what was going on in town, despite how wild things had become. We knew something was wrong. And we knew it had to do with the woman, you. We'd hoped you would return, but you didn't, and Dan got back into his work. We knew he was still bothered by whatever was going on between you and him. He was in emotional pain. I wanted to know if there was any way I could help. Everyone had sidestepped the business, because he wasn't opening up with anyone. Leyton was the only one who didn't act shocked about you. I figured it was because he was new to town so he didn't know Dan that well, just like Travis and I didn't. But then there was something about the way Leyton was acting that made me think he knew something about you. And if he did, I wanted to also. At some point, Leyton thought about Dan's wife, and I was shocked since no one seemed to know he had one.

"I don't just try to read someone's thoughts continually. I'd never get anywhere with that. I have to say something to them that might trigger the thought, if I really want to know something."

"Like a polygraph test, to get reactions."

"Right. I didn't straight out ask Dan anything about having a wife, but I just mentioned that he should get a wife sometime, and that's when he thought of you. I still didn't know if it meant Dan was considering taking a wife, proposing, or if you were already his wife. I didn't want to pry, so I asked Leyton if he thought Dan had a mystery wife, and he said he didn't know anything about it, but I read his thoughts and he did know Dan had a wife. Of course, why you were a mystery wife, and that you truly weren't married, that neither Leyton nor I knew. I never said anything to anyone. Not even Travis, because I knew there wasn't anything any of us could do to help the two of you out. Until now."

"I've never known anyone who has psychic abilities. Can you read my mind?"

Bridget smiled and shook her head. "I don't know why I can't with some people. Like they have natural barricades."

"Or are more evolved."

Bridget laughed.

"Does Dan know about your abilities?"

"Yes. So, don't worry about talking to him about it. I don't know if Dan has spoken to you about this, but we're hoping you will stay in Yuma Town, and find a home with us. Leyton Hill, the one we work for, wants to hire you as one of his agents. I know Dan wants you to be his deputy sheriff, but we wanted to make sure to let you know he's not the only one offering you a job. We all heard about how you took out those guys chasing after your vehicle."

Smiling, Addie hadn't known that everyone was lining up jobs for her in Yuma Town. "He hasn't discussed it with me, but that's probably because he knows I have a job to do."

"Find the mole? We'll all help you with that. We can't have, whoever this is, trying to gun you down."

"Thanks. And I want to thank everyone who came to our rescue."

"That's what we do. We take care of our own kind. This is a case right up our alley."

"The person who's responsible is a federal agent."

"And we have two retired federal agents who are helping with this. We'll do it."

"If I'm on the job, I'll have a better chance to learn who is responsible."

Bridget didn't agree, and Addie knew the agent didn't believe she would. Addie wondered if the others felt the same way as Bridget. They probably wouldn't want her to return to the job and this time be taken down by an assailant permanently.

She assumed whoever came for her in Yuma Town, if they did, they would be only the henchmen, not the one who hired the hit on her.

"I'll stay there for as long as it takes for me to recuperate."

Bridget smiled. "Good. We'll find the mole before you take off then."

That could be only a couple of days, if Addie's nerves weren't shot and she was perfectly healed physically. She'd love nothing more than to spend lots of time loving on Dan, which made her rethink where she'd be even in a couple of years from now.

"What makes anyone think I want to be in any dangerous line of work any longer? Maybe I just want to be a librarian."

Bridget laughed. "Somehow, I can't see you working

with books in a library. Reading tactical maneuvers, how to take down your opponent, that's what I can see. I hope you decide to work with us. You'd probably get to see enough of Dan anyway—"

The door opened and Dan stepped into the room. "She will never get enough of seeing me."

The ladies laughed.

"I offered her a job. Don't convince her to work for you. I'll give you some privacy." Bridget left the room and closed the door.

"I hope Bridget wasn't making you feel as though you have no choice about what happens next. Food's on the way. Chase and Travis are picking it up for us."

"Two of them?"

"We've been trying to work in pairs on this mission, especially after everyone has gotten some rest. Leyton and Bridget are pulling guard duty right now. We don't want anyone going out on their own in case the bad guys realize where we are and who all is with you. Will you stay for a while with us? Recuperate fully first?"

"Yes. You know I will."

Dan didn't know anything of the sort. She was unpredictable, and maybe he liked that about her too. His work was just as unpredictable. He wanted her to work where she wanted to, yet he hoped she would work with him, and he'd know where she was, what she was doing, and maybe he'd be with her on the assignment. If she was working for Leyton, she could be just about anywhere, and gone for long periods of time, trying to track down the bad guys. He wasn't sure he wanted to deal with that. Especially since, for ten and a half years, they'd already had that kind of an arrangement.

"Bridget told me what she could do—with mental telepathy."

"You're okay with it?"

"Yeah, sure. I think it's a great ability to have and maybe she can even use it to help us shed some light on this whole matter if we're able to take anyone hostage. I'm kind of surprised they haven't found us already," she said. "I don't want to have trouble at the hospital for the other patients or staff, but I'm really surprised they haven't tried to take me out here."

"We're watching the corridors, the fire escapes, and the elevator. No one who shouldn't be here has been here. We've checked everyone here, even family and friends visiting patients to ensure they really belong. The nursing staff, we verify, to make sure they're truly on staff at the hospital, and not like the nurse who had planned to use a hypodermic on you."

"I know the driver and one of the shooters in the car behind us were dead, but maybe in the crash, the other shooter was killed. He couldn't have been wearing a seatbelt because, like the other shooter, he was hanging out the window to fire rounds at me, then he might have been flung from the vehicle upon impact with the tree."

"And been killed. Now that sounds highly likely. That would mean that no one was left behind to report where we'd gone to, or that we had others rendezvousing with us. I'd say it was a good bet they'd try to track us down in Yuma Town then. I've called ahead to tell Stryker to have everyone on the lookout for suspicious characters. The perps won't know we're such a tightknit community that no matter how they try to blend in, they won't."

"Because we're cougars also."

"Right."

"That gives me an idea. I think, when I feel a hundred percent, I'd like to go camping—in the mountains."

Dan smiled. "Now, that idea, I like. I know a cave next to a waterfall that's just spectacular. It has a view of more mountains, the golden aspen in all its autumn glory, and the area is cougar-claimed territory."

"I'd like that." She sighed. "Whoever they send will probably think I'll be sitting in a house recovering somewhere. Or the medical clinic. If I were human, I'd never heal that quickly, and I'd probably be in a hospital for a week or more. Camping up in the mountains? No way."

Dan frowned. "I thought the idea was we could catch them up there unawares."

"Yep. Anyone they talk to will know just where we went. And the greatest thing about that, is that then a party can be gathered to take them out. I'd do the honors, but"—she shrugged—"I don't mind letting someone else do the dirty work this time around."

"You remind me of Tracey, Hal's wife. She was always in the middle of a shootout."

"And Bridget?"

"She saved Travis's life. If she hadn't come to take him into custody, thinking he was one of the perps who'd had a falling out with his partners in crime, he would have been dead."

"I like her. I know I'll like Tracey too."

"What do you think? Can you work for me as a deputy sheriff?"

She laughed. "You would be my boss. I don't know if I could handle that."

"You like being my boss," he said, smiling, realizing she might not like working for him. He had no trouble working for her in the capacity as her faux husband on an assignment.

Someone knocked on the door and Dan drew his gun.

"Just me," Travis said, "delivering hot meals."

Dan went to the door to get the meals and holstered his gun. "Thanks, Travis. See anything suspicious when you left the hospital?"

"No, but we had the idea that your rental vehicle is too conspicuous—shot out back window, fender damage. Chase is having it hauled off by the rental company, and he signed off as you. The insurance company you signed up with will pay all the damages."

"What about a police report?"

"You can fill out one when you get home, or Stryker can for you if you're too busy with Addie. It won't matter if they don't find the totaled car and the dead suspects in the event the men and other vehicles just vanished. There were rounds in the back of the last seat in the SUV, and that verifies someone tried to gun you down. We would have checked out the other vehicles last night, but figured we might have run into more of these guys and it was better to keep a united force here."

"Agreed. Okay, thanks for thinking of all this stuff." Dan set the tray over Addie's bed and helped her sit up so she could eat.

"You've had your mind on other things, and I don't blame you a bit."

"Addie's boss is sure to suspect she's going to Yuma Town to recover," Dan said.

"He will," Addie said, forking up some eggs. "The last time I was wounded, I left the hospital, and no one found me. There were rumors I had died, but, of course, those who had tried to take me out had to know they hadn't finished the job. My boss, Clinton Briggs, was shocked when I showed up six months later. I claimed amnesia. I don't imagine he believed me. I keep thinking there's a mole on the team, but what if it could be him? I've always liked Briggs, so I never gave it any thought. He's rough around the edges, but he's always made me believe he's one of the good guys."

"He'll wonder what happened to you then. How are we getting home?" Dan asked, figuring the guys had all talked about it and decided how they were going to do it. No one was really in charge in a situation like this. They were from multiple law enforcement agencies, and all that mattered in the end was that they all arrived home safe and sound to see their loved ones again.

"You'll ride in one of our vehicles. Kate will ride with you and Addie. Leyton will drive, I'll ride shotgun. Travis and Bridget will be our backup. Hopefully, we'll have no problem on the road home. Just in case, we have a disguise for the two of you. You'll stand out too much in your sheriff's uniform, and we have a change of clothes for Addie. And wigs for you both," Chase said.

Dan frowned at Chase.

Chase laughed. "It looks real, but it will make you appear like someone else. A blond. Addie will be a blond also."

"We need to discuss exactly why anyone would want you dead," Dan said to Addie. "If we knew the reason why, we might be able to thwart whoever is behind all this." He sat down to eat his breakfast of an omelet, slices of ham, and hash browns.

Chase pulled up a chair and had his notepad out in a flash. That's what Dan liked about his deputy, he was always on the ball.

"When did the first incident occur that made you feel that the attack on you was due to a mole in the organization?" Chase asked.

Addie sipped from her orange juice. "No one was supposed to know of the meeting I had with the courier. No one except our boss and the five men and the other woman on our team. Was it random that I was targeted? I really don't think so. I had a sixth sense I might be in danger that morning, so I took extra precautions and wore a steel-plated armor protection, when I normally don't. It's heavy and cumbersome, and hot. I was glad I'd worn it. It was the only thing that saved me from certain death."

"Did they catch the assassin?" Dan asked, forking up a bite-sized piece of ham.

"He was conveniently killed. No way to question as to who had hired him. I'm sure he didn't know that's what his employer had intended for him. He was found with a large amount of cash on him. Which looked like a plant, to me. I've never known an assassin to carry that much cash on him. Payment for a job is usually deposited in an offshore account.

And paid *after* the job is done."

"Who discovered him?" Dan asked.

Chase smiled at him. "I was trying to give Addie time to chew her food."

"Thanks, Chase." Addie finished her omelet. "A couple of our agents."

"So, one of them could have killed him and planted the cash on him," Chase said.

She buttered her toast and coated it with grape jelly. "Possibly, or it was someone else the person hired to get rid of the assassin, and he disappeared before the federal agents arrived."

"You weren't able to smell who had been close to the assassin when he died?"

Addie shook her head. "I was medevacked to the hospital right away. If anyone had witnessed what had happened to me, they would have thought I was dead. Or near death, I guess, because they hadn't put me in a body bag. My team members all said they thought I'd been a goner. When I'd recuperated enough, I slipped out of the hospital and disappeared."

"And came to see me, but didn't tell me what was going on, or tell me you were leaving again."

"I wanted to keep you safe," Addie said to Dan.

"I wanted to keep you safe."

Chase cleared his throat. "How did you slip out of the hospital? Didn't you have an armed guard outside of your door?"

"There was a chair outside of it, but no armed guard, no federal agent there to protect me. I knew something was wrong, and I wasn't waiting to get shot again. I didn't have my armored vest this time. I got dressed and slipped down the stairwell, afraid the whole time I would run into an assassin. I was more than just afraid, I was terrified. The one person I wanted to call was you, Dan, the only one I knew I could trust, but I didn't have my phone. They would have been able to trace where I was anyway. Before a mission, I have a storage locker setup nearby where I keep stuff for an emergency—cash, clothes, ID, anything I needed to make a clean getaway if I needed to."

"Why would you have something like that?" Chase asked incredulously.

Dan was wondering the same thing. Who did that unless they were either paranoid, or something like this had happened to them before.

"My dad was a former FBI agent, but he was killed coming home from a date. There were rumors circulating at the FBI that it had to do with a case he'd been working on. I loved listening to all his tales of heroism, and I wanted to be just like him when I grew up. He knew that, but he warned me that it was important always to have a way out if anyone targeted you. He wasn't talking about his fellow agents, but a perp he had taken down who had hired men to assassinate him. I always made it a point to have something like it nearby."

"My house would have been your safe house, but you didn't stay," Dan said, reminding her.

"I was healed up enough, and I was afraid if anyone learned where I was, it could cause real trouble for you...and for me."

"The case your dad was involved in when he died, what was that about?" Chase asked.

Addie finished her hash browns. "Dad had testified against a bank robber. I was eighteen at the time and went to see the man. He denied he'd hired a hit on him. I figured he wasn't going to tell me the truth and add more years to his prison sentence. Then he said the oddest thing—'You might want to look closer to home.' Of course, I asked him what he meant by that, and he shrugged. 'You're a clever girl. You can figure it out.' Closer to home made me think of my grandparents, but both were in a nursing facility by then. And my mom, but she left us when I was eight. I never heard from her again, and Dad never spoke about her."

"Was she involved with some criminal element?" Chase asked.

"She was an FBI agent like Dad. That's how they met—on a stakeout. But the police had stated it was a case of him driving home drunk from a bar after having a date there with a woman. And I never could learn anything differently."

CHAPTER 5

Chase relayed all the information Addie had given him and sent it to the Muellers to check out with their contacts at the Bureau.

Addie was sleeping again while they waited for the doctor to okay her release. Kate said she looked much better and was healing well, but just needed ample rest.

Dan liked the idea Addie had of camping out, but then he wasn't sure she could really manage that strenuous a trip in her condition. If she could do it, whoever was responsible for trying to have her killed would wonder how come the doctor's charts showed she was near death, but then could be camping in the wilderness.

Leyton and Travis were down in the lobby, watching for trouble.

Dan sat with Chase outside Addie's room to discuss what they'd learned while Kate and Bridget stayed in the room with Addie while she slept. "What do you think about the bank robber's story?"

"I checked the guy out and he was killed in a prison riot a few years back."

"Typical. Every prospective lead turns up to be a dead end." Dan rubbed his whiskery chin. He needed a shave.

"Bridget said Addie is bound and determined to return to the Bureau."

"I'm bound and determined to learn the truth before she does that. What about her parents?"

"Yvonne said she's looking into both the wife and husband's role at the Bureau, and trying to determine where the wife is now, if she's still alive."

"Okay, good. Want some coffee?" Dan asked.

Chase nodded. "Thanks."

When Dan returned with the two cups of coffee, he said, "What we need to know is why her mother abandoned her daughter and divorced her dad. I can't imagine the mother would want to have Addie killed. You know how family and friends are often suspects though."

"Yeah. Which means it's important we dig her up. And hopefully, she's still alive."

***

Addie saw the shooter, his coal black eyes staring at her as he began to shoot, the silencer muffling the sounds, and she cried out. Pain radiated through her chest, but female voices quickly reassured her.

She woke to find Kate and Bridget hovering over her, touching her, holding her hands.

"Addie, you're all right," Bridget said, she and Kate trying to wake her from the night terror.

Chase and Dan both bolted into the room with guns raised.

"It was just a nightmare," Addie said, feeling chilled all over. "I'm okay."

Dan rubbed her shoulder reassuringly. "About?"

"The time I was riddled with bullets. I dreamed I wasn't wearing a protective vest and every bullet hurt."

"You're really all right?" Dan asked.

"Yes."

The doctor came into the room and asked, "Are you ready to go?" He gave her information on what she needed to do for the next few days: no heavy lifting, no climbing or running, no sex.

She smiled at Dan. That was definitely on the agenda. The sex. And as soon as she could, she was going camping, to try and draw whoever came after her out. Carrying a backpack, climbing, and running came next. If whoever it was didn't come for her somewhere else first.

Whoever came after her, they had to keep him alive this time so they could question him to learn who was behind all of this.

She'd never suspected her mother could have had anything to do with this. Had she been involved in her dad's death? Her dad would never say why her mother left, only that they couldn't agree on key issues. Addie never could understand why her mother had left her with her dad either. Though she adored him. Weren't mothers supposed to love their children and have a deep maternal instinct?

Everyone left the room while Dan helped her to dress. He was her husband, after all, or at least he was taking the role seriously.

"Have you heard from your mother all these years?" Dan asked, fastening Addie's bra in the back.

"No. Not once."

"You don't think she had to change identities to protect you and your dad, do you, in the line of work she does as an agent?"

"Maybe. I don't know."

"Why would the bank robber say it was someone close to home? Was there anyone else it might have been? A nanny, a housekeeper?"

"A butler?"

Dan smiled as he helped her on with her socks and boots.

"No one. The bank robber was a career criminal. He was used to lying. He probably watched lots of cop shows and they say it's usually someone close to home."

"Over the years was your dad seeing anyone? Did he remarry, or was he engaged?"

"He was seeing other women. No, he didn't remarry and he was never engaged to be married. I think he still held a torch for my mother. Though he took down all her pictures, he had one of him and her and me, as a baby, in his desk drawer. My pen had run out of ink, and I was looking for one in his desk drawer and I couldn't believe he had kept the picture of her. Though she was dark-haired like me back then. I began searching through his drawers and found several more. He'd kept all of them. Even their wedding photos. None after I was a baby though. Still, that's not a man who has given up on his wife."

"Doesn't sound like it. I'm with your dad on that."

Addie pulled on Dan's spare black T-shirt. "What do you think about the doctor's restrictions on what I can do?"

"I wholeheartedly agree."

She pulled Dan into her arms for a light embrace and a kiss. And groaned. Her chest still hurt where the man had stabbed her.

Dan held her tenderly in his arms, very gently kissing her forehead, her cheeks, her mouth. "We'll see how you feel tomorrow. You rest all the way home."

"I think I'm slept out. Will you sit in the back with me?"

"Yeah. I'll also be the rear gunner if we run into the same kind of trouble as we did yesterday." He lifted the wig off the bed and handed it to her.

She pulled it on while he eyed the one for him. "Maybe we should switch."

He laughed and tugged his on. "How ridiculous do I look?"

"Chase was right. It looks natural. What about me?" She made pigtails out of the long, golden hair.

"Like you need to be a dark-haired beauty. *My* dark-haired beauty." He kissed her mouth, and took hold of her hand and headed out of the room, where Kate was standing with a wheelchair.

Addie wasn't about to object. She couldn't believe how tired she was. Dan rubbed her shoulder and helped her to get comfortably seated in the wheelchair, and then Kate pushed it to the elevator so Bridget and Dan could be ready to pull guns if they had to. Chase was downstairs already, watching for any signs of trouble. Leyton and Travis were getting the cars.

When Addie and her group reached the elevator, someone was coming up to their floor, and Kate pulled the wheelchair back away from the elevator, while everyone waited to see who emerged. A woman and a teen girl. They all gave a collective sigh, and Kate wheeled Addie into the elevator.

She pulled her to the back of the elevator while Bridget hit the main floor button, and she and Dan were ready for trouble. The elevator stopped on the third floor and an elderly man walking with a cane got on. Addie watched him warily though. He could be wearing makeup that aged him, and the cane could hold a sword. Or he could just be an elderly man visiting a patient. She hated to feel this paranoid, but after what had happened to them with the car chase and the business at the last hospital, she was right in feeling unnerved.

When they reached the main floor, Chase was there, watching the lobby. She saw Leyton and Travis with the vehicles, observing the parking area.

Travis opened the door to a black SUV for her. It looked like a Bureau vehicle, lots of room for all of them, and she could stretch out in the very last seat, resting her head on Dan's lap. What Addie loved was that someone had made a bed for her on the seat—blankets, a pillow, the drink holder pulled out and two cups filled with ice water in them for the two of them.

"Thanks," she said, not knowing who had gone to all the trouble.

"You're welcome," Bridget and Kate said.

Addie should have known.

"Be safe," Bridget said, and joined her husband in the other car, that would follow the SUV.

Addie climbed into the SUV's far back seat with Dan and got comfortable, her pillow on Dan's lap, though she knew if they had trouble behind them, she'd have to move pronto. If they gave her a gun, she'd be shooting out the back window with him. And she was a lot more rested up this time.

"How do you feel?" Dan asked, while Kate looked over the middle seat to check on her.

"I thought I was fine, until I got out of bed and dressed. I'm tired."

"Another nine hours of rest will help. We can pick up supper on the drive home, and when we arrive home, you can sleep all night," Kate said. "Where are you going to stay for the night, Dan? You shouldn't be at your house the first night. Not while Addie's still recuperating, if anyone comes after her there."

"The safe house for the first night," Dan said, "with Bridget and Travis. And anyone else who wants to come and stay to spell us."

"Leyton will be over after we get home," Kate said. "Probably Stryker will want to take a turn also. You know, he loves being your deputy, except when he gets left behind when all the action is going on elsewhere and the rest of the guys get to be there to deal with it."

"Yeah, but if something bad had happened at home, he would have been in the middle of it. And I trust him to get the job done."

"I agree."

"Speaking of which, I haven't heard from him in a while." Dan called Stryker and asked him if he'd witnessed anything suspicious.

"Yeah. I'm waiting for you to return to town first. Hal and I are just keeping an eye on things."

"What's happened?"

"A black sedan with tinted windows showed up at the motel some ways out from town. Since Calvin and Myrtle Dixon are cougars, they've been on the lookout for anyone out of the ordinary dropping in at their motel."

"And?"

"Calvin said two men pulled up, the one paying cash, and the guys got a single room. One pulled out his ID to register the car, and he had a family photo in his wallet. The man in the photo was him, along with three kids who looked like him, and he had a wife. If Calvin gets businessmen who are stopping at the motel, they always get their own rooms."

"Anything else?"

"He saw one was carrying a holstered gun. The other had something bulky under his jacket that could indicate it was a sidearm also. They were dressed casually, jeans, jackets, trying to look like they fit in, but they were wearing fancy shoes and watches, their hair cut government short."

"Would the feds be sending their own men for a hit, or someone hired to do the job?"

"Most likely someone hired to do the job. They could just be businessmen, good friends who are sharing a room on their way to somewhere else. But since Calvin's a retired state highway patrolman, he's good at profiling."

"Yeah, he is. Where are the men now?"

"Calvin said they're still at the motel. He said he figures if they're who we're looking for, they won't make a move until dark. They don't know that's the best time for us."

"Any other suspicious people running around town?"

"Two other men booked a cabin at Pinyon Pines Resort. Now, that's not a flag raiser in and of itself. They're driving a black sedan also. No fishing equipment, just one bag apiece, black leather. Shannon said she thought they could be carrying concealed weapons. She texted her mate already to let Chase know."

"Hell," Dan said. He didn't want Shannon and the kids in any kind of trouble.

"They're all right. These guys, if they're the ones we need to be worried about, are staying out of the town, as if they're afraid they'll be seen. They don't know that the places are all cougar run, and everyone is on the lookout for them," Stryker said. "I'm sure they're only waiting for the right time to learn if Addie is at your home. The Muellers moved into your home yesterday to conduct operations there. If anyone tried to slip in before you returned home, they'll have another think coming."

"That puts them at risk." Dan didn't like that bit of news.

"They've been doing this for a long time. It makes them relive the old days, and you know they're always at the firing range, keeping up their shooting skills. They're happy to do it."

"We're not returning there tonight. Addie's still tired and not fully recovered. We'll be staying at the safe house and Bridget and Travis will be there to help safeguard her."

"And Leyton," Kate said.

"And Leyton, and you, if want to take a turn," Dan told Stryker.

"Hell, yeah. Chase told me all the trouble you had. I just wish I'd been there to help out. Addie's an expert sharpshooter, I hear."

"Yeah, you definitely don't want to get in her crosshairs." Dan glanced down at his now blond wife. Her eyes were closed, but she was smiling a smidgeon, and he figured he was keeping her awake, but he had to know what the situation was like back home.

"No trouble leaving the hospital?" Stryker asked.

"Not so far. Hopefully, we'll get home without further incident in about nine hours. We'll keep you posted."

"I'll keep you informed if anything else happens here. I'm hoping the four guys, we suspect might be trouble, are the only ones who are coming here."

"Me too."

"Oh, and before I forget, Ricky and Kolby ran to the airport to pick up your Jeep. It's already in your garage."

"Hell, thanks."

"Okay, I'll talk later."

"Good luck."

"You too."

"Stryker said we have four guys who might be trouble," Dan told everyone in the SUV. "He's having folks keep an eye on them."

"Sounds good," Leyton said.

On the way home, they didn't see anyone following them who looked suspicious. They stopped for burgers and chicken sandwiches at a fast-food restaurant and everyone used the restrooms.

Dan was glad Kate and Bridget were there to be with Addie when she used the facility. He waited outside the women's room until Travis could relieve him, while Chase and Leyton ordered the meals. Addie was still moving more slowly than she usually did, and he didn't want her going anywhere without protection. She didn't seem to be bothered by the notion that she couldn't handle this on her own.

They all piled back into the vehicles, switching off drivers and ate their meals.

As professional as Chase was, Dan knew he was chomping at the bit to get home to Shannon and the kids, worried about their safety, if the men staying at one of the cabins was really trouble.

Then Dan got a call from Stryker and he put it on speaker this time.

"Don't worry about Shannon. Hal is there and Jack Barrington arrived unexpectedly. The two specially-trained cougar agents will take care of the situation there. They're posing as Chase's brothers, who came out to the lake for a visit," Stryker said.

"Good to hear it. Any other news?"

"No, everything's quiet in and around town. The guys haven't moved at all."

"Everything's been quiet for us. We were planning on getting in around nine, but with gas stops, bathroom breaks, and grabbing supper, it will be closer to ten."

"Unless anything major happens, we'll see you then."

Dan wondered if any of the bad guys had been

monitoring their progress and knew every step of the way where they were. He hoped not. If they did, they could relay to the men in place just where Dan and Addie ended up for the night.

Addie was lying down with her head on his lap again. And though he knew he had other much more important concerns to deal with, he couldn't help thinking about making love to her. He wanted the connection between them, to run with her as a cougar again, to be her mate for real. Knowing more of her background now, he wondered if her parents' divorce had made her wary of making a commitment to another cougar.

After a couple of hours' drive, she yawned and tried to sit up. He helped her up. "Are you feeling better?"

"Yes. Thanks. Much."

Kate was sleeping in the middle seat now and the dark had descended.

"No trouble?" Addie asked, resting her head against his shoulder, and he wrapped his arm around hers.

"None. I believe it would be too much to hope for that no one's going to bother us when we reach Yuma Town."

***

They were only about ten minutes from Yuma Town when Dan got a call from Stryker. He suspected it wasn't good news. "Yeah, what's up?"

"They're on the move. The two men at the cabin just left. I suspect they're going to your house. Hal is giving them a head-start and then heading over there. He isn't going to follow them. I'm already at the house."

"What if they don't go to the house? What if they're

planning to ambush us before we reach town?"

"Hal stuck a tracker on their car."

Dan smiled. "Okay, good show. What about the others?"

"They're headed out also. Calvin sent me a text saying they're headed into town. Hal tagged their car too. Jack Barrington's over there now too."

At first, Dan hadn't been sure about the CSF setting up shop in their town, figuring they would have issues over law enforcement matters. Leyton and his team were damn good agents, and he was glad to have them on board. Jack Barrington was on Leyton's team, the newest hire, and he had married his dispatcher and friend, Dottie. He was also combat trained, and he was another great addition to their town. Dottie had new babies, so Dan hadn't asked Jack to get involved. Though once the cabin was rented out to a couple of men who seemed suspicious, Jack had gone over to help protect Shannon and the kids. Knowing Dottie, she would have insisted Jack help out. Not that Jack would have wanted to be left out either. He was as hard-charging as the rest of their law enforcement officials.

"All right. And no one else who seems suspicious is hanging around town?" Dan asked Stryker.

"None that we've noticed. So far. Unless they change course, they're headed to your place from different directions."

"We'll be there in five minutes."

"You're not going to take Addie to the safe house first?"

"No," Addie said. "We go together."

"You heard the federal agent. We're doing this as a team. And no killing, if we can help it. We need to learn who sent them, and make sure they're the bad guys. If the Bureau sent them to protect Addie, us taking them out would be a disaster." Dan didn't want Addie with them in the heat of battle, if it came to that. He also didn't want to leave her off at the safe house if he wasn't going to be there. If they had already been there, then he would have stayed with her to protect her. "Kate and Addie, both of you need to hide until we arrive."

"Agreed," the ladies both said, and laid down on the seats.

"They're parking some distance from the house. I suspect they're moving into the woods around there on foot. Hal and Jack have already parked at the house and are inside with the Muellers," Stryker said. "I have a visual on one of the cars, no sign of the men. I'm moving into the house so we can gather there."

Chase was relaying the information to Travis in the rear car.

Leyton got a call and put it on speaker. "Mrs. Fitz is at the house, carrying boxes of pizza to make it look like they're having a party," Hal said.

"Mrs. Fitz? How did she know about all of this?" Dan asked, surprised as hell.

"You know her. She always seems to know things before we do even. She looks perfectly innocent, all smiles, greeting us," Hal said.

Dan shook his head. "She's full of surprises. Okay, wait for us before anyone takes any action. We see the one car. We'll pull into the driveway. Kate and Addie can remain hidden in the car. I don't want them leaving it, if the men are in the woods watching the house," Dan said. If his Jeep hadn't been parked in the garage, he would have driven this car inside. "We're pulling in now. Everyone ready?"

"Hell, yeah," Chase said. "I doubt they'll begin shooting at the lot of us. More likely, they'll wait until the 'party' is over, and then when the 'guests' all leave, they'll make their move."

"Or plan to," Dan said. "Come on. Let's go before the party is over." Dan leaned over and kissed Addie first and gave her one of his guns. "Be safe and stay here. Kate needs your protection."

"All right. Be safe yourself."

"I've got my gun too," Kate reminded him.

"Good, but stay hidden for now." Dan got another call from Stryker. "They're the bad guys. Calvin sent me a photo he managed to get of the two men at his motel just as they left. He sent them to me, and I ran them through the database. Both are known felons. Hal finally was able to take photos of one of the other men staying at the cabins, and he is also. Not sure on the fourth man, but if they're running together, I'd say it is a pretty sure bet."

"Okay, get the word out. *Now.* No clemency. No get out of jail card. We're taking them down. But, keep someone alive for questioning, if we can do it. Safety first though."

Then the men left the vehicle, and Bridget and Travis left theirs to enter the house.

Addie said to Kate. "Can you really shoot a gun?"

"Yeah, I've been taking a lot of lessons. I have a black belt in martial arts too, but I don't think my current condition allows for me taking anyone down that way. I usually do best with a frying pan in a pinch, but I've got my own gun, and I've had lots of target practice."

Addie smiled. "A frying pan? I'll have to hear that story. Okay, good. I have to tell you hiding like this isn't my favorite aspect of the job, but sometimes it's the most fruitful. I'd like to see what's going on though."

"Do you think the men have night-vision gear?" Kate asked.

"Yeah, they'd have to. It's a good thing we have our own built-in cat's night vision, but they'll be able to see as well as us. The only thing is they won't be looking for cougars."

"Do you think Dan will send some of the men out as cougars?" Kate asked.

"He's smart. I'm sure of it. I'd certainly do it."

They heard a cougar's cry in the woods—one that was meant to scare the crap out of the men, and the women chuckled.

CHAPTER 6

After stripping and shifting, Dan and Chase headed west into the woods in the direction of the men hunkered down. At least that's where they thought they might be. Hal and Stryker had taken off in the opposite direction, searching for the other two men. Leyton was in the house, keeping an eye on the SUV, rifle ready at the partially open window.

Inside the house, loud music was playing, the lights were on inside and out, except for the room where Leyton was serving as a sniper. It sounded like a pizza party was in full swing. He heard Mrs. Fitz laughing inside. Dan hoped Rick and Yvonne were safely inside too. Then he heard Travis and Jack talking loudly on the front porch as if they'd had too much to drink, or were trying to talk over the loud music.

"Dan wants to go fishing at Lake Buchanan tomorrow morning, if Addie's feeling all right," Jack said.

"As long as she has plenty of bedrest," Travis said, "she'll be as good as new. At least in another couple of weeks though, the doctor said."

Jack agreed. "I was surprised Dan wanted to have the party for her homecoming, but he said it would cheer her up."

Travis laughed. "Hell, if I were her, I'd send us all packing. No way can she get any rest at this rate."

"She's on heavy-duty painkillers and out for the count. I'm sure if she hears any of this, it'll be in her dreams," Jack said.

Running through the woods as a cougar, Dan saw one of the men then, the other not visible to him. Chase had moved away from him and vanished so they wouldn't both be seen together. The man was wearing camo gear and night vision goggles. Then Chase let out a blood-curdling cougar cry, and Dan smiled. Good way to rattle whoever he was after.

Dan still wanted to learn who they were working for, but he didn't want anyone taking the risk. If it was a matter of killing or being killed, he opted for taking them out.

Someone fired shots on the other side of the house. Dan thought it had to be one of the felons firing. He didn't think any of their own people were outside running as humans. At least that wasn't the plan. They always had to be ready for any eventuality, so the plan was always fluid. He hoped Travis and Jack were safely inside the house when the shooting began as he prowled toward the man sitting still in the brush where he had a clear view of the house.

Before he could reach him, the man removed his night vision goggles and looked through a device mounted on his automatic rifle. Thermal imaging?

He was looking at the car and getting set up to shoot at

it. He had to have seen Addie and Kate!

Dan leapt and pounced on the man, throwing off his aim. A burst of rounds hit the frame of the SUV, and Dan saw the man's blade as he tried to cut him. Dan went for the guy's throat, tore at it, and killed him. He had to warn the others, Kate and Addie were in danger in the car, if the rest of these men had thermal imaging gear and thought to look at the vehicle they were hiding in.

***

Several rounds struck the bottom edge of the SUV and Addie and Kate gasped. Addie feared she and Kate were in mortal danger out here. "They have to have thermal imaging equipment, Kate. We need to make a run for it. We're sitting ducks out here."

"I'll go first, and draw their fire."

"I think whoever hit the car is dead or he would keep firing. If any of them realize why he shot at the car, the others could focus on the car and see we're here and try too. Can you reach the button to turn off the overhead car lights?"

"Yeah, on it." Kate pushed the button. "Got it."

"Okay, we leave the car at the same time. I've got to be outside to do this, and you probably aren't able to run as fast as you usually could."

"You as well. Okay, on three?"

"Yeah, and leave the doors open. That could give us some cover if the men are at the right locations."

"Okay. One...two...three." Kate pushed her door open at the same time Addie did, and then Kate took a deep breath. "Ready?"

"Yeah, run."

Kate bolted for the house and suddenly the house went dark. Addie assumed that meant those inside were trying to protect her, but the men with night vision goggles, or thermal imaging, could see her too.

Three men burst out of the house—Travis, Jack, and Leyton.

Rounds were fired from the woods and Leyton grabbed Kate and hurried her into the house, his gun readied, just like hers was.

Addie fired a shot into the woods and someone cried out. She couldn't fire again because Jack was suddenly at her side, grabbing her up in his arms, and racing for the house as Travis fired shots in the direction the shooter had cried out. The next thing she knew, Dan was racing across the driveway as a cougar in the direction of the shooter.

She wanted to be with him, protecting his back, but Jack ran her inside, and gun readied, Travis followed Dan into the woods.

A cat snarled nearer the road and she wished the ones in the house would go outside and help the others out.

Then someone crashed through the back door and Bridget turned on the light, blinding the night-vision goggle wearer. He began firing indiscriminately and everyone dove for cover and then fired back from every direction all aimed at the assassin.

The man dropped his assault rifle and fell to the floor. An older woman rushed forward to move his weapon, and ensure he was dead. "He's dead."

Kate confirmed it.

"I'm Yvonne Mueller, and that's my husband, Rick,"

Yvonne said, pointing to the older gentleman. Both were armed to the teeth.

"Retired FBI," Addie said, making the connection, appreciating their help.

"Yes."

"Are you all right, Addie, Kate?" Leyton asked, wrapping his arm around Kate's shoulders and moving her to one of the couches.

"Yeah," both Addie and Kate said.

Dan ran into the house through the back door, shifted, dressed, armed himself, and looked around frantically at all the people there. When he saw Addie sitting on the couch, gun in hand, he rushed across the floor, and lifted her off the couch. "Are you okay?"

"Yes, thanks, Dan."

"We got four men. If there are any more than that, we need to be ready. My house has been compromised. Leyton, I know you don't work for me, but I want you to take Kate home. She's had enough excitement for the last couple of days. We don't want that baby coming prematurely. Hal, you need to be with Tracey and the babies. Jack, same with you. Go home to Dottie. Rick, Yvonne?"

Chase headed inside, and Dan was glad to see he was fine. He shifted and got dressed too.

"We'll return home and keep trying to learn what we can from our friends at the FBI from there," Yvonne said.

"Any word yet from them?" Dan asked.

"Not yet."

Stryker said, "Mrs. Fitz headed home through the woods, saying she'd call once she arrived home."

"She should have waited for us to take her home," Dan said. Then he got a call. "Okay, good. You're home safely." When he ended the call, he said to Addie, "She lives in a Victorian house through the woods near me, which is why I didn't see her car. She must have carried the pizzas from her house."

"Travis and I will secure the house, if Bridget and—" Stryker paused when they heard a car park out front.

An older man came inside. "Hell, I missed all the shooting. I'm Calvin Dixon," he said to Addie. "My wife, Myrtle, and I are owners of the motel on the outskirts of Yuma Town called Cougar Country Motel. Glad to meet you. We finally get to meet Dan's mystery wife."

She raised her brows at Dan.

"I swear I didn't say anything. Mrs. Fitz, the widowed woman, who owns the bakery in town, and our party pizza delivery lady, started the rumors. She saw you entering my house when I wasn't home. Imagine my shock upon returning to find you in my bed, needing medical attention. Then more rumors were flying when Kate had to come by the house."

"Sounds like my mate," Bridget said, winking at Travis. She'd never let him live it down that she'd had to rescue him while she'd been on an assignment.

"We'll take care of the bodies too," Stryker said.

"Where do you want me? With Stryker or to ride shotgun with you, Sheriff?" Calvin asked.

"Why don't you follow us," Dan said, and carried Addie out to his own Jeep, glad it was still in mint condition in the garage.

"I'm headed home to check on Shannon and the kids,"

Chase said.

"Okay, thanks, buddy."

Bridget got in the Jeep with Dan and Addie, and Calvin followed behind them as they headed for the safe house.

"You'll need to tell us who all was on your team, who you think is the most likely suspect, and we can narrow it down from there," Dan told Addie. "I remember an Asian dude, the petite blond, and the prematurely gray-haired guy."

"I will. Did all the men have thermal imaging equipment out here?"

"Just the one I took out. He had been concentrating on the house, then he must have thought to check the SUV and saw two prone bodies. I didn't have time to pounce and kill him before he shot off any rounds, but he lost his target when I knocked off his aim."

"Thank God for that."

"The other man you shot?" Dan asked her.

"Yeah? He was firing at Kate and me."

"You took him out with one shot. Have you had sniper training?"

"Yeah. I was pretty good at it."

"Hell, you're a crack shot. We could really use someone with your talent in the sheriff's office."

"With the Cougar Special Forces Agency too," Bridget hurried to say.

Addie chuckled. "I never thought I'd have two law enforcement agencies fighting over me."

"We help each other out," Dan said. "If you want to work for one and the other agency needs someone with your talent, we'll share."

He noted she wasn't biting at the opportunity to put a bid in for either job. She was about as stubborn as him. She wanted to work for the FBI and resolve this. He damn well hoped that she'd quit them after that and return to them. As friendly as everyone was here, they'd had their fair share of situations requiring rescue missions, and dealing with issues requiring deadly force. Mostly though, when the suspects were cougars.

The shooters' vehicles would be examined for any more clues about the men and who they worked for, though they were career hitmen, so Dan was sure they wouldn't discover anything that would help, either on their person, or left behind in their vehicles. He hoped they'd have better luck with Rick and Yvonne's FBI sources.

As soon as they arrived at the safe house, Bridget and Calvin went inside to make sure it was all clear. Then Calvin came out to signal everything was okay.

"I'm so sorry about your house, Dan," Addie said, as he helped her out of the car.

"The repairs won't take long at all. All that matters is that everyone who should have, lived, and everyone who shouldn't have, died. I doubt we could have gotten anything out of them anyway, as far as useful information. Though I wish we'd had the chance to try," Dan said. "Did you want anything before you go to bed?"

"You," she said, pulling him toward the stairs.

Bridget smiled at Dan.

He knew this was a side no one ever saw of him, yes, protecting damsels in distress, but not protecting one who was an FBI agent, and his pretend mate.

"See you in the morning," Dan said to Bridget and Calvin.

"We've got you covered," Calvin said.

They certainly weren't used to him slipping off to bed with a woman he was protecting, instead of being in charge, giving orders, and planning the whole operation.

He flipped on the switch in one of the bedrooms and the overhead light came on.

"Thank you for soliciting everyone's help," Addie said, pulling off her clothes, and he hurried to help her.

"We wouldn't have done anything differently. Are you going to be all right with sharing the bed with me?"

She smiled up at him. "I will be a very growly cat if you don't."

"That's all I needed to hear. I just didn't want to hurt you in the middle of the night." He hurried to remove his clothes as she climbed into bed naked. He looked over the area where the man had cut her, but it looked like it was healing, no infection, still red, the stitches holding. It would still take several more days to heal to the point where he felt she was out of the woods as far as infection went, or that she could do any vigorous exercise.

"I'm fine," she said, "and I know what you're thinking. And no. It's not going to take long before we can have sex."

He chuckled. "I was thinking of running as cougars and other kinds of vigorous workouts." He didn't want her to think that all he saw in her was a woman he could make love to.

He climbed into bed and moved close to her, cupping her face, kissing her cheeks, her eyes, and then her lips.

She kissed him softly back, and he knew then she really wasn't ready for anything very vigorous. "Can you rest against me?"

"I can try. I want to." Instead of placing her front against him, she moved around so they could spoon. When he pulled her in close to his body, she sighed. "This is so nice. I've wanted to do this since I saw you. Feel your arms wrapped around me. Just cuddling. Until I could work up to more. Soon, though. I'm not waiting long. I've been wanting to see you. Desperately."

"Same here, honey. I tried to pretend you didn't exist. That you're just a figment of my imagination so I wouldn't be thinking of you all the time. To get on with my life without you. It's never worked for me."

"Good. I wouldn't want to think you weren't holding up your end of the bargain. Just so you know, I was aware you were keeping Dottie company."

He smiled. "Been checking up on me, eh?"

"I told you. You couldn't be seeing anyone, dating, or marrying. It would have been too dangerous for her. Then I learned about the guy she hooked up with, Jack Barrington? And that he was the real love of her life, so you were off the hook and I didn't have to order a hit on you."

Dan laughed. "I thought I was just supposed to sign on the dotted line to divorce you."

She chuckled. "There's divorce. And then there's...divorce. Besides, I'd learned they'd been together before she moved back to Yuma Town and had his kids. I helped him to learn about it."

"Why, you minx."

"Just doing my job as a good, honest, upright public servant. And keeping you out of trouble."

He chuckled.

"I missed you. If it hadn't been for the hit on me six months ago, and now this, I would have returned sooner to see you. I hadn't planned to get you involved in all of this."

"Since the moment you targeted me at the Hamburger Stop, I became involved. And I'm still your husband."

She sighed. "You have no idea what we're up against."

"I agree."

"It could get deadly."

"Most probably."

"I don't want to lose you. Not as a faux husband, and an agent undercover, but you."

"I don't want to lose you either, which is why I'm in this for the long haul. We'll figure this out, take down the bad guys, and you can work for me."

She laughed. "All you want is another warm body at the sheriff's office."

"I want your warm body right here with me whenever we're off the job."

"Writing out traffic tickets on the job."

"Hell, Stryker would be grateful if you chased down the really bad guys, and he continued to help rescue cats from trees."

She laughed. "Oh, I bet he'd love to hear you say that. He seemed upset he couldn't be in the thick of things. I think if he always got to rescue cats from trees, he'd really be ticked off."

"It's his fault. He's really good at the job."

She chuckled and ran her hand over Dan's arm wrapped around her. "I missed this with you."

"Ditto, honey." He sighed. "What will your boss think of you not showing up for work or reporting in?"

"After I returned to work following six months of hiding out and recuperating the last time, I'm sure he'll figure I'll do the same thing this time."

"I can't believe he's unaware that something's wrong with his organization. With the team. He knew you were injured both times, right? Then you disappear? Does he even have anyone looking for you?" Dan couldn't believe what was going on with her team and no one seemed to care.

"I had to see the Bureau psychologist when I returned, to determine if I could go back to work. She okayed me. I have to tell you I've been having trouble with night terrors. It won't be any picnic for you. I might wake up screaming or beating you. I might even go for my gun."

"Huh." Dan slipped out of bed.

"Sounds like I might be a little too rough on you?"

He smiled and retrieved his gun that he'd loaned to her from where she had set it on her bedside table. "I'm going to just keep them safe over here. Out of your reach. Just in case."

"Smart man."

"I don't want them too far out of reach in case we have more trouble." He settled back in bed with her and pulled her close. "Did your boss even question you about where you were or what had happened?"

"Sure. I told him I had amnesia at first. He suspected I was lying. I told him the story repeatedly, and almost had myself believing it. Then I figured if he was the bad guy, he'd have already gotten rid of me."

"Unless he figured by keeping you close, he could keep an eye on you, and the next assignment you had, get rid of you then. It would have just been a case of the suspect murdering you. No involvement from anyone on the team. Or so it would look."

"Which means I must know something that they don't want to get out. I can't figure out what though. I told my boss we had a mole on our team. I was hoping for all the backup I could get on this. He didn't agree and said it was just one of those things that happens. Someone let it slip about where the meetup was going to be. Someone overheard. Or even I made the mistake. I went over it a million times in my mind, but I don't see where I would have. I don't go out drinking with people, don't talk about my business with anyone. I didn't tell anyone about the meeting."

"Except you talk to me."

"You didn't know about that meeting. It couldn't have been you."

"Good to know."

"Yeah, Dan. I know you're one of the good guys. All growly and ready to protect my back, no matter what. I trust you with my life."

"You just didn't trust my life in your hands."

"You don't know how ruthless these people are."

"I think I have an inkling."

"Well, yes, now you do." She sighed. "There are five other members on the team. We've only worked together for the past six months. I don't really know any of them well. We don't socialize. I don't know if they're married, have families, whether they go to church, or play softball. I don't know anything about them at all."

"Okay, well, we need to give their names to Yvonne and Rick and they'll try to track down as much as they can about them. Do you suspect any one of them more than any of the others?"

"No. Not really."

"I would say that the likelihood it was just a mistake, something that just happened could have been a possibility, until you returned to work and someone tried to kill you on another courier mission. Was it related to the one six months earlier?"

"I didn't think so, but now I'm wondering if it did."

He wondered about Addie's mother too. "What if your mom's disappearance had something to do with her trying to protect you and your father from the work she was doing?"

"I would say no. That was so many years earlier."

He wasn't going to dismiss it. "Get some sleep, honey, and we'll talk about it some more tomorrow."

What he wasn't expecting her to do in the middle of the night was to begin rubbing her soft body against his, kissing him, wanting to make love.

CHAPTER 7

Dan was up bright and early, eager to get somewhere with this case while Addie slept. He couldn't believe she'd wanted to make love to him last night and he'd resisted, momentarily, but when she got all growly with him, reminding him of her divorce option, he had obliged. Happily.

He loved her. And he was glad she had been feeling well enough to make love, but he worried that's why she was sleeping so late this morning—she'd overdone it.

Bridget gave him a warm smile and handed him a cup of coffee. "Is Addie still asleep?"

"Yeah. Where's Travis?"

"Talking to Stryker out front. They didn't want to disturb the two of you." She set a plate of pancakes on the table. "She must have been feeling better last night."

"Yeah, but you have creaky, damn box springs." Dan sat down to eat. "Is anyone else joining me?"

"Uh, we noticed on the box springs, but we're glad she's

feeling better. We already ate. I'm just serving as the kitchen staff this morning until everyone's happily fed."

"Thanks, Bridget. What are they discussing? I guess everyone's been keeping me out of the loop or I would have gotten some traffic on my phone by now." He took a bite of the pancakes smothered in blueberries, butter, and maple syrup.

"Unless it was an emergency, or you had a need to know right that moment, no one wanted to disturb you. Not when you were...mostly sleeping with Addie."

"She couldn't keep her hands off me. I had to do something to help her get back to sleep."

"It's true," Addie said, coming down the stairs. "Boy, did those box springs make a racket, particularly with our sensitive hearing. I hope we didn't disturb your sleep too much."

Bridget smiled. "We were on guard duty, so it made life interesting. I picked up some clothes for you at one of the stores. You're about my size, so they should fit. As soon as you're feeling better, Dan can take you shopping for some things."

"Yeah, sure thing. I hadn't even thought of that. I need to pick up some things from my place too," Dan said.

"Would you like some coffee?" Bridget asked Addie.

"Yeah, sure, thanks."

"Sugar, cream or milk? Half and half?"

"Hmm, yes."

Dan rose to take Addie in his arms and kiss her while Bridget made her a cup of coffee.

"Are pancakes all right?" Bridget asked.

"Yes, ma'am, if they look like Dan's."

"Coming right up." Bridget set her coffee on the table.

"Thanks, Bridget." Addie kissed Dan back, her arms wrapped around his neck, her breasts pressed against his chest.

He swore she wanted more loving. If they didn't have this business to deal with, he would have hauled her back up to the bedroom. He led her to the seat next to him instead.

"What's been discussed while I was sleeping my life away?" Addie sipped some of her coffee.

"Nothing. I just got down here and other than talking about noisy box springs, that's about all we've discussed."

Addie smiled.

Bridget served her a plate of pancakes.

"They've been holding all of my calls so I wouldn't disturb your sleep last night."

"I'll let the guys know you're up and can come in and talk about any news they have. This place was really quiet last night." Bridget joined Stryker and Travis outside.

Then the three of them came inside and sat down at the coffee table while Dan and Addie finished up breakfast and then moved into the living room.

"I think we should call your boss and tell him the trouble you've had," Dan said to Addie as they sat next to each other on the couch.

"He'll say it's all in my head, or that it's my fault somehow."

"There are too many of us involved who know what went down. Don't mention us. Just let him know your guard detail standing outside your door vanished and you weren't staying."

"You talked to my boss. Briggs? Right?"

"Yeah, to get him to tell Leipheimer to let me into your room to see you. He said I had five minutes. I was grateful when I had a lot more time with you. I began to think that either he was a lot more sentimental than I thought or that it was odd. The nurse came to give you a shot, and I asked about the agent serving as your guard, but she said there wasn't one. And the men coming into the room after that weren't security officers. What if Leipheimer wasn't an agent? What if, when he handed me the phone to talk to your boss, I didn't even speak to Briggs? Just some random guy?"

Stryker handed her a burner phone. "I suspect they know you're here still. Not exactly where. I agree with Dan. Talk to Briggs and see what he says about this. He might not even realize you're alive, and were taken to the hospital, or any of it."

"If they hadn't wanted me to live, why would someone have taken me to the hospital?"

"Maybe it was someone else? A bystander who called it in? Then what could the ones who want you dead do about it?" Dan asked. "Nothing, until you were alone in a hospital room all drugged up."

"And the agent outside my door?"

Dan shrugged. "He might have been legitimate, and someone killed him, or he was paid to leave. Or he might have been a fake. I didn't ask to see his badge. I just assumed if he was standing outside your door acting like a federal agent, that's what he was. He didn't ask to see my ID either."

"You were dressed as a sheriff, cowboy hat and all."

"Yeah, but see? By wearing the right clothes, we all assumed we knew what the other was claiming to be."

"All right." Addie took the phone and called her boss. When he answered, she put it on speaker. "Sir, it's me, Addie Steinacker."

"Where the hell have you been? What the hell happened with you as far as picking up the information from the courier? You just pulled another disappearing act? This is the last straw, agent."

She looked at Dan with an expression that said she told him so. "You know an assailant killed the courier using a dagger on him before the courier reached me, don't you? I heard his cry and I ran to check it out, afraid the courier was being attacked. He was already dead by the time I reached him. I chased down the assailant and he managed to stab me, but I got a round off and killed him—point blank shot to the temple. Paris and Dirk were there seeing to the courier. The armed assailant had the manila envelope, which I assume contained the information we were after."

Briggs didn't say anything.

"Okay, listen, I couldn't have left there on my own if I'd wanted to. I was completely out of it. Someone had to have called 911 and I was picked up and taken to the nearest hospital before anyone could finish me off."

"All I know is the courier never showed up. You vanished. The information was gone. There were no bodies at all—no one stabbed, no one shot."

Stryker was shaking his head. Dan was rubbing her back, but Addie didn't act in the least bit flustered.

"Dirk and Paris didn't tell you what happened? Dirk

yelled at me to wait for backup, but he didn't leave Paris with the dead courier to provide backup either."

"I'll talk to both of them and check out the hospital where you were staying."

"Don't bother. Two faux security officers and a pretend nurse tried to kill me there, but I'm sure you won't find them either. Or any record of my stay there. I never saw any of it on the news, so I imagine cleaners came and scrubbed the place. Oh, and I suppose you didn't have an agent named Leipheimer guarding my room."

"I've never heard of him and I couldn't assign anyone to your room for your protection when I didn't know that you'd been taken to a hospital, now could I?"

"Either we've got a mole on the team, or you're the one orchestrating this," she said, still fully in control, holding her temper.

"Or you need long-term psychiatric care."

"Well, since I've found witnesses who can testify to what they've witnessed, that theory won't fly."

"Where are you now? I'll have someone pick you up and bring you in. If what you say is true, I'll put you in a safe house."

"Thanks." She hung up on him and handed the phone to Stryker. "I told you it wouldn't help. He didn't believe me the last time either."

"Because he's involved? Or because these people are covering their tracks so well?" Dan asked.

"Notice how he asked where she was?" Travis said. "If he already knew, he wouldn't be asking."

"Unless he's pretending he doesn't know," Stryker said.

"I don't think he knew," Bridget said. "I think he was furious with Addie for not bringing in the information, maybe even fearing she had other plans for it. I got the impression he really hadn't thought she'd been in trouble."

"I agree with you," Addie said. "I still can't completely put my trust in him, but I think the business with the hospital and that he didn't know the agent who was guarding my room, said a lot. And though he sounds like he's in denial about the existence of a mole, or that I'd been hurt, I'd bet a year's worth of wages he's going to check out the park and see if he can find any evidence of foul play."

"Will he send someone else out to look for clues?" Dan asked. "If he does, and he sends the wrong person out, they're liable to find no evidence at all."

"No. He's pretty hands on, and in a situation like this, when it's possible we really have a mole, I suspect he'll investigate it himself. And check out the hospital too."

"What if he's in danger for investigating this on his own?" Bridget asked.

Addie motioned for Stryker to give her the phone and called her boss again. "When you look for evidence that I'm telling you the truth, watch your step. They followed me here, and we had a shootout. None of them lived, that we know of. They're professional hitmen. These guys mean business and if you're not the mole, I don't want to learn you vanished too." Then she hung up on Briggs again and handed the phone back to Stryker.

Stryker smiled. "If she's done being your pseudo-wife, Dan, she can be mine."

"Wow, between all the job offers, and now pseudo-marital offers, I seem to be a hot commodity. You all must not get a lot of excitement around here."

"You have no idea," Bridget said.

"You're hot, all right," Dan said. "And *not* on the marital mart. We have a contract."

Someone knocked on the door and Travis and Bridget headed for it together. Stryker, Dan, and Addie pulled their guns out.

"Just Yvonne and Rick," Travis said.

Dan waited to holster his gun until they were inside the house and Travis had locked the door.

"Any news?" Dan asked.

"Have we ever," Yvonne said.

Bridget got everyone fresh coffee as they settled in the living room.

"I talked to my boss," Addie said, updating them on that front. "He didn't know I'd been stabbed or taken to the hospital. Only that I'd vanished and the courier had too. He's going to investigate it."

"Sounds like there's really a breakdown in your department," Rick said.

"Yeah, and we have some shocking news. Your mother, Alicia Shields, is your boss's boss," Yvonne said.

Addie's jaw dropped and tears sprang into her eyes. She couldn't believe her mother had been so close to her as far as the job situation went, yet had never reached out to her.

"Then we need to get hold of her and tell her what's going on. If Briggs didn't have anything to do with your injuries, then surely, Alicia hasn't either," Dan said.

"I wonder if that's why I was selected for this task force,"

Addie said. "Maybe that's why I was even hired on at the Bureau. Both my father and mother were agents."

"And because she trusts you," Yvonne said, then sipped her coffee.

"Why not get hold of you then and let you know that she knows you're working on the task force?" Stryker asked. "And, hell, why wouldn't she know what's going on with you? You'd think she'd have an eye on you."

"Briggs said contracting out to a 'civilian' to serve as my husband wasn't his idea."

"Then it was your mother's idea?" Dan asked. "Who all did she have on the list of names for possible candidates?"

"They were all former military—Special Forces. I turned down the first dozen because I was looking for—"

"Me," Dan said, sitting up taller.

Everyone laughed.

"You were number thirteen on the list. Then Hal, Stryker, and Chase were listed after that. Even Leyton was on the list."

"I can't believe I was on the list and you didn't reject him first. Or that my brother was on the list too. Though back then I didn't even know he was my brother. Were the others cougars?" Stryker asked.

"No. Dan was the first on the list who was a cougar."

"She still would have chosen me over the rest of you guys," Dan said, looking as serious as could be.

"I wasn't on the list?" Travis asked.

Bridget punched him in the shoulder.

He laughed.

"What I want to know is why your mother would have

set this up for you to have a pseudo husband who wasn't an agent," Yvonne said.

"I think we have our answer already. Either your mother, or someone else higher up, suspected there was trouble in the Bureau and wanted to get someone who was highly combat-trained, but also who wasn't part of the Bureau, to watch over Addie in the event there is a mole," Dan said.

"We have a number for Alicia Shields. It's a private number, so she might not answer it, if she doesn't know who's calling," Rick said.

"She might not take the call even if she does know who is calling," Addie said, annoyed with her mother for dropping out of her life, even if she thought she was protecting Addie and her father. If she pulled Addie in to do this job and now Addie's life was in danger, that didn't make any sense.

"Why would she pick potential pretend husbands for you who weren't cougars?" Yvonne asked.

"She knew I wouldn't accept any of them, probably, but no one else would know that."

"Once they knew who it was, he would be in as much danger as you," Travis said.

"Only when I was injured and dropped into his life again." She squeezed Dan's hand, loving him for being so patient with her.

Dan got a call from Ricky Jones, one of the boys Hal had taken in to work on his ranch, who was a fairly newly turned cougar and former informant for his wife while she was working to locate animal traffickers.

"Yeah, Ricky, what's up?"

"Hey, Sheriff, Kolby and I were looking over the crime scene. Yeah, yeah, I know we're not supposed to be over at your house, but no one's paying any attention to it while they clean up the mess the shooters made of it and replace your back door and—"

"Did you find something?" The kid was a great kid, and he wanted to be in the same business as Tracey and now Hal were. When he was older, Dan was sure he'd do a super job. Getting to the point of the matter was always an ordeal with Ricky.

"Yeah, you know, there isn't any yellow tape showing a crime scene, but my brother and I used our noses to search all over the place and we found a piece of paper half buried by leaves. You know, people just tromped all over the place, removing bodies, and just made a mess of everything and so it's no wonder no one found it."

"The piece of paper? What did it say?"

"It had a name on it. The grass and leaves were damp and so, you know, the note was damp and the ink is blurred but I could still make it out and all that was on it was a name: Alicia Shields."

CHAPTER 8

"It doesn't mean your mother was involved in hiring the men to take you out," Dan said to Addie, feeling terrible for her and ready to take out her mother, if she was responsible for the attempted hits on Addie.

Addie shook her head. "I know she didn't. Why would the piece of paper be found lying on the ground? Why wouldn't the assassin have it in his pocket? And why have it at all? The name isn't hard to remember. He wouldn't need to carry it with him. I doubt assassins carry information with them that would identify who hired them. At least, none that I've ever dealt with have."

"Then it's a setup to put us on her trail. Maybe so we'd go after her next," Dan said. "Give me her number. I'll call her. I was on her list. She must have seen something in me that told her I could keep you safe."

Addie snorted.

Dan raised a brow and smiled a little.

"I don't mean that you couldn't keep me safe. You did. But that my mother wished it?"

"That's what we need to find out." Dan took the phone number for Addie's mother and called it. He got an answering machine. Naturally. "Hello, I'm Sheriff Dan Steinacker of Yuma Town, Colorado, and I'm working with your daughter, Addie. For now, I'm keeping her—" The message machine cut off. "Hell."

"Message machine?" Addie said.

"Yeah. She's sure to know my number so if she doesn't return the call by tonight, I'll call her back. Did you learn anything else?" Dan asked Yvonne and Rick.

"Still working on leads. We've got a couple of people checking into several queries we had. The men were known assassins. Why they would want Addie dead is a mystery. Why not just kill her anytime?"

"After I was targeted the first time, I disappeared for good. I had only been back at the job for two days, had another courier meeting, and the same result—an assassination attempt on my life. I never had any trouble before this."

"Then it has to be something to do with the last two assignments you had," Rick said. "That's when everything changed for you. Not when you began working with Dan. Unless the person who arranged for that to happen knew it would come to this and so set the plans in motion early on to have a protector for you."

"Did anyone ever try to convince you to leave the Bureau?" Yvonne asked.

"No, and I've enjoyed working for it. It's just been the

last six months, and really just these two cases, that have made me reconsider working for the Bureau. If every assignment you get, someone's targeting you, there's no fun in that."

"These are the only two cases you've had when you were targeted," Dan said.

"True. In the past, I always had the upper hand. I was targeting the perp, and getting my man, or woman, as the case might be."

Someone unlocked the front door and everyone pulled guns.

Leyton smiled, walked inside the house, and locked the door. "Glad to know everyone's on high alert. How are you feeling, Addie?"

"Much better," she said. "Thank you. How's Kate?"

"Good. She went in late to work today. No emergencies." Leyton took a seat on one of the chairs and they filled him in about Addie's mother and the note Ricky had found.

Chase called Dan from the sheriff's office after that and he put it on speaker. "We've got a problem. That pesky reporter from Denver, Carl Nelson, was snooping around, heard gunshots fired, and was looking for a story."

"Just tell him we were hunting on my property. Was he on my property? Arrest him for trespassing if he's still around."

"Will do if I see him around your place again. He left after I spoke with him. He was eyeing the work being done on your place to repair things. No one was talking to him about anything. Not that anyone working on the repairs really knew what had gone down."

"Hell, I thought he wouldn't ever show his face around here again after all the trouble we had with protecting Shannon from being his front-page news story."

"Don't I know it. I thought we'd run him out of town for good, but he just happened to be driving through town when he heard all the gunfire."

"Wait, you know him. If he heard the gunfire, he would have hunkered down to watch what was going on."

"Okay. I'll check it out. If he left his scent in the area, then what?"

"He could have been video recording the whole thing."

"Not without a camera equipped with night-vision ability." Chase paused. "Hell. He could have taken video of us fighting the men as cougars."

"Removing the bodies. Not reporting it. Find out where he is now!"

"And arrest him?"

"Yeah."

"We've also got a single car wreck out by Dottie's place. Do you want me to take care of it too?"

"I'll get on it," Stryker said.

"Thanks, Chase, Stryker, for helping to hold down the fort on the sheriffing business." Dan's thoughts were so tied up in the business with Addie, it was hard to think of anything else.

"That would be great. If Stryker has a minute, there's a cat in a tree he can rescue too," Chase said.

Dan smiled.

Stryker shook his head. "Chase is doing some real

deputy sheriff business and I'm stuck getting a cat out of a tree." Stryker rose from his chair. "I'll look for Carl Nelson while I'm at it."

Dan swore Stryker liked how a couple of their older cougar widows always asked for him, even if he pretended not to want to waste his time over it, knowing perfectly well the cats would get down on their own.

"Keep me posted, and while I'm rescuing a cat, if I see anything suspicious with regard to Addie, I'll call it in." Stryker left then.

"We'll keep looking into the Bureau situation," Yvonne said and Rick agreed. They left then too.

Leyton leaned back in his chair. "If anyone needs to do anything else, run errands, or whatever, feel free to. Kate's working at the clinic now, and I'm free to do guard duty. Unless you need me to take down a reporter."

"Chase will call up everyone to make them aware we've got a potential ticking time bomb running loose. Unless Carl tore off for Denver, my bet is he's still here looking for more details. I'll give him credit for that, at least. He's a good investigative reporter. Only we sure as hell don't need him reporting on anything here."

"Agreed," Leyton said.

"I need some more groceries," Bridget said. "Is there anything you'd like, Addie?"

She shook her head. "We'll probably be returning to Dan's house soon, won't we?"

"Only if we have some extra firepower," Dan said. "I think for now, even after we get the house repaired, we should stay here. The likelihood that someone else would come for you at my house would be greater."

"I can't believe you're a brunette, after Mrs. Fitz said she saw a blond enter your house," Leyton said.

"A wig. I was incognito. I'm glad she was fooled then."

"She has an eagle eye. I'm surprised she didn't realize it wasn't natural," Bridget said. "I really expected a blond too." She grabbed up her purse and headed for the front door when someone knocked. She pulled out her gun and continued to the door. When she looked out the peephole, she shook her head. "Speak of the devil, it's Mrs. Fitz, Florence Fitzgerald, bringing pastries from her shop, no doubt, to learn more about what's going on." She opened the door. "Why, Mrs. Fitz, how lovely to see you again."

"After last night's escapade, and knowing you'd all be here, and with so many dropping in and out, I thought I'd bring by some cupcakes, cookies, and other pastries to celebrate having a new cougar in town."

"Thank you," Bridget said.

Dan knew Mrs. Fitz wanted to come in and meet the mystery woman, since she left last night before she could do so. He should have said no to it, but she always knew the gossip of what was going on in town even before they knew it. She could be a valuable resource.

"Bridget was on her way out to do some grocery shopping. Come on in, Mrs. Fitz, and have some coffee with us," Dan said.

"Oh, my, certainly, thank you." Silver-haired, and always smiling, Mrs. Fitz hurried to join them while Bridget grabbed a couple of chocolate-chip cookies, thanked her, and left.

"This is Addie, my guest, and as you're well-aware,

we've had a bit of trouble. She's a federal agent with the FBI," Dan said. "She's been injured and we're taking care of her."

Mrs. Fitz's blue eyes widened. Then she hurried to offer the treats to everyone, like the perfect hostess would.

Addie selected an apple turnover and thanked her.

Leyton declined. "Kate said she's eating for two, but I wasn't allowed to."

Everyone laughed.

Travis helped himself to a chocolate-frosted, chocolate cupcake.

Dan thanked her, but said he'd have something later. He needed to get down to business. "All right, so Chase has put out the word that we need some help locating that reporter, Carl Nelson. He might have gotten some video of us as cougars last night when we had so much trouble at my house."

"Oh, no," Mrs. Fitz said.

"Right. That's bad news. Everyone usually ends up at your place sometime or another, so if he shows up, let us know, but don't let on you're calling us about him."

"He was there this morning already. He asked me a million questions. I told him I'd tell him anything I learned, but that I didn't know what had happened. Which is why I came by here bearing treats, in case he's watching to see where I go. Of course, I'd never tell him anything you didn't want him to know, which is why I wanted to learn what it is you want me to share."

"Thanks, Mrs. Fitz. It's a dangerous business," Dan said.

"Absolutely. What is it that you want me to say?"

"Just that federal agents are involved, and it's an

ongoing investigation. Which is the truth."

"What about Addie's identity?"

"No. We'll keep quiet about that."

"All right." Mrs. Fitz slapped her lap, a smile stretched across her face. "I'm going to get out of your hair so you can take care of this business." She stood, then leaned over and gave Addie a hug. "Welcome, dear. I hope you're going to stay around for a while longer this time."

Dan stared at Mrs. Fitz. She couldn't have known Addie was the same woman who came to his place six months ago.

Mrs. Fitz smiled and whispered conspiratorially to them. "Something you might want to know about me. I'm a former CIA operative. So was my husband, Ralph. We were both retired. I know everything that goes on. It's hard to let go of all the training I've had in the business. If you run out of treats, let me know and I'll drop them off, being that you might not be able to leave here for the time being." She smiled brightly.

Dan swore everyone was gaping at her, like he was, but then he thought she had to be teasing.

Leyton escorted her to the door so he could lock up after her. "CIA," Leyton said, smiling at her.

"Yeah, who would have thought it." She smiled up at him. "Having the bakery was my dream occupation once I left the Agency as well as being among my own kind again. Your secrets are safe with me." Then Mrs. Fitz patted him on the chest and left.

"Well, hell, I wondered why I always liked the old gal," Dan said, figuring she was telling the truth.

"Maybe she's got some friends in the CIA who could

check this out," Leyton said.

Dan got a call from Chase and put the phone on speaker. "Yeah, Chase?"

"Ricky and Kolby are out at your place looking around for Carl's scent, and they found he'd been all over the place. We can't determine when exactly though. Last night? Or sometime today?"

"All right. That's what I figured."

"It's okay if the boys are out there looking for any other evidence, isn't it? They didn't want to get into trouble with you."

Dan snorted. "They think to ask now?"

Chase laughed. "Yeah, I know."

"Mrs. Fitz just dropped by with some treats and gave us a heads up on Carl. He's trying to learn what he can about what went on last night." Dan told Chase what the story would be. "She also dropped a bomb. She says she's a retired CIA operative."

"What? Do you believe her?"

Dan got another cup of coffee to go with a vanilla cupcake covered in maple frosting. "Knowing Mrs. Fitz, I wouldn't be surprised. She seems to know so much of what's going on way before we do, sometimes. She seemed to realize Addie was the one who came to see me, and that she hadn't really been a blond."

"Well, I'll be. She was helping to cover for her, even back then."

"Seems like it."

"Way to go, Mrs. Fitz," Chase said.

"I'm still shocked at the revelation. Have you seen any

sign of Carl?" Dan asked.

"No, but since the call went out, I've been hearing from tons of people who either have seen him or who have fielded his questions."

"Okay, well, keep me posted."

"Will do."

When they ended the call, Dan called Addie's mother again, but it just went to voicemail.

***

"Until the next storm hits, I think I'll lie down for a while." Addie couldn't believe the woman who had brought pizzas to the shootout last night was Flo, her mom's old friend, and that now she was operating a bakery in Yuma Town. She never would have connected her with the name Mrs. Fitz, or Florence Fitzgerald. Her mom had only introduced her as Flo and that was it.

"Need any company?" Dan asked.

She chuckled. "Tonight. For now, I think I'll sleep better, alone."

"All right." Dan turned to Leyton. "Do you have a less squeaky bed?"

Leyton laughed. "The one I used at the end of the hall is nice and quiet."

Addie said, "We're moving to it." Then she disappeared upstairs. She hated feeling this out of it, just like the last time when the assassin had tried to kill her.

She had business to take care of too. She found a home phone in the bedroom and used it to call Mrs. Fitz's Bakery. "Hello, Flo? It's me, Addie. It's been a long time since I last saw you. What do you know about my mother?"

CHAPTER 9

Ricky Jones owed everything to Tracey and Hal Haverton, but also to so many others in Yuma Town. They had saved his brother's life. And they'd saved his. Here, all he'd been was an informant, dreaming of being an agent who took down wildlife traffickers just like Tracey did. And then Hal too. He liked what the guys in the sheriff's office got to do too. Then Leyton and his agents came along and he was torn between doing their kind of work: taking down murderous, rogue cougars. Though he still was a bit miffed that Leyton had swept Kate off her feet. Well, and he'd had a giant crush on Tracey too, while he worked as her informant, before he'd been turned, and Hal had mated her. See? The agent always got the girl.

Maybe Ricky could be the sheriff someday when Dan retired. He loved being a cougar. Newly turned still, though he and his brother were getting a lot better at controlling their shifting. He loved the townspeople who had welcomed him and Kolby into their hearts, since they'd had no family left of their own.

He was curious about the woman Dan was protecting. He'd seen Mrs. Fitz and she said the beautiful woman was an FBI agent. In the worst way, he wanted to see her. He didn't think he could do that kind of work. Not when he was newly turned. Living and working among the cougars, no problem.

For now, though, he and his brother were running as cougars in the woods around Dan's house to try to locate where the news reporter had trekked. He wanted in the worst way to find something useful for Dan and the she-cat. He missed doing the clandestine work for Tracey.

Ricky and his brother could look for clues in the woods a lot easier when they were cougars with their noses to the ground. They had to do ranching chores on Hal's horse ranch after that, so they had to do this quickly and then come back tomorrow and search some more.

Even though they were working at the ranch to earn their keep, everyone had been teaching them hand-to-hand combat and weapons' qualifications training for when Ricky and his brother were old enough to work at law enforcement pursuits. They loved the horses though too. As long as Ricky didn't have to babysit all the new Haverton babies, he was fine. Of course, when the kids were older, he was all set to teach them how to ride.

Then he heard someone walking around the woods, the leaves crunching beneath his feet. He went to see who it was, figuring it was Chase or Stryker. What he hadn't expected to see was the reporter with a gun in one hand, and a camera hanging from around his neck.

Ricky held very still, half hidden in the brush, but he should blend in perfectly with his surroundings if he didn't move. Then Kolby came running out of the brush, and Ricky couldn't warn him in time to watch out for the armed reporter. He knew his brother had come in search of him and knew he'd get shot. Ricky leapt as far as a cougar could as the reporter fired off a shot.

Ricky slammed into him, taking him down to the ground, the man crying out. He still had hold of the gun and lifted it to shoot Ricky. Ricky knew Hal and Dan would want to kill Ricky for what he was about to do. The reporter fired another shot and the bullet slammed into Ricky's chest. Ricky bit the reporter's wrist, hard, drawing blood. The reporter yelled out and dropped the weapon, but Ricky collapsed on the man. Ricky had been hit and he was just beginning to feel the excruciating pain. Ricky knew he would be in *so* much trouble now.

Kolby was there in a heartbeat, the reporter managing to get the gun again, but Kolby bit the reporter in the wrist this time as he fired another shot off, but the bullet pinged against a nearby tree.

Ricky hoped that would be the end of the reporter grabbing for his gun again, his own strength dwindling.

Ricky knew the reporter believed he was fighting for his life in the face of a couple of man-eating cougars, so he didn't blame him. If he had been the reporter, he would have reacted in the same way. Ricky's head seemed to suddenly weigh a ton, and he dropped his head on the man's chest, unable to hold it up any longer.

The reporter had passed out. Maybe from sheer fright.

Maybe from being bitten.

Kolby moved in beside Ricky and began licking his cheek, trying to stir him. He stared at his brother, but even his eyelids grew too heavy, and he finally just shut them, grinding his teeth against the pain in his chest.

This was one problem with being in law enforcement. Even if he wasn't there quite yet. Taking a bullet that hurt like hell wasn't something he really thought he could get used to. Saving his brother's life? He was always on the front line for that.

***

Dan got the call from Chase that shots had been fired at Dan's home and he said, "I'm on my way." He raced up the stairs to tell Addie he was needed at his place, worried the assassins were targeting the workmen.

"I thought it was another assassination attempt, someone believing you and Addie were at the house, but Ricky was shot. The ambulance is here. Just meet us at the clinic," Chase said.

"What happened?"

"Carl shot Ricky."

"The damned reporter? What the hell? Did you read the bastard his rights? Is he in jail by now? How is Ricky?" Dan said, "Just a second."

Addie was sitting up in bed. "What's happened?"

"That reporter shot Ricky, the boy who works for the Havertons at their ranch. I'm running over to the clinic. Ricky should be there soon."

"I'm coming with you."

"Are you sure?"

"Yeah, I'm not going to sit in bed forever. I'm feeling better. I can rest afterward."

Dan put the phone on speaker and set it on the table while he helped Addie get dressed. "Okay, tell me exactly what happened." He suspected Ricky had found Carl and told him to get off the property, maybe threatened him when the man wouldn't listen to him, and Carl shot him.

"No, I didn't read him his rights. Ricky bit him."

"What?" Dan couldn't have heard Chase correctly. A wind was blowing outside where Chase was and making a lot of noise on the phone, despite how good their hearing was.

"Yeah, Ricky and his brother were running in the woods as cougars."

"In broad daylight?"

"It's heavily wooded around your home and no one was supposed to be there, other than us."

"Carl shot Ricky?" Now Dan understood why Chase hadn't read Carl his rights. He could still charge him with trespassing and endangerment to wildlife. "How bad is Ricky?"

"Kate's working on him. We won't know until she comes out of the operating room. Kolby is pacing around the hallway ready to bite Carl again, only fatally this time. I just arrived at the clinic."

"You said Ricky bit him."

"Yeah. The first time, to make him drop his weapon. He was going to shoot Kolby. Ricky had to make Carl drop his weapon, which he did, but not before he shot Ricky. Then when Kolby came to Ricky's aid, Carl picked up the gun again, and Kolby bit him this time. He said he'd do it again too."

"Hell. If there's one person I never wanted to see again in Yuma Town or anywhere else, for that matter, is Carl Nelson."

"That makes the two of us. I'm calling Tracey and Hal now to come see Ricky and talk with Kolby as soon as you're here."

Dan and Addie got in his Jeep and he roared around to the next street over where the clinic was. "We're at the clinic, just getting out of the Jeep."

"What about Addie?"

"Yeah, she's with me. She didn't want to be left behind." Dan escorted her into the clinic and met Chase in the lobby.

Ricky's brother, Kolby, saw Dan and hurried to speak with him, wiping tears off his cheeks. "I'm so sorry. I'm...I'm sorry."

"We protect our own," Dan said, squeezing his shoulder. "You were trying to help. Carl is at fault over this. Hal and Tracey will be here shortly."

"They'll want to kill me too."

Chase shook his head. "You did what you had to do. Any of us would have done the same."

Kolby gave a derisive laugh. "You would have terminated him."

"Probably," Chase said, "after having dealt with Carl before."

"Where's Carl?" Dan asked.

Chase motioned to room one. "He's handcuffed to a bed. And we've got all his video and camera equipment. And his phone. Travis came to pick it up and learn what information he has on us. The nurse has seen to Carl. Kate's still working on Ricky."

Dan frowned as he headed for Carl's room. "Ricky's going to pull through though, isn't he?"

"We won't know until Kate tells us the prognosis," Chase said, his voice full of worry.

"He'd better," Dan said, and stalked into Carl's room, but Addie stayed outside in the hallway with Kolby.

Chase remained with Addie to protect her, in case anyone showed up at the clinic who shouldn't.

"Buchanan told you what happened to me, didn't he?" Carl said, his eyes narrowed, his wrist bandaged, and an IV attached to his other hand.

"He sure as hell did. You were trespassing on my property—again."

"Hey, I know when there's a story to be found. And you are shit deep in trouble. Dead men who disappear in the middle of the night. The shootout. Trained cougars to do the killing. I got it all on tape in a safe place, so you're not covering this up. And this?" Carl raised his bandaged wrist. "This is all the rest of the proof I need."

Dan smiled at him, only the look he gave him was dark and foreboding. "You couldn't leave us alone, could you? And now you'll pay the price. Believe me, I never wanted this. Ever. You're here and stuck with us."

Carl frowned. "I told you. I already sent the video to my boss, so if you're thinking you can eliminate me too and no one will miss me, it isn't happening."

"If what you say is true, you're going to have to do some fancy talking to convince your boss you're a lunatic, or making the joke of the century."

"I won't do anything of the sort." Carl looked as pigheaded as ever.

"Fine. You'll change your tune sooner or later." Dan read him his rights, charged him with trespassing, shooting protected wildlife on his property, littering, disturbing the peace, resisting arrest, and anything else he could throw at him. The problem wasn't the video now as much as it was that Carl would become one of them and then what were they to do with him? He knew Carl would retract what was shown on the video if he had sent it to someone, because he couldn't afford to have the word get out about cougars attacking people in Yuma Town. Not now that he was one.

Hal and Tracey had been happy to take Ricky and Kolby in because Tracey had already been working with Ricky on her cases. The boys were good kids, got themselves in trouble sometimes, but they always had good intentions. But Carl? He was always out for himself, trying to make a name for himself, trying to make a fast buck off other people's misfortunes. Everyone hated him.

"Littering?" Carl asked. "You've got to be kidding me. And I didn't resist arrest. I was wounded and wanted medical attention in case I had rabies, so I wasn't resisting arrest."

"Littering? Shooting rounds on my property? A round cutting into the bark of two of my favorite trees, injuring them, the casings left on the ground. Resisting arrest? Chase said you wouldn't give up your camera. He had to confiscate it. If there's nothing damning on it, we'll return it to you."

"Damning for you, maybe," Carl grumbled. "Which means you'll wipe it clean."

"If you've already sent the damning video off to your

boss, then you have nothing to worry about if we wiped your disks clean. We're not going to do that." Not unless he really did have video of them attacking the men on his property. Even if Carl was going to be one of them, they couldn't let him keep such damning evidence, in case it fell into the wrong hands.

"Is this really necessary?" Carl said, raising his manacled wrist up.

"Yeah. We'll have a guard on the door at all times. You're not a very popular guy around here, so you're going to have to work damn hard to make some friends."

Carl smiled. "That's not the kind of business I'm in, unless I use my charms to help get a story."

"Tell you what, you're a damn good investigative reporter. Once you've decided you want to work for us, you can help us uncover the truth of what happened last night. You'll work for us, not in Denver any longer."

"Not happening. Tell Chase to return my phone so I can make my call."

"Get some rest. I'll be seeing you later." Dan left the room. "I want either you, Chase, or Leyton on his door at all times."

Leyton smiled at him.

"Hey, I know you don't work for me, but your mate works here, so you have a vested interest if Carl goes nuts with the shifting into a cougar sometime today or tonight."

"Yeah, I agree. I'll take the first four-hour shift. I want to go home with my mate tonight. Kate's been having trouble sleeping, unless I give her back rubs," Leyton said.

"Been there, done that," Chase said.

Dan looked around, feeling panicked when he didn't see Addie.

"She's with Kolby seeing Ricky. He's come out of surgery and is still in intensive care, but Kate said they could go in and talk to him, make him feel loved. I already told him he's not in trouble for what he and his brother did," Chase said.

"Okay, I'll give him my two-cent's worth then." Dan headed for the intensive care unit and called Stryker. "Hey, if you're free later this afternoon, I need you and Chase to guard Carl at the clinic. Leyton's helping too. Have you heard what has happened?"

"Yeah, Chase called me when you were in talking to the bastard. How is Ricky?"

"I'm going in to see him in intensive care now. Leyton said he'd take first shift, so you and Chase can work out the rest of the schedule for tonight. Travis can rotate in if Leyton says he's fine with it."

"Okay, I'll give Chase a call."

Dan walked into the room and Addie joined him, giving him a hug. "Kate said he should pull through. No running as a cougar for several days. No heavy lifting. No running around investigating things. He has to have bedrest for three more days after he leaves the hospital in a couple of days."

"That's damn good news," Dan said, feeling relieved.

Kolby shook his head and folded his arms. "He's always finding a way to get out of work."

"Better than if you had been shot, right, Kolby?" Dan said, though he knew Kolby was just trying to find some humor in a frightening situation.

Kolby gave him a crooked smile. "Nah." His eyes were

still watery, as if he hadn't come to grips with the news that his brother was going to live and would be fine.

"You've got a great brother, you know," Dan said. "And he's got a great one in return. Keep sticking up for each other. You'll both go far."

"What about the bastard who shot him?" Kolby said, all growly.

"Carl? Unfortunately, we're stuck with him. Don't expect any apology from him either. I'm sure he'll want the two of you to apologize to him for what he'll become. Or he'll want you dead. It depends on how well he takes the change. We don't see it very often, but sometimes a turned human will have to be taken down."

"Who's going to take him in to teach him our ways?" Addie asked.

"We may have to draw straws on that."

"That bad, eh?"

"Yeah. We might just have to leave him in jail for a while until we can decide who will take him in to teach him all about us."

"What about any video recordings that he took of that night?" Addie asked.

"Chase confiscated all his equipment, but Carl said he already sent off the video to his boss. Now, it's possible he sent it off to someone or somewhere else for safekeeping while he was continuing to investigate what had gone down last night. He's too thorough in his work to send something that he hasn't worked on and polished to the nth degree before he's turned it in. It doesn't mean he doesn't have a duplicate hidden somewhere in case someone took the original away from him. I'm hoping we can learn the truth and confiscate it once he realizes his life is changed forever and he's one of us. And how much danger it would be for anyone to learn what we are."

Hal and Tracey hurried into the room and while Tracey held Ricky's hand, Kolby told them in his words what had happened.

"And Carl is still alive?" Tracey growled.

"Yeah. You don't want to take him in like you did Kolby and Ricky, do you?" Dan asked, even though he knew their answer would be hell no.

Ricky opened his eyes, though he looked groggy still. He glanced at all the people standing in the room, but then his eyes widened when he saw Addie. Then he gave her a big smile. "You're still...available, aren't you?"

CHAPTER 10

Chase met with Dan and Addie in the lobby, with news about the camera and Carl's other possessions. "Travis said he found the video Carl took of all the action that night: you, tearing into the one killer as a cougar, some of the guys firing rounds, others running as cougars. All of it. It wasn't real obvious as to who the people were, especially since they were camouflaged, and of course, he wouldn't have a clue who the cats were. We're the only ones who would know that. Certainly, the recording isn't clear enough to really identify the men. Since he took a video of several of the scenes, I thought we all might want to look at them to see if we find any more evidence of anything."

"He wasn't just passing through when he heard gunshots ring out then," Dan said, realizing Carl hadn't been telling the truth.

Chase frowned. "That's what he said."

"It isn't true. It would have taken him too long to get

there and set up. I had to take down the first man when he fired at the SUV. Carl had to have been there, already set up, and taking the video, if he caught me on video taking the man out."

"Hell."

Dan pulled out his phone and called the Denver newspaper and put it on speaker. "Hi, this is Sheriff Dan Steinacker of Yuma Town. I'm calling to check on the credentials of a Carl Nelson. Does he still work as an investigative reporter for you?"

"He quit the paper some years ago. *Yuma Town*. Yeah, after he said he had a big story in Yuma Town and then nothing came of it, the boss was furious. It was all hush-hush, but in truth? I think he fired him. Carl Nelson isn't there causing trouble and claiming he's a reporter for us still, is he?"

"He's been causing trouble all right. Thanks so much for your time."

"Anytime, Sheriff. He had to turn in his credentials, so if he's saying he's working for us, he's lying."

"Thank you." Dan ended the call and said to Chase, "Did he have any newspaper credentials on him?"

"Not that I saw. We all just assumed he was still working for the Denver paper."

"Why would he be at your place at that particular time?" Addie asked. "How would he know we were headed to your place when we weren't even there? Or that there would be some action that he could record? Why else be there? If he no longer works for a paper, who does he work for?"

"I think we need to talk with Carl again." Dan, Addie, and

Chase headed for the room, but Leyton wasn't outside the room.

They rushed to reach it and pulled open the door. Leyton was trying to pin down Carl, the newly turned cougar, and yelled, "Someone get a tranquilizer!"

So much for questioning Carl now.

***

The nurse handed Dan a syringe and while Chase and Leyton held Carl down, Dan injected the cat. Addie figured she and Dan might as well return to the safe house. They weren't going to be able to get anything out of the man, well, cat, now. Not for some hours.

Instead of trying to chain him to the bed, they brought in a large cage, muzzled him, and put him inside to sleep for now.

"We should declaw him too," Leyton said, showing off his battle wounds.

Knowing Leyton wasn't serious, they all knew it was dangerous for a cat to have its claws removed, and no way to climb into a tree to protect itself from wolves or other predators.

Kate came in to take care of Leyton's claw marks, even though the nurse could have done it.

Addie smiled at her for taking care of her mate. He kept kissing her while she tried to bandage him, and Addie thought they were a cute couple. It was interesting to see how growly the cougars could be toward others who could be dangerous, but so affectionate toward their mates.

Stryker was frowning at the two of them, and she swore he was interested in Kate himself. He and Leyton were twin brothers!

"We could throw him in the jailhouse and then you don't have to waste a bed on him," Chase said. "He'd be more secure, can shift at will, and have a bigger 'cage' to roam free in."

"Yeah, let's do it." Dan said.

Kate handed them bandages for Carl's wounds for when he shifted back into his human form.

The men hauled the sleeping cat in the cage out to Hal's pickup and then they took him to the jailhouse. Several of the men carried the cage into one of the cells. Once they set it down, Chase and Dan pulled Carl out of the cage and laid him on the bed, then they removed the cage. Leyton, Chase, and Stryker would take turns staying at the jailhouse to guard him.

"Let's return to the safe house," Addie said.

"Bridget and Travis will help with guard duty there." Dan told everyone where they were going. "I need to pick up a bag of clothes and toiletries, and we need to do some shopping for you."

They quickly made stops at a drugstore and Millicent's Mint Julep Boutique, then headed to his place to pick up a bag of his things. The workmen had finished the work on the house and had already left.

"It's a beautiful home, love the woods, and view of the mountains. I'm glad the men were able to restore it to its former glory. You wouldn't even know someone had crashed through the back door and bullets had riddled the front."

"The cougars in town do a good job. We've always got someone who has the skills we need."

She followed him into his bedroom. "Hmm, I like the large bedroom and bath."

"We'll have to try it out as soon as it's safe to return here." Dan finished packing a couple of bags, and they left the house to get back in the Jeep.

"I need to talk to you about something else," Addie said when she and Dan were in the Jeep.

"This sounds ominous." Dan glanced at her, then pulled out of his driveway.

"Mrs. Fitz knows my mother. I'd seen her several times when she came to the house to see my mother before she took off. I never saw Mrs. Fitz again either. I thought they were...well, kind of friends. Maybe they were business associates. Now I don't know. I called Mrs. Fitz and asked her what she knew about my mother. I wasn't sure she'd tell me anything, if it was all supposed to be some big national security secret."

"And?"

"Alicia isn't my mother. My real mother died in a car accident when I was twelve-months old. Somehow, I survived. Alicia took the place of my mother. She was a faux wife to my father, and then she left when I was eight because her contractual obligation was up. Dad didn't need her and she didn't need him. I always wondered why I stayed with my dad, who was warm, kind, affectionate, and everything my mother was not. The photos in Dad's desk drawers make sense now. They were all of him with my mother, my real mother, when they were married, and of them holding me until I was about one. After that, no more pictures. My dad and Alicia were in a pretend marital relationship like us."

"It's not the same with us," Dan said, and she reached over and squeezed his hand. He smiled at her. "I need you in my life. We might have had a contractual agreement to begin with, but even from the very beginning, it's meant more to me than you can know. I'm not divorcing you, or ending the contractual obligation in any way. I want this to be real between us. As real as it has been, except without the long absences. I can really do without those."

"You're not getting tired of me yet?"

"Are you kidding? You should know all the plans I have in store for us, when we're not taking down assassins."

She chuckled. "Like?"

"Remember when we were coming here, and we had the notion of camping up in the mountains, staying in a cave, running as cougars?"

"You still want to do that?"

"Yes. I'd like to find resolution in this, but I still want to do that with you."

She looked out the window. "You don't think you'll have the seven-year itch and then take off, like my mother, uh, pretend mother did?"

"No. If I have any itches, you'll scratch them and make them go away."

She smiled and ran her hand over his groin. His cock jerked beneath the jeans, and she smiled again. "I hope no one else has plans for us, because I want you in that soft, non-squeaky bed when we reach the safe house."

"If anyone has plans for us, they'll have to wait."

He parked at the garage, and they got out of the Jeep, with bags in hand, then approached the house.

Bridget opened the door for them. "After I returned home from shopping at the grocery store, I heard all the news from Travis about Carl and Ricky." She eyed the shopping bags Dan was carrying into the house. "Oh, good, you managed to get some shopping done."

"It will tide us over for now. Yeah, it's a mess, as far as Carl being turned, but Ricky will be okay. Do you and Travis want to take Carl in?"

"I don't even know the man, but from everything I've heard Chase say about him, no," Bridget said. "Not only that, but we can't be watching him when we go on missions. Hal and Tracey have that big ranch and they can put him to work mucking stalls and with their foreman, Ted Weekum, and Ricky and Kolby, they can all keep an eye on him."

"They said no."

"Then a stay in a jail cell sounds like his only option unless someone else wants the chore," Bridget said.

Addie snagged Dan's hand. "We're going to take a nap. See you in a bit."

"Sleep tight."

They hurried up the stairs and when they reached the blue room and shut the door, Dan began helping Addie out of her clothes. He unfastened her black lace bra and then pulled off her panties. "I remember that first time we made love," he said, kissing her bare shoulder blades as she unbuttoned his sheriff's shirt. "I was envisioning red panties and a bra. But black is just as sexy."

"I knew you'd want to seal the deal, Sheriff," she said, running her hand over his badge attached to his belt, then tugging at his belt to unfasten it. "And I sure wanted to."

He combed his fingers through her hair in a loving caress. "Hmm," he kissed her breasts, his hot lips pressing against them, his hands cupping her bare buttocks.

She licked his nipple and he quickly sat on the bed and started pulling off his cowboy boots. She helped him with the other, and yanked off his socks and tossed them in the air before they landed on the carpeted floor behind her.

Before he could stand and pull off his jeans and boxer briefs, she pushed him back against the mattress and pressed her body between his legs, rubbing his arousal.

He pulled her higher and spread her legs so she was straddling him. "Hmm," she murmured against his chest, liking the way he was resting between her legs, even if he was still wearing his soft jeans, his hard erection straining for release, his hands running over her thighs, and moving over her buttocks.

He was so sexually attuned to her, and it made her blood run hot. Their pheromones were wrapping around each other's, calling for a mating, for release, for the connection.

Her heart was pounding as she rubbed her body against his, but this wouldn't do. She wanted him inside her. Now.

She moved back and began yanking off his jeans, but it meant climbing all the way off him. As if he didn't want her to get away, he dragged her to the mattress, and as quickly as he could, he rose off the bed, shucked his jeans, and then his boxer briefs, and moved his naked body over hers, between her legs.

And he began to kiss her jaw. She felt herself grow wet for him, and she wanted to feel him thrusting deep inside of her. He licked her breast and suckled on a nipple. God, he felt good. Wanting to touch him in a way that said she'd claimed him too, she speared her fingers through his hair, scratching lightly at his scalp. Groaning, he moved his body against hers, rubbing his cock between her legs, teasing her. Then he began rubbing vigorously and she thought he might come outside of her if he didn't hurry and enter her, just like she was going to come at any second.

"Oh," she cried, gripping his strong, muscular shoulders, and he slid into her and thrust, making the whole bed move, banging against the wall.

It was as bad as the creaky springs. They couldn't stop now. He only smiled and she laughed, but then they concentrated on the business at hand as he deepened his thrusts. He pulled her legs over his shoulders, and she felt her world come apart. "Omigod..."

"You're all right?" he suddenly said, easing up.

"Yes, finish this or I'm terminating you."

He smiled and thrust harder, her buttocks slapping against his thighs. The headboard kept hitting the wall. Bang! Bang! Bang! Faster! Bang-bang-bang!

And then slower. Bang...bang...bang. He pulled nearly out of her, then thrust again and again, and the headboard kept up the rhythm, finally ending when he found release. He sank down on top of her and kissed her cheeks.

"Hell, woman, you are never leaving me."

She laughed. "We need to move the bed away from the wall though if we do this again here."

"I'll have a couple of the guys help me. I don't want you moving anything." He laid back on the mattress and pulled her into his arms before covering them with the blue sheets and blue quilt. "You're incredible."

She rubbed her cheek against his chest in a cat's way that said she thought he was too.

She could deal with mated life if it was always like this with him. He had never acted toward Addie in any way like her dad and the woman who had pretended to be his wife whenever she and Dan were together. It had been so infrequently that she wondered if it would be different if they saw each other every day, day in and day out. The same old routine. Oh, sure, give a speeder a ticket, give a hunter hunting out of season a ticket and a fine, take care of a car wreck. Would living together be boring? Then again, couldn't she use a little bit of a boring life for now?

What she loved was that she was already making real friends. Cougar friends. And she wanted to help them like they'd helped her. She could see a whole new life for her here. Only if she could resolve this situation. She didn't want them to have to deal with her issues, worrying that innocents could be caught up in the crossfire. Better that she was gone, dealing with this on her own. Dan had a job here. He was sheriff. They needed him. Even now, she was taking him from his duties. She was certain if she even hinted at leaving the town, he'd be against it. Probably the whole town would be.

Could she solicit Mrs. Fitz's help if Addie decided she had no other choice but to leave Yuma Town and learn what was going on with regard to her? She sighed and cuddled with Dan. She hoped he'd understand, though after the last time she'd left him, she'd felt bad the whole six months she was gone. She knew she'd done the right thing by him, keeping him out of her conflict, but she still felt bad that she'd involved him in any of this in the first place.

Now she didn't know what she was going to do as far as who she could trust. Her pretend mother had to have tried to protect her by setting her up with a man who could very well be her mate someday. Even if Alicia had never told Addie the truth, which was understandable because if she was living the lie because of her job, telling an eight-year-old the truth would have been way too risky.

And, even if Addie was wrong, she still felt her direct supervisor was one of the good guys. That made her wonder if Briggs had learned the truth about what had happened to her out in the field that had made her run for her life? Had Alicia learned what had happened to her?

Her pretend mother had never even called Dan back.

And what was the deal with Carl, the fake reporter?

***

Dan was lying with Addie in his arms, soft, cuddly, perfect for him in every way, yet she *wasn't* his. And she might never be his, he thought with regret. Her eyes were closed, she was relaxed, but she wasn't sleeping, and he knew she was thinking about her situation, mulling over everything that they'd learned, and was trying to sort out who the mole was, who wanted her dead.

He was thinking about it too, having nightmares about it, trying to sort out what was happening, from what was just a dream and what was real. He was thinking about her too, about the long-term, about being with her for the short-term. About not being apart again.

He knew, until they resolved the business with the assassin, she could never leave her old life behind, never begin anew.

He caressed her bare arm, wishing they already knew the truth and they'd put this whole business to rest. And that she'd feel they had enough feelings for each other that she'd make a go of it with him. He didn't want to be with anyone else.

She seemed to like the townspeople, everyone she'd met so far. He'd seen the way she smiled at the couples who had found their chosen mates. Yet she was holding back from having her own happiness. He worried it went deeper than the business that people were trying to kill her. That she didn't know how to have a loving, long-term relationship with a guy because she'd never seen her parents have one.

They had been like Dan and her—a contractual agreement, except for him, and it seemed for her, that's where the similarity stopped.

Knowing she wasn't sleeping, he leaned over and kissed her forehead. "I want to be mated cougars, to marry you, to make this for real. I understand if you feel you have to wait until you resolve what's going on with you otherwise, but don't think for a second that I'm going to let you run off to do this by yourself either."

She rubbed her hand lightly over his chest, but didn't say anything. And then he felt a tear drop on his chest, and then another.

"Aww, honey." He wrapped her tightly in his arms and held her tight. "We'll get through this together. I promise. But together. You've been the Lone Ranger long enough. You have me now. And a whole town full of cougars at your beck and call. We'll have your back, as we know you'll have ours."

Addie burst into tears.

Aww, hell. What had he said wrong?

CHAPTER 11

Addie couldn't believe Dan had made her soar with the eagles when he was making love to her and had declared he wanted her to be his wife, and now she was boohooing all over his bare chest. She couldn't help but feel so many mixed emotions where he was concerned. She wanted to be with him, loving him as her cougar mate, and to settle down in a place like this, with real friends and family. Was she just using the business of the assassination attempts on her life as a means to push him away? And because she didn't want to get hurt like her fake mother hurt her and her dad when she left them, even though the woman had never been close to either her or her dad?

She'd still been her mother for seven years. Maybe Alicia had been afraid to become emotionally attached to her or her father, knowing it was just a job and it would be easier that way when she left.

Alicia had been the only mother Addie had

remembered. And Alicia had done her motherly duties while Addie had been growing up, taking care of her when she was sick, helping her dress, and feeding her when she was little. Even teaching her so many things, taking her places like the zoo and the parks when her father had to be away. Addie loved to read because Alicia had read stories to her all the years she was growing up—until she left. Those were the good times she remembered with her.

What if, never having had a real, loving mother, Addie wouldn't know how to be a good mother either? Was that something they were born with, or was it learned behavior? She liked kids, so she supposed she was equipped with mothering genes. She didn't know for sure.

Poor Dan was upset because she was crying on his chest, and he didn't even understand what was upsetting her. She didn't even know herself. She was just one big jumble of emotions. And she was never like this. She could always shut off her emotions, except whenever she was with him. He turned on her other needs—for companionship, for loving, for pleasure—even in the trivial things: eating, sleeping, and running with him. And the major stuff: fighting the bad guys with him at her side.

Yeah, she had fallen for the sexy cougar all the way.

Before she analyzed them any further and changed her mind, she blurted out, "I'll marry you."

He laughed and tightened his hold on her, kissing her forehead in a loving way. "Somehow, I expected a different scenario when I asked you if you'd like to be my mate and you accepted."

"If you have to think on it..." She was serious. If he was

changing his mind already...

"Hell, no. You made the oral commitment. I've made it, and I sure didn't know what to expect when you convinced me to be your pretend husband ten and a half years ago, but even then, I wanted something more between us."

"Benefits."

He laughed and caressed her arm further. "You have to admit the benefits have been damn nice."

"Yeah, they have. You might have been thirteen on my list, but you were the magical number. The perfect one for me. I wouldn't be alive now if you hadn't risked your neck to rescue me. I really hadn't expected you to come to my aid like that, or for the whole town to help out."

"As soon as you called me and sounded so weak on the phone, I was trying to learn where you were. Then I was on my way. I'm sure everyone wanted to know what I was doing, running off in such a hurry. As much as we were separated, I couldn't stop thinking of you. Admittedly, I wanted to stop thinking of you, because I didn't want to be holding onto something that could never be between us—marital bliss, a normal life together—but it wasn't working. I wanted you. I wanted this. You here. With me. Never leaving for months on end. Unless I was with you. I had to stick it out, come hell or high water. The truth is—I love you, and I could never give you up."

She sighed and kissed his chest. "I knew I was in love with you from the moment you said you wanted benefits if you were to be my pretend husband."

He chuckled.

"You don't think we're being too rash, do you? Maybe

we should wait and see if after living together for a few months, we don't get tired of each other, or annoyed with one another over bad habits, or something."

"No. We've had a practice marriage for ten and a half years already."

"Ha! And how many times have we seen each other over all that time?"

"Not enough. Not every day and every night like I wanted. Never enough. Not waking up to you so we can make love. Not making love before we go to sleep. Not having some afternoon delight on an extended lunch break."

She smiled. "You sure have a one-track mind. I might not be the perfect mate, doing all the things you might expect of a mate." She couldn't help worrying she wouldn't measure up. That, after a while, she'd turn out to be just like her pretend mother.

"You're perfect for me just the way you are. We'll take it a day at a time. Love each other, help each other, deal with this business until we resolve it. We'll be together when we do it."

"We don't have to do the wedding stuff. It seems like a waste of money, time, and energy."

"We'll do whatever you want to do. I'm happy to just go before witnesses. Jack and Dottie did that. Then we had a marriage celebration for them here later. I'm happy to do it any way that makes you happy. When can we tell everyone that we're mated for certain?"

"Are you eager to claim me as your territory?"

"Hell, yeah. Stryker's waiting in the wings if you decide to dump my butt. And you heard Ricky."

She laughed. "All right, anytime is fine with me."

***

They slept for a few hours, and when they got up, it was pouring rain outside. Travis and Bridget were talking to Leyton downstairs about a case they had to go on. Addie hated that, because of her, everyone had been putting their own workloads on hold.

"Yeah, we've got to take this guy down. We still have the situation here with Addie," Leyton said to Travis and Bridget. "Which of you wants to go with me to take this cougar down? Or I can ask Jack if he wants to."

"I will," Travis said.

"Hey," Dan said, walking down the stairs with Addie, "if you all need to go, we'll be fine now. Addie's feeling much better and we can call on some others to help out if we need them to. I don't want you to be short of manpower on your mission, putting yourselves at risk."

"The job will only take the two of us," Leyton said. "Before we go, we'll help you move the bed."

Dan smiled at Addie. She felt her face go up in flames.

The guys went upstairs to move the bed.

Bridget got Addie a cup of coffee. "Leyton isn't what you call subtle sometimes."

Addie laughed. "Well, we were making rather a racket up there. We've agreed to be mated. We're not sure about the marriage details for now, but we're committed to each other for real."

"Omigod, yes!" Bridget gave her a big hug. "I'm so happy for the two of you."

"I worry about this business with me though."

"We're serious about all of us helping you with this. That's what we do. All for one and one for all. We wouldn't have it any other way. We're trained for it, just like you are. The feelings go deeper with us because we're cougars."

The guys all came back downstairs.

Bridget was smiling. Travis raised a brow.

"They're mated. Isn't that wonderful?"

Travis and Leyton looked at Dan as if he didn't know the news, or were surprised he hadn't already shared it with them yet.

Dan laughed and wrapped his arm around Addie's shoulders. "All I can say is it's about time."

Chase called Dan and he put the phone on speaker. "What's up?"

"Carl shifted back into his human form and he's wanting to talk to you, not just us lowly deputies."

"I'll be right over."

"I'm going with you." Addie wasn't worried about anyone planning a hit anytime soon, not after whoever it was who had planned this had lost four more men. She assumed they'd sit tight for a while to come up with another strategy. She even had the thought that maybe no one believed she was a threat any longer if she wasn't on the job. On the other hand, she wasn't on the job and they'd come after her, so that pretty much ruled out that conjecture.

"Did you want me to go with you too?" Bridget asked.

"No, you're fine. Just do whatever you need to do," Addie quickly said. They couldn't all be guarding her always. Eventually they'd let down their guard. Sure, everyone would be wary of newcomers to town, and be watching for anyone showing up unexpected that they didn't know, but having a full-fledged guard detail couldn't go on forever. Not that she felt comfortable running around by herself for now. If Dan had to take care of business without her, she would welcome someone else serving as her backup.

"Okay, we're out of here," Leyton said, and Travis gave Bridget an endearing kiss.

That's what Addie had with Dan, the same shared looks, the same compelling need to be with her mate. Her mate. She couldn't believe she'd agreed to be his partner for always.

Then Leyton and Travis were out the door.

"Are you sure you don't want me to come with you?" Bridget asked. "Now that everyone else is gone, and I don't have anything else to do, I wouldn't mind seeing what Carl has to say."

Addie smiled. "Yeah, sure. Carl might not talk to us either, but we can visit."

"One or two vehicles?" Dan asked.

"I'll ride with the two of you unless you want to talk in private about anything," Bridget said.

"Come with us. Save some gas." Addie suspected Bridget would rather be with them to watch their backs and in on the action, than sitting at home waiting to hear from someone. Plus, she was probably just as curious as Addie was to see what happened when they saw Carl, a newly turned cougar. Not to mention the business about him having been at Dan's place to catch all the action from the beginning.

Bridget smiled and grabbed her gun off the dining room table. "Gotcha. I'm always up for carpooling."

***

At the jailhouse, Stryker and Chase were waiting for Dan to arrive. Stryker was leaning his butt against one of the desks, arms folded across his chest. "Hope you get more out of him then we could."

"I was all for using torture," Chase said, knowing Carl could hear everything that was being said, even though the door to the cells was closed. Now that he could hear like a cougar, he would be listening to everything they said.

Unless, they spoke in hushed voices or went outside to talk.

"It may come to that," Dan said. "Come on, Addie." He suspected Carl knew something about Addie and all this business. He figured she should help to question him, unless Carl refused to speak to her or in front of her.

Bridget waited in the offices with Chase and Stryker, while Dan opened the door to the jail cells and followed her in and closed the door behind him.

Carl was sitting on his bed, head in his hands, elbows resting on his legs, looking down at the floor like he didn't know what kind of a mess he'd gotten himself into. He quickly looked up and narrowed his eyes at them.

"Still want that call?" Dan asked, escorting Addie to the cell.

"Hell."

"Believe me, I never wanted you to be one of us. I'll tell you right now, you'll have a time of it with shifting. And unless you want to be caged, studied, and have tests run on you in some science lab for as long as you live, you can't tell anyone what happened to you."

"Don't you think I know that?" Carl growled.

"I'd think so, you're a clever guy, but sometimes someone who's newly turned needs to be warned." Dan shoved his hands in his pockets.

"When are you going to let me out of here? I assume you don't really intend to press charges for all that minor stuff."

"You'll be here as long as we feel you need to be."

"You can't—"

"We can. We run Yuma Town, so we go by our rules, our way. Which means, bottom line, you cause any more trouble for us, you're a dead man."

Carl snorted, but Dan knew from the expression on the man's face he knew he was in serious trouble, and Dan wasn't exaggerating.

"Rogue cougars are taken down permanently," Dan clarified. "We can't risk having anyone learn of what we are. And now you can't either. Unless, like I said, you want to be someone's science experiment and find of the millennium."

"I got it already. How do I get out of here?"

"First, we must have a family willing to take you in, teach you the ropes, and monitor you until you get your shifting under control. No one is stepping up to the plate. Face it, Carl. You're not well-liked at all. I can't force someone to take you in. I imagine it's going to take some time to place you."

"Like I'm a damn foster pet?"

Dan smiled. Then he frowned at him again. "A foster pet would be well-loved. If you cause any trouble, the word would be to terminate you. Just remember that. Maybe Roger and Millie Haverton, who run the newspaper in town, could take you in."

"Some small-town newspaper?" Carl snorted.

"The cat lady, the widowed Mrs. Sorenson, is always taking in strays. Maybe she'd think you were a worthwhile cause," Dan said.

"I'm allergic to cats."

Everyone smiled. "I'm sure whatever allergy you had to them was knocked out when you became one of us. Now to business. Who are you working for?"

"I'm a news reporter for the Denver Press."

"See, Carl? This kind of attitude is going to keep you here. Try again. You left your job four years ago."

Carl looked at the floor again.

"Okay, next question. You said you heard shots fired and stopped at my place to see what was going on. The date and time stamp on your video, and the fact you recorded a cougar taking down the one assassin, meant you were in place before the shooting began."

Carl eyed him for a moment, then glanced at Addie.

"What do you have to do with all this?" Dan asked. "I'm asking real nice right now in front of the lady. I won't when she leaves."

"Tough guy act."

"You saw me kill the first assassin with my cougar canines. You know it's not an act."

Carl's eyes widened. Dan was sure he still couldn't quite wrap his mind around anyone being a cougar shifter.

"We have enhanced healing abilities, if you didn't realize it. Which means I can keep tearing you up real good and allowing you to heal and start all over again."

Carl looked up at him, skepticism written all over his face.

"Check your bandages. If your deep, cat bite marks haven't healed all the way by now, they should be well on their way."

Carl unwrapped his wrist and stared at the bite marks that were still red, but the tears had begun to heal much faster than humanly possible. He just stared at the wounds in disbelief.

"Tell me what we want to know. Why you knew to be at my house before we arrived and were already set up to take the video. Why none of the assassins knew you were there and took you out. Because they did know you were there. To my way of thinking, you were part of their team, video recording the assassination to prove they did the job right. Only they didn't get it right and the good guys won out. Except now you're one of us and you can't be on their team any longer. And frankly, we don't want you on our team either. I'm just surprised we didn't catch you out there at the time. You were damn lucky."

"I was fired from my job at the Press. All right? I had promised them the story of a lifetime. I knew there was something wrong with you people. I'm damn good at my job, digging up the truth, investigative reporting, uncovering the story behind the story."

"Except for with us."

"Yeah, well, without the story, I was canned. Without a paycheck, I couldn't focus on you or this place any longer. I've been freelancing since then and several of my jobs have taken me out of the country. I was approached by a woman, no name, who said she worked for a federal agency. She wouldn't say which one. And she said she needed me to go to Yuma Town to watch your house, and video record the agents taking down the occupants. After the last time we had our showdown, I was eager to take on the assignment. An even bigger incentive was she said you and some of your cohorts were home-grown terrorists, but they needed a videographer who could show the takedown for future training exercises."

"And to prove the 'terrorists' resisted arrest and had to be taken down permanently?" Addie asked.

"Who are you?" Carl asked, glowering at Addie.

"A federal agent. I'm with the FBI, and those men who were sent to kill me? They would have taken you out once they had the video recording. We have a mole on the task force I'm working on. Dan has been my undercover husband for ten and a half years. It wasn't until six months ago that someone started targeting me. If you're as good as you say you are, and you think you can help us investigate who's behind this, I'm sure Dan would give you some leniency. We might even find someone willing to take you in."

Carl looked at Dan to see his take on it.

"If you can help us, I'd consider it. Did you send the video off to anyone?" Dan asked.

"No. I was supposed to hand it over to one of the agents, only they weren't agents, from what you say."

"Right. They had long felony records, hitmen, every one of them," Addie said, leaning a little against Dan.

"Be right back." Dan should have thought of it before, but Addie needed to have a seat and he was going to get a chair for her. On second thought, if Carl could behave himself, he'd let him out of the cell so they could sit on the couches and chairs in the breakroom of the sheriff's office since this was going to take a while. "If you'll behave yourself, we can take a seat in the breakroom where we can be more comfortable."

"Yeah. I'm not going anywhere," Carl said, sounding resigned, but Dan still didn't trust him.

Dan let him out, and then they walked back to the door and he unlocked it. "We're sitting in the breakroom to discuss this. All of us," he told Chase, Stryker, and Bridget.

Everyone moved to the breakroom that Dottie had redone with some of the stolen money they'd recovered. She'd hated the breakroom, and always thought it should be a nice getaway from the stresses of the day, and even afforded them a nice place to visit with guests there. Dan and the rest of the sheriff's office employees loved it.

A curved black table and black chairs offered enough seating for eight. A black and white kitchen, the upper cabinets white, the lower ones black, fridge, stove, microwave, and dishwasher looked super high tech and suited their purpose. The newly furnished and decorated breakroom gave the sheriff, deputies, and dispatcher a place to cook while taking lunch and supper breaks, breakfast even, for those pulling overnight duty. A large picture of a cougar sitting on a rock with his mate overlooking Carver Falls decorated one wall. On another, all those who worked for the sheriff's office were pictured in their cougar coats: sheriff, deputies, the dispatcher.

"What if Carl shifts?" Stryker asked, leaning against a

wall, looking ready for action.

"He'll behave himself. We're armed to protect ourselves and he knows that," Dan said.

Bridget took a seat on one of the comfortable black chairs situated around a glass coffee table, her back to the kitchen. Chase sat at the kitchen table. He and Bridget were situated so Carl couldn't make a move for any of the knives in there, though Dan didn't believe he was combat trained and was certain the guy was smart enough to know if he moved toward the kitchen, he could be put down before he took a few steps.

Dan sat with Addie on the sofa across from where he motioned for Carl to sit in the corner, barricaded from making a move. Other than a small table situated between another sofa and the chair he was sitting on, he didn't have anything he could easily grab as a weapon.

"Tell them what you told us, in case they didn't hear what was said." Dan knew they would have heard, but he wanted Carl to repeat what he said to learn if he varied his statement much, or if he had his statement down pat, rehearsed, in case things hadn't gone as planned.

"They planned to kill you then," Stryker said after Carl finished sharing his story, stating what Dan believed was obvious, but it didn't hurt for Carl to hear it from others, confirming the truth of the matter.

In other words, they had saved Carl's life.

"Hell," Carl said. "If the assassins planned to kill me, then they probably still want to."

Everyone smiled.

"Well, you don't need to look so damned happy about

it."

"They didn't kill you, and we saved you, so show a little gratitude," Chase said.

"Yeah, but now I'm one of you! A werecat. And I can't even do my job now because of having these damnable urges to shift into one."

"We're cougar shifters," Addie said. "Not werecats. Describe what the woman looked like who hired you to video record the shootings."

"Dark-haired, but she was wearing a wig. Her eyebrows were much lighter. She was wearing eye pencil to darken them, but I could tell. In my stuff, I've got a photo of her."

"A photo?" Addie looked at Chase.

"Where?" Chase asked, standing.

"It's in the driver's side door panel."

"We have your vehicle impounded behind the sheriff's office. I'll check it out." Chase left the breakroom.

"How did you manage to get a photo of her without getting yourself killed before you even took on the assignment?" Addie asked.

"I have a friend who does some freelancing too. He took the picture when I went to the meeting in Forest Park. Even though she was supposed to be one of the good guys, I wanted proof concerning who I'd met, just in case anything went wrong. I don't like all this cloak and dagger stuff."

"Yet, that's your business," Addie said.

"Uncovering it, yeah. Living it, no. Well, except when I'm digging around for the truth." Carl turned to Bridget. "I know who all the others are and why they're here. Who are you?"

"Cougar Special Forces agent. My mate and I work for a

local agency that takes down rogue cougars."

"Like me if I don't behave."

"Yep."

"What's this all about then? If you're not terrorists, why would anyone be out to eliminate all of you?" Carl asked.

"We were escorting Addie here. She'd been wounded by more of the same kind of thugs," Bridget said. "We were trying to get her safely here, but we were attacked at Dan's house."

"Has anyone tried to contact you—" Dan paused. "I guess we have your phone." He smiled for making the slip. "I just wondered if the woman, or one of her cohorts, had tried to get in touch with you to see what went down after the whole incident. We haven't seen anyone else in the area who looks suspicious."

Stryker brought out Carl's phone. "No one's called. You can imagine she believes everyone died—and I mean, the bad guys, Carl."

"Let's keep it that way," Dan said.

Carl sank against the chair a little, looking relieved.

Chase stalked into the breakroom and handed the disk and camera to Addie. "I figure if anyone knows who she is, you will."

Addie inserted the disk into the camera and began scrolling through the pictures. When she came to one, she frowned. "Paris Pepion. She's on the team I've worked with for the past six months. She and Dirk Carter were my backup when the assassin knifed the courier and took off." She showed the picture of the woman to Carl. "Is this the woman who hired you?"

CHAPTER 12

Dan's phone rang, and he pulled it out of his pocket while everyone in the sheriff's office breakroom looked at him. The caller was listed as unknown, and he answered, "This is Sheriff Steinacker."

"This is Clinton Briggs, and I need to speak with Addie, if she's available."

"You're her boss?"

"Yeah."

"All right, just a second. You guys watch him, will you?" Dan asked Chase, Stryker, and Bridget, motioning to Carl.

"Yeah, he moves, we take him out," Chase said.

"Good deal." Dan and Addie left the breakroom and walked into his office and shut the door. "Briggs wants to speak with you."

Addie took the phone and sat at the sheriff's desk, putting the call on speaker.

Dan took a seat on one of the chairs opposite his desk.

"Yes, sir? Did you learn anything that will prove I'm not crazy?" Addie asked.

"First, the scene where you were to meet the courier was clean."

"I told you cleaners had to have showed up and taken care of things."

"I haven't finished," Briggs said curtly. "Trace amounts of blood were found in the soil. The problem is, we can't prove it's the courier's because his body vanished."

He believed her.

"And it wasn't your blood, which we have on file. As to the hospital, it's as you said, no one knows anything. Which is just incomprehensible. When I dug deeper, I found a doctor who said he was told not to say anything to anyone about the matter because an attempt had been made on your life and whoever it was would try again. That it was a federal matter and no one was to say a word about it. The doctor, and the nurse who assisted, were in the operating room working on a gunshot case when you must have had all the trouble at your hospital room. They confirmed a federal agent had taken a position at your door, serving as your guard. The receptionist said she remembered the deeply-concerned sheriff coming to see his wife, and the room number she had given matched the one you said you were staying in."

"You know I was telling the truth."

"It appears that way. Assassins, missing bodies, well, I have no clue what's going on."

"We have other news." Addie wasn't sure if she should tell her boss everything, but if he was involved, he already knew all this anyway, and he would still plan to get rid of her.

"Your boss is my mother, only she's not really my mother."

"I talked to her about what was going on. She did tell me she had served as your mother for some years."

"Seven, and then she took off when I was eight. What is this all about?"

"I don't know. I really thought you'd been faking all this business, six months ago. I knew you didn't have amnesia and I'd discovered you had gone to Yuma Town to visit your undercover husband."

Addie frowned at Dan.

"Then you vanished from there. I thought you just wanted to be with him, that you'd had some kind of mental breakdown on the job and needed to get away. It happens. I let on that I believed your amnesia story."

"Okay, so the two agents assigned to be my backup, Paris and Dirk, they were there when the courier was killed. Or at least they were with him when he was dead. Dirk didn't come with me to provide backup. I raced after the assailant, and well, he got the best of me at first, but I killed him. Now there's an investigative reporter who took—" she paused. She couldn't mention the video recording. They had to destroy it. She had to mention his tie in with Paris. "...who was hired to take video of the assassins killing Dan and me at his house. He was told that the assassins were federal agents who were after terrorists. Dan's arrested him for trespassing, and learned that the woman who hired him was Paris Pellion. A friend of his took a picture of him speaking with her, and of him taking the deal."

"Then you need to turn this reporter over to me, and we'll see what else we can learn from him."

Dan was shaking his head vehemently, saying no.

She knew that. Carl would shift and be a cougar in Brigg's custody. What a disaster.

"I'm sorry to say he died shortly after that. One of the assassins was told to kill him after the job was done, we're certain, and he'd been shot. After he was questioned, he died of his gunshot wounds. We couldn't find the video recordings he took, if he even managed to get any."

"And the assassins?"

She looked to Dan for his help. They'd have to turn the bodies over to the feds.

"At the morgue. All known hitmen," Dan said. "The feds are welcome to them."

"I'll send a team to pick them up," Briggs said. "They'll be coming from one of our offices located closer to you and should be there in a couple of hours."

Was he in on all this after all? Had he pretended to investigate her situation, already knowing full well everything that had gone on? Was he having the bodies picked up to hide what he'd been responsible for?

"I hate to do this, Addie, but until we can verify that everything you say is completely true, I'll have to ask for your resignation. You'll have to turn in your badge and gun."

She ground her teeth. She supposed she knew this was coming. "You'll have to get it from whoever took them from me before or after I ended up at the hospital. All I had were the bloody clothes I was wearing."

"All right. I'll check with the hospital then. Men will come and take the bodies today."

"What about Paris and Dirk?"

"I'll question them, but so far as I know, they said that you were to meet with the courier and disappeared. He never showed up, and they returned to the office and reported you'd done your vanishing act again."

"And of course, you knew then they were lying through their teeth."

"I'll speak with them."

"And let me know what's going on."

"You're off the case, out of the Bureau, Addie. We'll handle this from here on out."

"Thank you for your service." She hung up on him, and tried calling Briggs's boss. When a woman identified herself as Alicia Shields, Addie nearly dropped the phone. Out of habit, she said, "Mother?"

"Oh, Addie, dear, I'm so sorry. I can't tell you how much I wanted to keep you and your father safe and how terribly I failed."

Tears stung Addie's eyes as Dan came over to hug her.

"What's...what's going on?" Addie asked her.

"Your mother, God rest her soul, had unearthed something big. She was working with the Bureau when she met and married your father. They were very happy for the five years they had together. Someone discovered she'd learned about dirty coverups, and she died when you were only a year old."

"She was murdered."

"In a car wreck, made to look like an accident. Luckily, you survived. I was assigned to be your father's wife and your mother, to learn if he knew just what she'd gotten involved with. In the seven years we were together, I never discovered anything that he knew about. I was told my time there was terminated. You have to believe it was the hardest thing for me to leave you, even though I was trying not to fall in love with you, knowing I could never be with you after your dad and I separated. Then something he did alerted some of those in power that he'd known just what Cecilia, your mother, knew, and that got him killed."

"I didn't know about any of this. Is this why someone is targeting me now?"

"That's what I suspect. I had you moved to this task force over ten years ago so I could watch over you."

"If you've been watching over me, then you know all that's happened to me."

Alicia gave a bitter laugh. "After the fact, but barely any of the details. Briggs has told me what he's learned."

"And Dan?"

"I know you. You had to make your own choice. Dan probably won't remember me, but I met him some years earlier when he was just finishing college and Army Reserve Officer Training Corp requirements, and he came to a job fair at the college. He stopped and talked to me while I manned the FBI booth. Most boring job ever, but I said if he ever wanted a job with the Bureau, look me up."

Dan was frowning.

"He said he had an army obligation, but he'd think on it. I followed his career, and that of his friends, Stryker, Hal, and Chase, who joined him at the booth, telling him he'd look good with an agent's badge. They were all cougars, strapping young men, already weapons trained, and they were going into the military. Then I had the idea of setting you up with a faux husband for some of your missions, to watch your back, not trusting just any agent to watch out for you. And you picked him."

"The first dozen were human."

"Exactly. You don't think I could have found that many cougars who were qualified, do you? I only knew about the four men because they all came to my booth and I took their cards and handed them mine."

Addie looked up at Dan. He nodded, as if he recalled the incident.

"And see? I was right. He's protected you when no one else in the Bureau could."

"Leyton Hill was listed too."

"I met him later. Tell Mrs. Fitz I want her to watch out for you."

"She told me you weren't my real mother."

"I told her to tell you, but privately, so you could decide who to share the information with. And the Muellers? They can stop searching into my background. Concentrate on Paris and Dirk. I think you know they're involved in this."

"And Briggs?"

"I'd be careful around him. I can't believe he didn't know what was going on with regards to you. I'm in charge of several task forces. I can't be everywhere at once. He's got half the number I have, and, well, suffice it to say, I'm not at all happy with his job performance."

"He's taken away my badge and gun."

"I told him to."

Addie frowned, still not sure she trusted Alicia. "If you know I'm telling the truth—"

"You're a target, Addie. And I don't want you murdered like your parents were. We'll learn the truth and take these people down. You settle down with that sheriff and stay out of trouble."

"What if they keep coming for me here? I'm endangering everyone's lives that I touch."

"As soon as Briggs and I spread the word that you're no longer working for the FBI, whoever's responsible will believe you're no longer a threat."

Addie had a hard time believing that. She also wanted to learn who had put out the hit on her mother and father, and her now. She wasn't going to sit back and pretend none of it had occurred.

"I've got a call I've got to take. If you need to call me, just use this number. We'll talk later."

Addie didn't believe Alicia really meant it. She had told her all she was going to say on the matter and Addie was done with being involved. But Addie wasn't.

She handed the phone to Dan and said, "Do you believe she intends to talk to me later?"

"No."

"Do you remember meeting her earlier?"

"Yeah, I sure do, but I never paid attention to her name. Stryker, Hal, Chase, and I joked about being FBI agents later. As cougars. Once we finished our army obligations, we were returning here, though Chase ended up being a sheriff in Oklahoma for a while and lost his wife and child, and returned here finally after I convinced him to come home."

"I'm so sorry to hear that."

"Yeah, he was out on a call, and his family was

murdered. He was really broken up over it."

"That's horrible. I'm glad he returned here to be among family and friends."

"Just like you."

"I'm sorry about mentioning Carl being hired to take the video recordings."

"You recovered nicely on that one. As long as they don't ask to see Carl's body."

"You don't think it's a mistake to turn the hitmen's bodies over to the feds?"

"No. And good riddance. We have all the records on them in duplicate. Of course, we'll only give them the two we had to shoot. The two we killed as cougars are already buried."

"Good. I didn't even think of that."

"They don't know how many were here, unless they were involved. I'd love to hear them ask where the other bodies are."

"Let's talk with Mrs. Fitz," Addie said. "I want to see if she knows more about my parents' deaths, and her take on what Alicia said as far as everything else goes."

"I take it you don't trust Alicia."

"Do you? I don't trust anyone that I worked with there any longer."

"All right. Let's take Bridget back to the safe house and I need to have Stryker return Carl to his cell."

"He told us everything."

"He still needs to have someone take him in."

"Us?" Addie asked.

"Not in a million years." Dan walked Addie back to the

breakroom and said to Carl, "Stryker will return you to your cell when he needs to. There's no rush. If he can behave out here with you guys, he can stay out. If he shifts, he has to go into the cell. Or if one of you has to run out, he returns to the cell."

"I told you everything I know," Carl said, fuming.

As if that earned him the right to get out of jail free. "Right. We still have to find a family who will take you in," Dan said.

"What do I have to do to get out of here?"

"Whatever it takes."

"I'll help you investigate this business. You said yourself I'm good at this."

Dan agreed. He wouldn't turn down anyone's help with this, if he thought they might really be of assistance. "You can use one of our computers, if you think you can help with this case, as long as someone's watching everything you're doing."

"I can stay here," Bridget said. "Your deputies can do whatever work they need to do, and I'll monitor Carl. I'm really good at research too. And I'm just as armed and dangerous as the rest of you." She patted her gun.

And she could read minds. As far as Dan knew, she rarely used her talent, careful not to intrude on what others were thinking, but in a case where they didn't trust the person, she was handy to have around, if she could read the person's mind.

"In a couple of hours, we have some men coming over to pick up the assassins' bodies at the morgue. Do you think you might be able to talk to them and learn who they really are?" he asked Bridget.

Bridget smiled. "Sure thing, Dan."

He was never sure about asking her to do anything with her ability because she wasn't his asset, though as a cougar, she was willing to help anyone out who needed the aid. Also, he knew she hadn't told everyone about what she could do. Not everyone would feel comfortable about knowing she could read their minds. He wondered if she had already known what was up with Addie when she'd come to his house six months ago. As a cat, she had to be curious, and he wouldn't blame her if she had tried to learn for herself the truth of the matter from reading his thoughts. If she had, she'd never let on, and no one seemed to know about it, and for that, he was grateful.

"Where will you be?" Stryker asked Dan.

"Picking up some pastries at Mrs. Fitz's place since we've already run out," Addie said.

Stryker nodded, knowing they had business other than pastries in mind.

"I thought we could get Ricky a pastry too, and drop it off and check on him," Addie said, walking out with Dan to the Jeep.

"You know that kid crushes on every new she-cat he sees in town."

Addie slipped her arm through Dan's. "I'm already taken."

"That's for damn sure." He got her door.

"We don't have to get him a sweet treat. I just thought it would be nice because he and his brother were trying to help us out."

"Of course, we can. No problem there. I just wanted you to know as soon as you give it to him, he's going to see more into it than you mean."

She chuckled. "I'm *way* older than him."

"He likes the older cougars."

She laughed.

When they arrived at the bakery, Dan swore he could pack on the pounds just smelling the sweetness emanating from the place. Mrs. Fitz had all kinds of fall and Halloween candy on display in the windows, from pumpkin to Frankenstein petite fours, and cakes.

"Omigod, this place is so cute and just heavenly." Addie hurried into the shop where a dozen people were sitting at round tables big enough for four people, giant lollipops hanging down from ribbons tied to white trees. The whole place was washed in white, showing off the bright candies. "I want to buy out the whole store."

Mrs. Fitz heard the bell jingle their arrival and came out wiping her hands on a hand towel, all smiles, until she saw them.

Dan swore it was the first time he'd ever seen her smile visibly slip. She knew they were here for business. "We came to pick up something for Ricky to cheer him up."

"And for Kolby for helping save his brother," Addie added.

"Right."

"And we ate all the goodies you brought earlier, so we wanted to get more for tomorrow." Addie smiled and leaned down to look at all the sweets under glass.

"Why don't you come back here while I finish pulling

some things out of the oven. I've got a couple of girls working for me who can man the front while you pick out what you'd like." Then, all smiles, Mrs. Fitz walked them back into the kitchen.

When they were in the kitchen, Dan noticed nothing was baking, that everything was clean.

She had them sit at a small table, and she said, "What is it you want to know?"

"What was my real mother, Cecilia, involved in that got her killed? And then my father knew about and ended up the same way as my mother? I'd like to know what it is that they think I know that has put me at risk," Addie said.

"I don't know. Really, I don't, or I would have told you before this. I want this resolved as much as you do. I love it here and everyone in the town. I'd protect anyone, if I knew any more than that."

Dan said, "You knew who I was seeing—that I was undercover as her husband."

"I knew Addie, yes. I knew the situation with her parents. No more than that. Alicia was my friend and she often told me how hard it was to maintain her objectivity where you were concerned. She and your father were no match, but you were a darling. I have to admit I wanted to take you home with me instead. Alicia couldn't believe it when you applied to the academy and joined the Bureau."

"So, she didn't have anything to do with me getting where I did in the organization?"

"Are you kidding? You were top of your class because you were that good. Of course, as cougars, we pride ourselves in doing better. Our enhanced cat abilities really help give us the edge. Other than that, you did it all on your own."

Addie looked visibly relieved to know that someone hadn't helped her get through the training or score so well based on family ties.

"Is there anything you can tell us, even if you don't think it's relevant to the case?" Addie asked.

"I said that Alicia and your father's agreement was terminated and that's why she left, but the truth is—and I hadn't wanted to mention it—but your father was seeing another woman. It's understandable since Alicia and he only had a Bureau marriage. That meant the end of the contract between them though and Alicia was recalled."

Addie frowned. "He never married anyone after Alicia left."

"No, but he was seeing a number of other women. The truth of the matter is, they were Bureau plants, all of them investigating him to learn if he was involved with whatever your mother had gotten herself into. They had no intention of marrying him. A couple of male agents befriended him for the same purpose—to learn if he knew anything."

"Does Alicia know what it was my mother was involved in?" Addie asked.

"Alicia was your mother's handler. Even though she and I were best of friends, we didn't discuss the particulars of the job. We worked for different agencies, and we wanted to continue working for them. All I know is that she was your mother's handler before your mother died. And she was your dad's wife for Bureau purposes. Beyond that, you would have to ask Alicia, but I highly doubt she will tell you anything that's classified."

"What about the Muellers digging into this?" Addie asked, sounding concerned.

"They will understand the risks."

"In other words, if they learn what my mother knew, they could be targeted too."

"Yes."

"Thanks, Flo, for sharing with us." Addie turned to Dan. "Are you ready to pick up some treats and see Ricky?"

"Yeah, sure." Dan suspected Addie believed Mrs. Fitz truly didn't know any more than she said she did, but Addie was worried about the Muellers. Sure enough, as soon as they bought two boxes of pastries from Mrs. Fitz and were headed over to the clinic, Addie said, "I want you to tell Rick and Yvonne that they don't need to dig into this any further."

"Are you sure? You know they're capable of dealing with any fallout, particularly since the whole town is on high alert."

"Yes, I'm sure. They're retired. They've left that cloak and dagger business behind. These are their golden years, and they shouldn't have to spend it fearing for their lives."

"Not only are they glad to help, they feel they have a greater purpose in life by taking part in this venture. Not to mention they wouldn't want to feel left out because they're older cats. If you insist, I'll tell them to call their search off."

She frowned at Dan. "You're making me sound like I'm putting them out to pasture."

He shook his head. "I just know them, and I know what it would be like for me if I were retired and the new sheriff asked if I could help. Just like Calvin, the retired highway patrolman, got involved. I don't think I've seen him more eager and willing to take part in anything as much recently as when he thought he could help take down the bad guys."

"All right, but just warn them, okay? Tell them I said not to keep looking if it's too dangerous."

"Will do." Dan knew they'd continue to look into it. Not only had they felt more alive than they had since the last time they had helped on a case, but working as a team with each other, always brought them closer together again. Dan got on his phone after he parked at the clinic. "Hey, Yvonne, Addie's worried about you digging into this case and wants you to call it off." He put the phone on speaker so Addie could hear what she had to say.

"Tell her we're fine. Oh, you have this on speaker. Addie, we're fine. And we've got some news." Yvonne paused. "She's listening in, right?"

"Uh, yeah."

"Okay, Addie's mother learned the assistant director was corrupt, involved in money laundering, off-shore accounts, racketeering, and murder. She was gathering evidence while working her real job. She told Briggs, who was working with her and he said he'd tell his boss. Then she was quickly dispatched."

"And nothing was done about her allegations," Addie said.

"No. It was swept under the carpet, but a couple of people had overheard what was said and they kept quiet."

"And Addie's dad?" Dan asked.

"He didn't seem to know anything about it, but then he was with an agent, female, posing as his girlfriend, and they were out drinking, and he spilled the beans to her. And he was murdered."

"What has this got to do with Addie?" Dan asked.

"Within the past six months, someone got word she had the critical information that would put several people in jail. The assistant director has retired and is in his seventies now, but some of the fledgling agents who were involved in the cover-up still work for the Bureau. They'd all go down if she shared the information."

"I don't know where any of this information could be. I didn't know any of this, not until people started trying to kill me."

"This all happened, starting six months ago," Dan said. "What happened differently for you?"

"I was supposed to get information from a courier about bank robbers who had hit several banks in the area."

"The job could have been a means to send a hit on her," Yvonne said, "and have nothing to do with any real mission."

"True. Did anything happen to you that makes you suspect something triggered this?"

"My apartment was broken into. Several other places had been broken into also. I didn't feel I'd been targeted."

"Possibly, they were random, or the others were done to make it appear as though the same people broke into all the places. Was anything missing?"

"A set of keys. They were just a bunch of old keys I had that I kept meaning to go through and get rid of. You know, like suitcase keys to luggage I no longer owned. A safety deposit key that I found that I'd lost, and had to pay for. They had to change out the lock on the box, so the key would no longer work on it. Stuff that I should have tossed a long time ago."

"Why did you notice it was missing?" Yvonne asked.

"It was sitting in a desk drawer and was on a dragon key ring, something my dad had given me when I had a fascination for everything dragon. It was heavy, so I just used it for all the random keys I'd gathered up and meant to toss."

"Nothing that could be important to the investigation?"

"No. Except for being irritated at losing the dragon key chain, I figured the thieves would have a fun time figuring out what anything belonged to, and they would be worthless to anyone."

CHAPTER 13

Dan was at a loss to figure out what was going on. Then Bridget called him while he and Addie were at the clinic and he was hopeful it would be good news.

"Okay, we have some news. We dug up some information about what Addie's mom, Cecilia, had been working on. Now, if we could find the evidence wherever she might have hidden it, or Addie's dad had hidden it, maybe we could get somewhere with this," Bridget said. "Does Addie have any idea where he might have had the information she'd gathered and then stored it that no one would know of?"

"Everything was sold off. I didn't keep any of it. Not when I was moving around so much."

"Except you used the storage facility to retrieve things that you used to vanish the first time you disappeared after you were shot," Dan reminded her.

"Yes, but other than some of my dad's things—

weapons, another protective vest, a safe house of sorts, well, just stuff, I don't remember anything else that would have been evidence of an incrimination."

"No one knew of it, right?" Dan asked.

"No. That's why it was still there when I went to it."

"Was there any secret hiding place in the storage unit? Was it part of a storage facility, or on private grounds?" Dan asked.

"It's privately held land, but it's mine."

"Then anyone could have found it," Bridget said. "And gone over it with a fine-tooth comb, looking for it."

"It was under a company name that we used. Remember, it was our way out, to vanish, so that no one would discover it. No one. It even has a kitchen, bathroom, and loft bed, if I needed to really hide out. We just called it a storage facility, but it's more like a combo storage and safe house."

"Where is it? We need to search it, just in case," Bridget said.

"Cheyenne, Wyoming. It's not a place where my family ever lived and we never told anyone. We would go through there on our family vacations—after Alicia was gone, and my dad would tell me every time what supplies he had and what they were for. He never said anything about having any evidence of wrongdoing at the FBI. It requires numerous passcodes to get in."

"Then when are we going?" Bridget asked.

"I'm coming," Carl said, as if he would be invited to tag along.

"We're seeing Ricky in a minute and then we're heading

out of here," Dan said.

"You're not going alone," Bridget said.

"No. We'll take a guard force with us," Dan said.

"And I'm coming. Leyton and Travis are off on a mission. I'm not going to sit here and do nothing," Bridget said.

"All right, you're coming," Dan said.

"And me," Carl said. "If we find evidence of wrongdoing, I can give it to the press. I might not work for one of the newspapers now, but I still have a lot of contacts. I can reach them, and we can turn the evidence over to them and they can run the story."

"All right," Dan said, hoping he wasn't making a grave mistake in bringing him with them. "We're going in to see Ricky at the clinic, and then we'll make arrangements to leave."

Addie was carrying the pastries into the clinic and then they entered Ricky's room. Kolby was sitting there with him, talking away. "Whoa, what's this?" Kolby said, taking the box of treats and looking them over.

"For the two of you," Addie said. "How are you doing, Ricky?"

"Much better, thanks." Ricky picked a chocolate pastry from the box. "These look great. When can we go back to investigating things?"

"No time soon," Dan said. "You're staying in bed for another couple of days, and some more time after that when you return to the ranch with Hal and Tracey."

"What about that reporter? Did you lock him up and throw away the key?" Kolby asked, grabbing a blueberry pastry.

"He's at the jailhouse," Addie said.

After they spent a little time with Ricky, Dan told him to behave himself and then they left. Dan started organizing some people to come with them in another vehicle, just in case they needed the backup.

"What if we find nothing there that will prove what my mother had discovered?" Addie asked.

"Then we don't. If we do find something there, maybe we can stop this now."

"What about Carl? Won't he be a problem? He won't have a lot of control over his shifting. What if he decides he wants to sell the story to the highest bidder?"

"He won't be able to. We'll be with him at all times. Someone will always have an eye on him." Dan got a call from Mrs. Fitz, and said, "Yes, have you got any news?"

"No, but I heard about that reporter."

"Yeah, he's now one of us and we have to find him a foster home until he has more control over his shifting."

"I'll take him in. If he doesn't know how to bake, I'll teach him. I have all the weapons training I need to keep him in line, and if push comes to shove, I can take him down as a cat," Mrs. Fitz said.

"Are you sure?" Dan was really surprised she'd want to take him on.

"Yeah, I can use another baker, and in the business I was in, I was often the handler. I'm trained for it, and it'll be fun for me. I'll have someone to talk to. Maybe later, he can work for the newspaper, if the Havertons wouldn't mind hiring him. In the meantime, I'll take him in."

"Okay, right now he's going with us on a mission, but

when we return, I'll turn him over to your care. And thanks, Mrs. Fitz. We sure appreciate you stepping up to the plate to help out." Dan hoped it wouldn't be a mistake. He could see her teaching him to bake and him burning all her pastries. Or turning into a cougar in the middle of the kitchen while he was supposed to be baking treats.

"You're welcome, Dan. Anything I can do to help."

Dr. Kate's receptionist, April Hightower, told Dan before they left the clinic, "You told us to be on the lookout for those FBI agents. It looks like they're here—dark suits, black SUV, side arms under their jackets. I was just in the breakroom, and saw them getting out of the vehicle."

Dan got on his cell and called Chase. "I need you and Bridget here at the clinic pronto. I'll need you to watch over Addie. The feds are here to pick up the bodies at the morgue." Dan didn't want Addie to go down to the morgue in case the men had plans to eliminate her if they saw her.

"We're on our way."

Dan escorted Addie to the breakroom. "Stay here until Chase gets here."

"If these guys are trouble..." Addie said.

"If you hear shooting down in the morgue, you can come down and rescue us."

Addie shook her head and hugged and kissed him.

Dan heard April talking to the men and telling them where to reach the elevator to the morgue. "Stay here. I don't want Kate down there, just in case."

He needed to wait for backup, but he wasn't risking Kate's life if these guys weren't legit. Dan headed for the stairs and saw Bridget and Chase rushing into the clinic.

"Addie's in the breakroom, Chase. Stay with her, all right? Bridget, with me."

He and she raced down the stairs to the basement, but Kate was already there. Damn it.

Kate greeted them and they saw the two men in black suits waiting for her to release the bodies. One of the bodies was lying on the autopsy table.

Dan recognized one of the men as the agent who had suddenly vanished while supposedly guarding Addie's room. Dan said under his breath, "Leipheimer."

"What's the trouble?" the other man asked Kate, eyeing Dan in his sheriff's uniform.

"What the hell happened to you?" Dan asked Leipheimer, pulling out his gun. "You were supposed to be protecting Addie at the hospital."

Leipheimer held up his hands in truce. "Hey, Sheriff, I'm one of the good guys, all right? My relief came and I left."

Even though that could have been a reasonable explanation and his replacement was a bad guy, and Leipheimer was perfectly innocent, Dan thought both men looked and smelled nervous. Why be nervous around a local sheriff, when they were FBI agents? Unless the men really weren't federal agents, or they were so new on the job that they were just worried they'd screw up their assignment. Why send two men who were both new?

Then he recalled what Briggs had said—he didn't know Addie was in the hospital so he hadn't sent anyone to watch over her room.

"I need to see your credentials." Dan motioned to the bodies. "These guys posed as FBI agents and we need to make sure you guys are the real deal."

They showed him their ID and it looked legit. "Now give me the name of your boss so I can verify he sent the two of you and you can take the bodies. Can't be too cautious you know."

The men looked at each and Bridget pulled out her gun and yelled, "They're not federal agents!"

Kate ducked for cover behind the autopsy table. Dan hadn't wanted to shoot the men, certainly not with Kate in the morgue. "Let me see both your hands!"

Both men reached into their suit coats and they drew their weapons. Dan and Bridget dove for cover behind the autopsy table, not a whole lot of cover, but more than the men had. He thought about shoving it at them, but the wheels were locked in place, and they'd lose what little cover they had, even if he ran the table into the men. They fired at the men from the sides of the table, taking them both down as the pretend agents' rounds ricocheted off the metal tables. A couple of their rounds struck the corpse on top of the autopsy table.

"Is everyone all right?" Dan asked Kate and Bridget, pissed that this business would continue and put his whole town at risk.

"I'm fine." Bridget ran to check out the men, kicking their weapons aside. Then she knelt, and pronounced, "They're dead."

At the same time, Dan went to help Kate, who looked a little pale, lying close to the floor, out of harm's way. "Yeah, I'm fine," Kate said, "as long as the corpses don't start shooting back."

Smiling, Dan helped her up from the floor. "Glad everyone's fine. Except for those two." He helped Bridget find any more weapons on the two men, another gun a piece, knives. "Fake badges, fake IDs."

"The man who called you about these men coming, is he involved in this?" Bridget asked. "Or did these men arrive—"

"What the hell," Chase said, barreling into the room with his gun out.

Addie was right behind him, ready to shoot someone. She frowned at the two dead men. "Don't tell me—they're not really FBI agents."

Kate was already getting DNA samples from them, and Bridget took pictures of their faces.

"Hey," Calvin said, coming into the morgue, then spied the dead men on the floor. "Hell. Who are they? There are two men upstairs who say they came for the bodies. April wanted me to check out the situation because she heard all the shooting right before the new 'feds' arrived."

"Send them down." Dan hoped the hell these guys were legit. "Can you run by the sheriff's office and ask Amy to give you the fingerprint kit and bring it back here?"

"Yeah, sure," Calvin said.

Dan wanted to make sure they could identify these men once the feds took them away.

CHAPTER 14

When the two agents arrived at the morgue, they were facing an armed Addie, Chase, Dan, and Bridget.

"That's how we do business here in town," Kate said, asking to see their ID while the others held their weapons on them. Twenty minutes later, Calvin joined the party with the fingerprint kit and Chase took the fingerprints of the dead men.

"I'm calling Briggs and if he's not your boss, you're dead men. Just saying." Dan got on his phone and talked to Briggs. "Okay, tell me something you know about each of the men that imposters won't know."

"Having some trouble?" Briggs asked.

"You're damn right we have. The body count went up from two to four."

"Iverson has a chipped front right tooth from playing a game of baseball with some of the guys. He still needs to get it capped. And Rogers has a new baby girl and he carries a picture of her in his wallet. All the guys give him a time about it because he doesn't have one of his wife."

"Okay, thanks." To the one man, Dan said, "Open wide." Once he saw the chipped front tooth, he figured the men were the right ones this time, but he asked to see Rogers's pictures in his wallet.

He looked a little red-faced and showed a picture of an infant all dressed in pink.

"No picture of your wife?" Dan asked.

"She hates having her picture taken. But I've got one of her with the baby on my phone."

Dan didn't need to see it, but he decided it wouldn't hurt. When he saw the picture, he nodded. "They're both beautiful. Tell her so. Okay, the bodies are..." Forgetting about Bridget, he glanced at her.

She nodded, letting Dan know the men were the real deal, after she'd read their thoughts.

"They're all yours. All four of them."

"You guys mean business," Iverson said.

"Yeah, and so did they," Dan said, showing them the arsenal the men were carrying.

"All we've got to say is we want to get whoever's behind this as much as you do," Rogers said. "We take care of one of our own." He glanced at Addie as if to say he meant her.

"No longer an agent," she said. "Not until this is all over and cleared up."

Dan sure as hell hoped she didn't want to get back into the business once they knew who was behind this and stopped them. He was happy serving as the sheriff of Yuma Town and he had no intention of trying to become an agent with the FBI to join Addie.

Addie came to take his hand and smiled up at him. "I'm not leaving, no matter what happens with this business."

He let out his breath, relieved.

"We'll give you a hand with the bodies," Chase said, and then he and the rest of the men hauled the bodies in bags to a refrigerated unit to take them back to their headquarters.

"Thanks," Iverson said, shaking Dan's hand.

Rogers did the same thing.

"Good luck," they said to Addie.

"Hope we catch these people," Rogers said. "Or you do."

Then they were off and Dan was glad they were able to take care of all the bodies. So was Kate. She didn't have dead bodies in her morgue very often. The ones they had to eliminate in the past—they'd buried.

"Don't anyone tell Leyton what happened here today," Kate said, looking sternly at everyone gathered there. "He's got to concentrate on his mission, and he and Travis need to remain focused. No one was hurt, other than the bad guys, and I'll tell Leyton what happened when he and Travis have taken down the bad guy. All right?"

Everyone agreed.

Her cat, Sheba, wound around her legs, and she leaned down to pick her up. "Glad you weren't in the morgue with us."

That was the thing about having a cougar-shifter clinic. Sheba was loved by all the shifter patients and the hospital staff and welcome there.

"We need to head out to Cheyenne to investigate that storage facility," Dan said. He called Stryker and gave him his orders. He deputized Calvin and another couple of men to help out with sheriff duties. It was late afternoon when Dan and the others picked up Carl. Then Dan, Addie, Carl, and Bridget got on the road, while Chase and Hal came to ride shotgun in a second vehicle.

"I heard there was another 'incident' involving the taking down of more men posing as federal agents," Carl said.

"Yeah, just once, I'd like to have someone who was still alive to question at the end of all the shooting." Dan glanced at Bridget to learn what she knew about the men from listening into their thoughts. He wasn't sure she wanted to discuss it in front of Carl, but she could say she'd tell him later if she didn't.

"All I know is they were trying to figure out how to come up with a story that would fit, then they assumed the only way they could get out of there with the bodies they'd come after was to shoot their way out," Bridget said.

"They wanted to get rid of the evidence," Dan guessed.

"Yes, and that someone higher up is really furious already over the botched-up job. They were worried they'd fail too."

"Which they did and earned their just rewards," Addie said.

"They weren't worried about us as much as about a boss who would eliminate them if they made a mistake?" Dan really thought they were nervous about them learning they were frauds before they could leave with the bodies. Leipheimer, or whatever his real name was, had to have been shocked to see Dan arrive at the morgue.

"Yeah, imagine that? They must take us for pussy cats, not wild cougars," Bridget said.

"Their fatal mistake," Addie said.

"Okay, so just how did you come by all of this?" Carl asked Bridget.

She smiled sweetly at him. "I can read minds."

Carl stared at her. Then he smiled. "Sure, you can."

"Earlier, when you and I were doing research on the computer at the sheriff's office, you were thinking how hot I was. Don't let my mate know you think that, by the way. You might think you're a real lady's man in Denver, but in our part of the world, we were born cougars. You're newly turned, and trouble."

Carl's ears turned red.

Everyone was quiet for a long while.

Then Addie let her breath out and asked Carl, "Which newspaper do you plan to send the information to if we do find evidence of wrongdoing within the Bureau?"

"*The Washington Post*. I have a friend there who's an investigative reporter. She'd gladly take the case on and present it to her editor."

"An old girlfriend," Bridget said, as if trying to prove to Carl she really could read his mind.

Dan was glad she was with them on this trip.

Carl frowned at her. "Yes, an old girlfriend, but if I have a story, I'll send it to her. She investigates it and writes up the story. And then she pays me as her source."

"We can't have anyone see you, Carl, just in case you can't stop the inevitable and have to shift. Which is why we brought the cage for you in the hatchback. Not to confine you because we're afraid you'll hurt us, but because others will wonder why we've got a cougar riding as a pet in an SUV," Dan said. "That means trying to get in touch with your old friends isn't going to work."

"Even if I contact her by text or email? That's usually the way we got in touch. If I turn into a cougar, you can text on my phone as me. You can send her the information. Whatever works. Just use me as your contact."

Addie was really shocked that Carl was working with them on this. She still worried he had a hidden agenda. Though in his current situation, she supposed he finally realized he needed their help to get through this all right.

"I can't believe I can hear so well, or smell scents I couldn't before. Will I have better night vision?" Carl asked.

"Yes. When those men were wearing night vision goggles," Dan said, "we didn't need them."

"Even when you're human?" Carl asked, in awe.

"Yes. Just like you have an enhanced sense of smell and of hearing now while you're human."

"Okay, that makes sense. What if I get injured? I can't go to a human hospital. I can't believe I'm calling anything human-run as if I were an alien. I guess I really am."

"As a cat, your DNA only shows cougar DNA. As a human, you only have human DNA. If you end up in a hospital, or in a zoo, no one could tell you were a shifter," Addie said.

"A zoo? Oh, great."

"Or a big cat refuge," Addie warned.

"The problem comes if you shift in front of humans," Dan said. "Now, we do have someone who has volunteered to take you in. And you're fortunate for that."

"Oh? You said no one likes me. Why would anyone agree then?"

"Mrs. Florence Fitzgerald. She owns the bakery shop and she's willing, no reason really given," Dan said.

"You're kidding," Addie said, not believing the retired CIA agent would take in a new cougar as disagreeable as Carl had been. Then again, he seemed to be trying to fit in, to help out.

"Okay, so what do I do? Live at her house? Serve up desserts?" Carl sounded like this had to be a joke.

"Bake."

"Hell, I can't cook. Even making microwave dinners can prove to be a mistake. Why do you think I have so many girlfriends?"

"You know, Carl, the more I hear you talk, the less likeable you are, and you were at the bottom of the barrel already," Addie said.

"Hey, I have to eat, don't I? I guess someone else will have to offer to take me in. I suppose the paper wouldn't be so bad to work for," Carl said, sounding like he was changing his tune about working for a small, local paper.

"Mrs. Fitz is it for now," Dan said. "You're lucky anyone offered. She'll teach you to bake and you'll stay in the kitchen. Hopefully, you won't turn while you're there, but if you do, she has an office off the kitchen and you can sit it out in there. Also, that way none of her human patrons will see you. I can imagine a whole lot of human patrons dashing out of there in the face of a cougar racing through the dining area. If you even pulled a stunt like that, one of us would come over and tranquilize you and stick you in a cage, for the safety of the patrons, even if the cougars knew you were safe to be around."

Carl was quiet for some time. Then he suddenly asked. "Do you think the people who hired me will be coming after me too?"

"Yes, I'm sure of it," Addie said. "If they hired you and their men are all dead, they might feel if you're alive, you could compromise the situation. They wouldn't want to risk a loose end like that. I'm certain they planned to eliminate you at Dan's house after you video recorded the situation. Even though you hadn't known the woman's name, see how you were able to point out the woman from a photograph? If you think you're safer on your own out there, think again."

"I wasn't thinking of leaving and hiding out somewhere else. This business with the shifting means I'm not going anywhere. I'm sorry about nosing into your business before," Carl said to Dan. "About all of it. I was just hell-bent on a story, and yours looked like it had so much promise. Now I know it did, only it isn't one I could ever tell."

"You need to apologize to Chase and Shannon."

"I will."

"I've talked to Chet Kensington, one of Bridget's friends, who is an agent like her, Travis, and Leyton. He has a safe house in Cheyenne. He's on an assignment right now, but by the time we reach his place around noon tomorrow, he should be through with the job and join us. He's eager to help us with the search," Dan said.

"Are we driving through the night?" Addie asked, hoping they would. She kept worrying if something was in the storage facility, someone would learn about it and remove it, if they could find anything.

"Yeah. We'll take turns driving in shifts. Except for Carl. He could turn into a cougar and we can't have that. And not you either, unless you feel up to it."

"I'll take a shift," Addie said. "I feel fine now. Did you tell him we're bringing a brand-new cougar?"

"Yeah. Since he's never met Carl, I filled him in on who he is and what's happened. Which is why he's eager to help. Though it's usually not their job and he had to ask Chuck, his boss, if it was okay to work with us on this."

"Chuck okayed it?" Addie asked. She hadn't met the man either and she was glad they'd have a local cougar agent who could aid them.

"Yeah. He's a good guy."

The drive was quiet the whole time, no issues. She almost felt as though this was wasted manpower, but she knew better. Even if nothing happened, it was better to have more manpower than not enough. Not only did they have to protect each other, if they should get into a firefight, they had to protect Carl. He wasn't allowed to have a gun, not after shooting Ricky, though he hadn't known the cougar was a boy. Still, he wasn't one of them. He'd have to prove he could be there for them, as they were for each other. He had to prove to them he could be trusted, and he was one of the good guys.

"Is Mrs. Fitz single?" Carl suddenly asked.

"Yes," Addie said, smiling. And about twenty-five years older than Carl. At least Flo knew how to use a gun too, so if Carl did anything threatening, she knew how to handle him.

As much as Addie would like to believe he was completely committed to them, she couldn't. Not yet.

"Do you mind if I sleep back here?" Carl asked.

"Go ahead," Addie said. "We'll all be taking turns."

They'd driven about five hours, when they stopped again for gas and this time grabbed some burgers. Carl suddenly said, "I've got to return to the car. In a hurry."

Addie headed out with him. "Are you going to shift?"

"Yeah, and I'm fighting just stripping out here in the parking lot." He finally managed to get into the car. They had parked it next to a grassy area. Everyone parked on top of the building like it would kill them to walk, so the parking spaces out there were empty.

He was suddenly shifting and lying down on the very last seat.

Addie opened the windows. "Don't get up and don't look out the windows. Everyone's bringing their food, and yours, to the car. We'll be on our way again. Just stay down."

He made a grumbly, growly noise, and remained hidden.

"How's he doing?" Dan asked, as he climbed into the passenger seat, and Addie took over the driving.

"Growly. Can you blame him? We can completely control our shifting. It makes all the difference in the world. He's a slave to it when he's probably used to nothing or nobody dictating to him. Total life changer."

Bridget said, "Here's your dinner, Carl. I got one of those Styrofoam containers so you can use it as a dish. Though I guess Hal brought you a food dish too for when you turned all cat on us." She poured water in a water dish and set it on the floor for him. "You should be all set. Sorry you weren't able to eat your meal before you had to shift."

Carl gobbled up his burger, drank some of his water, and settled down on the seat.

They drove for hours before they heard Carl moving about in the backseat, dressing.

"How are you feeling, Carl?" Addie had been sleeping in the center seat, Bridget driving, and Dan keeping an eye on things as a passenger in the front seat, after rotating drivers.

"Well rested. Having weird dreams of fighting with another cougar."

"Just don't get into a real one. You haven't had all the lifetime experiences with being one and learning to playfight." Addie unbuckled her seatbelt, leaned forward, and kissed Dan's cheek. "Want to lie down for a while? I'll take over guard watch."

"We'll pull in and get gas up ahead." Bridget called to Hal and told him the plans. Then they pulled into the next travel center, a couple of cars gassing up, a couple of more parked next to the travel center.

Everyone took bathroom breaks, gassed up the car, and Addie switched with Dan so he could get some rest. She was looking forward to sleeping in a bed with him tonight, hoping they didn't have squeaky beds at Chet's place.

Then they returned to the cars. It was six in the morning, and they still had six hours to drive. No sign of anyone following them so far. Addie and everyone else was grateful for that.

Dan woke after about four hours and asked if Addie wanted him to take over the driving, but she said no. She could make it and they'd already made another gas stop an hour ago when they'd switched drivers. They should make it to the storage facility without having to stop again.

Bridget said to Carl, "Quit thinking about how you're going to get yourself out of this mess. You're stuck with us."

Addie smiled. She loved how Bridget could read minds.

"Yeah, well if you were suddenly thrown into a situation like this, you'd be thinking the same thing."

Addie figured he assumed Bridget had guessed how he was feeling, but she knew Bridget had to have read his mind and was warning him he had to change how he viewed the situation or get himself into further trouble.

"I'm not going rogue," Carl grumbled.

"Not a morning person?" Bridget asked, cheerfully.

She seemed to be and so was Addie. She liked her and was glad to have found so many cougar friends here.

"Not a cat person."

Everyone laughed.

"Okay, I don't get something. Well, a lot of somethings, but how can Hal and Tracey Haverton own a horse ranch when they're cougars?" Carl asked.

"They bred and raised them," Dan said. "If a human raises an animal, feeds him, and takes care of him, the animal learns to trust him. He smells both the cougar and human side of Hal and Tracey and the others. Well, and us. The problem would be if the horse wasn't afraid of a wild cougar. Cougars are territorial. They smell enough male cougar shifters to know to stay out of the areas where we live."

"Do you have sex as cougars?" Carl asked.

"Lots more fun as humans," Addie said.

"Though having kits can be easier for a mother than as

a human," Bridget said.

"A woman can bear cougar kits?" Carl asked, sounding shocked.

"No. She shifts into a cougar first! Jeesh. Okay, so it's really, really rare, if doable at all that a cougar shifter gets a human pregnant. I've never heard of it happening with a cougar," Bridget said, "but I've heard of a wolf shifter that happened to."

"Wait, wolf?"

"Caracal cat, coyote, jaguar. We've heard rumors of polar bear shifters in Alaska, but that might not be true. We've only ever met a caracal cat shifter, but the family we had seen said they'd run across a wolf shifter pack. They call themselves *lupus garous*. And one mated a part coyote, part wolf."

"Anything's possible then."

"Yeah, just be careful of having sex with a human and not being protected. The offspring doesn't have all our abilities, but some. You'd have to turn the mother, possibly. And if you turn one person, it could prove disastrous. They might have a whole family that would then need to be turned."

"And it snowballs. Gotcha. Good thing I don't have any family."

"Or friends," Bridget said.

"I have friends. Not close friends. Associates. What if I have a girlfriend? Cat girlfriend?"

"Then you need to take precautions not to have kids."

"Or else, you'd take care of me, right?"

"Right," Dan said.

"What about divorce?"

"Marriage, divorce, it all can happen. We hope that if you find someone, it's for life," Addie said.

"But you don't think it's likely." Carl sounded a little blue that no cougar female would want to have anything to do with him.

"Just remember, Carl, you're prickly. You've lived off other's woes. You did everything for gain at others' expenses. You created all kinds of trouble for us in the past, and more recently. And you're a brand-new shifter. That means trouble in and of itself. It also means you'll have to work extra hard to change your way of thinking if you want to make any inroads with the she-cats," Dan said. "You'll have to prove you've become a new man."

"I can't cause trouble for you any longer. Not without outing myself."

"Correct, but your attitude has to change. Maybe the right she-cat will come along and voila, you have a total change of heart. It can happen. I had no intention of finding a male cat to mate. I just rescued Travis and that was it. We were so perfect for each other, I was just glad he was one of the good guys," Bridget said.

"I'll have to meet a cat from out of town," Carl grumbled.

"You'd be better off sticking around here," Dan said. "There are more of us to help you out. Though we don't advertise who we are, I haven't heard of another town run specifically by cougars. You'll be safe here. Happy? If you want to be."

"Why were you running around with a gun on Dan's

property?" Addie suddenly asked.

"Hell, I recorded cougars killing people. I worried they'd still be hanging around the property. They're territorial, you know. Did you think I'd just shoot pictures of them if any of them attacked?"

"See where that got you?" Addie asked, and smiled.

CHAPTER 15

When they finally arrived at the safe house, Chet met them outside. "All the she-cats are taken, I suppose," Chet said, eyeing Addie, since he knew Bridget had mated Travis, and Leyton had hooked up with Kate.

"Addie and I are mated," Dan confirmed before she could say so.

Typical alpha male cougar, but she loved him for it. She noticed Carl appeared to be taking mental notes of what to say and do to learn if a she-cat was available. He'd learn. He was smart.

"And this must be the reporter," Chet said in a disagreeable way.

"Yeah, I'm the reporter, Carl Nelson, and I swear if you all will let me, I'm trying to make amends." Carl offered his hand to shake Chet's.

"Chet Kensington." Chet shook his hand. "And I take down rogue cougars."

"I've heard. I won't turn rogue on you." Carl spoke with conviction, but they never knew what would cause a newly turned cat to suddenly turn rogue. Past history? Unable to deal with their cougar half? They weren't sure.

"Good. I'd have to be the one to take care of it." Chet turned to Addie. "Where's this land and the storage building?"

"Here." Addie pulled out a map she'd drawn to show him where it was located. "There are no real identifying marks for the property and it's on a dirt road. Just land as far as the eye can see. A river runs through it and it has trees, but all of the land out there is undeveloped."

"Weren't you ever worried that someone might break into the building when no one was there to take care of it?" Chet asked, motioning for them to come inside the house. "I made hamburgers on the grill for everyone."

"It's out in the country, way off the beaten path. So, no. It's built like Fort Knox. On the outside, it looks like an old metal building. Inside, the walls are made of reinforced concrete block, a roof built of the same material. A metal roof covers it to disguise the fact it's so reinforced. Dad must have really worried someone might find it and access what was inside. I always knew it was secure, but I just believed he was afraid someone would break in and steal his weapons cache and then use it to commit crimes."

They all fixed up their hamburger buns the way they liked them, Addie adding a little mustard and mayonnaise, pickles, lettuce, and grilled mushrooms to hers. She watched as Dan loaded his with mushrooms and cheddar cheese. That looked good too. Once everyone was done, they sat out on the back patio to eat.

"Now you think there might be more than the weapons inside?" Chet asked.

"Maybe. Why else build it like that? Hidden from prying eyes, the location so secret, no one would ever know about it, under a different name? Anyway, Dad was extremely law-abiding. He never jay-walked even, always went the speed limit, even when I missed the school bus and I was running late for school. He always went in the 'Enter' door, and always exited through the door labeled 'Exit.' He never wanted to give anyone access to his weapons and aid a criminal in committing felony crimes."

"I don't blame him," Dan said. "I'd be concerned with leaving weapons unattended like that."

"They're in a secure vault in the hidden basement," Addie said.

"Wouldn't people have learned what he did?" Dan asked.

"All cougars helped him build it and only parts of it. No one person ever saw the finished product or what went inside. Except for Dad and me."

"All right. Well, if everyone's ready, let's go." Dan sounded eager to find what they'd come for and return home.

They'd taken bottled water with them for the trek they'd have to make to the building, wearing hiking boots and backpacks.

She thought Dan didn't like being out here with her without the protection of the entire town of cougars. Not for himself, but for her and the others. She wished they could resolve this so he and she could go anywhere they liked without worrying they'd get into another firefight.

It took them half an hour to reach the land, traveling fifteen miles on dirt roads, and finally coming to a fence where they had to park the vehicles.

"It's isolated all right," Chase said. "Beautiful."

"And a two-mile hike from here," she said.

"How did you manage when you were injured the last time?" Dan asked, helping to push the barbed wire aside for everyone to make it through. Then Chet held it apart for him to make it through.

"Kate took care of me at your place, and then I slept for several days at the storage facility. It's fully equipped for living for a time—septic tank, electricity run underground, solar panels, a well. It has a bathroom and kitchen. And Dad added a cellular repeater system to boost a signal out here."

"If you hadn't led us here, I doubt I would have found it," Chet said.

"I rarely come here. Well, never, except this time and the time after my Dad died, and when I was wounded and feared for my life. That means no trails are left behind, not like they would have been if I came here often."

They finally spied a building that looked like a partially rusted old storage building. Trees, shrubs, and wild grasses had grown up all around it. It definitely looked abandoned.

"No critters living inside, right?" Carl asked.

"Maybe a spider or two. It's well-sealed off."

She moved to the only thing about the building that looked secure. The door—solid steel. She used a code to get into another box behind that and another code to unlock the door.

"Are there any boobytraps inside?" Bridget asked.

Dan smiled at her, but Bridget looked serious.

"Dad had considered it, but he was afraid we'd come here and find dead bodies rotting away. Or one of us would trigger a boobytrap accidentally. Because of that, he never wanted to set them up."

She entered the building and turned on the lights, then locked the door behind them.

Storage lockers lined two of the walls. A bathroom and kitchen were at one end of the building. A loft above was equipped with a bed and extra clothes for her.

"All these lockers are damn secure," Chet said, examining them.

"Made of heavy duty steel." She used a password for the first one and opened it, revealing non-perishable foods. Then she unlocked all the rest so everyone could search through them for any clues as to why her parents and she had become targets.

"Where's the entrance to the hidden basement?" Dan asked.

"I'm not finding anything in these," Bridget said. "Just tons of cash, clothes, passports, and IDs."

Hal and Chase were searching the kitchen and Chet was looking up in the loft for any hidden compartments. "The floor looks like it's more substantial than it needs to be up here," Chet said. "I'm looking for a hidden compartment in the floor."

"We'll be in the basement," Addie said and led Dan to the last wall locker, unlocked a panel in the side, and entered a password.

Bridget and Dan were watching her, and she smiled, knowing they were as in awe about this place as she was. Then she had an idea. "You know, once I'm done being target practice, or even before that, this place could serve as a safe house for any of us in the law enforcement agencies—the Havertons', the sheriff's office, and the Cougar Special Forces."

"This would make one hell of an ideal place to store some of our gear," Chet agreed.

"I'm all for it," Dan said, "and I know Tracey and Hal would agree."

"I definitely am up for it," Hal said.

Addie heard a click, telling her the movable shelf unit in front of them was unlocked, and she pushed it open to reveal steps down into a basement. She turned on a switch, and she climbed into the locker and down the steps.

"Wow," Bridget said.

Chase and Hal quit searching in the kitchen and came to check it out. "I want one of these in the house," Hal said. "Cool hideaway. Not sure what I'd use it for. Wine cellar, maybe."

Chet continued to look for a hidden compartment in the floor up in the loft.

The basement was all painted in white, fluorescent lights making it appear bright and not dark like a dungeon. Storage lockers filled two of the walls.

"Same as before?" Bridget asked.

"Yeah, only the one three doors to the left on the south wall has the hidden vault." Addie used codes to get into the first two keypads, then pushed the storage shelf in and it opened to a massive vault.

She turned on the lights in there, and inside, they got to look at all the weaponry—assault rifles, handguns, rifles. Everyone admired the weaponry while Addie began opening all the other wall lockers for everyone to search through.

Dan asked her, "You've never come across any papers or anything that seemed out of place?"

"Dad had maps of everywhere, though some of it might be a little outdated, with new roads not marked in areas. He had tons of city maps. Even so, I would have just used my GPS and not bothered with the paper maps, for the most part."

"I found some thumb drives in a secret compartment in the back of the bedframe," Chet hollered from upstairs.

"I found some in the false bottom of a can of cleaner," Carl said from the kitchen.

Addie hadn't realized he hadn't come downstairs with them.

Everyone continued to look for anything else, like it was an Easter egg hunt and they each needed to discover their own treasure. She hadn't realized her dad had hidden anything anywhere. She guessed he thought he'd keep it secret from her and she'd stay safe. She wished he'd told her and she could have exposed the corruption in the ranks.

She just hoped that what they'd find on the drives would really reveal enough to help put some people behind bars and stop people from coming after her. She was looking over the bare walls, not believing she'd find anything, but her dad had been so clever, what if it was right before her eyes and she just didn't see it?

Hal and Chase were taking apart weapons, looking for anything hidden inside. She couldn't imagine her father would hide anything inside one of them that would make the weapon inoperable.

Then Bridget said, "Uh-huh," and pulled two flash drives from the butt of the rifle. "Your dad was really brilliant."

"We're behind on the job," Chase said to Hal.

"We have as long as it takes to search every square inch of this place," Dan reminded them.

Addie agreed with Dan. She didn't want to find anything in haste, and then leave what could be the most vital information behind.

"Does anyone have a laptop or a cable that can connect to our cell phones to check and see what's on the flash drives?" Bridget asked.

"There's a laptop underneath the kitchen table. And a gun," Addie said. "There should be a cable in one of the storage cabinets upstairs that can connect with your phone, if you'd rather look at the contents that way."

"Okay, I'll gather up all the thumb drives and see if there's anything on them." Bridget glanced in Hal and Chase's direction. "Since I found mine." She smiled at them and they chuckled.

Then Bridget headed up the stairs. "I'm getting the laptop and if you guys will toss me your flash drives, I'll check and see what they contain. If nothing important, we're back to square one."

Addie sure hoped they'd find something. She continued to look at the walls while Dan was checking for secret compartments in the tile floor.

The other guys didn't find anything in the weapons and had put them back together, then replaced them in their wall lockers. They began looking for any hidden compartments in the floor. Chase paused at the wall lockers. "Are these attached to the walls?"

"I believe so. They don't seem to move at all when you open the doors," Addie said.

"I'll check just to be sure." Chase began trying to move them from the first one on down the line. "All secure, wait, this one isn't."

"I'll give you a hand," Dan said, coming to help him. They pulled the wall locker away from the wall, needing Hal's help too.

And stared at the steel plate hiding a compartment in the floor.

It wasn't locked and Dan pulled it open. They'd hit the mother lode. Or at least, it appeared that way if all the metal boxes down there contained what they'd hoped for.

"How are you doing up there, Bridget?" Addie asked, going over to see what all the men had found in the floor.

"It's all your mother's photos and documents of what she found. What did you find down there?"

The guys were all hauling out the files, and Addie began opening the metal boxes. "Looks like the original documents detailing all kinds of shady deals that went down," Addie said, pulling out a file and flipping through the documents. "This is going to be bad news for some agents. We need to go through all of this before we leave here and see who all it lists to discover if Alicia or my boss, Briggs, were involved."

"We need to send it to my contact with *The Washington*

Post," Carl said. "Hell, I even know someone with *The New York Times*. We're not friends. Far from it. I sort of stole his girlfriend. Unintentionally. She just liked me better than him. It didn't last, but to get a breaking news story like this? He'll bite."

"Give it to him to send it," Addie said. "I'd rather this be sent before we even leave here in case we have any trouble along the way."

"You've got Internet out here?" Carl asked.

"Sure do. It was important for me to keep up with what was happening in the world when I came here. That's how I knew no one had reported that the courier had died, that I'd been hurt, none of it, the first time I came here."

"Yeah, got it," Bridget said.

The guys began hauling the boxes of files up to the main floor, and Addie sat at the table to scan through the documents, looking for names of everyone involved.

"We'll need to scan all these documents and send them too," Addie said. "Just in case none of this is documented on the flash drives."

"I saw a scanner in one of the wall lockers," Dan said, and went to retrieve it. He set it on a long narrow table.

"Here, I'll scan them once Addie looks them over," Chase said.

Dan joined her at the table and considered the documents she'd already gone through. "You're a fast reader."

"Scanner, but I also have a really good memory."

"Photographic?" Dan asked, raising his brows.

She smiled.

"Hell, we want her working for us," Hal said.

"No, with our agency. You failed to mention that little skill set," Bridget said, smiling at her.

"I never think about it. It's so automatic."

"We need her in the sheriff's office," Dan said, taking a stack of the papers for Chase to scan.

Though Addie liked the idea of taking down rogue cougars, or apprehending wildlife traffickers, she wanted most of all to stay and work with the sheriff's office. She could help out with the mundane and anything wilder. For now, she needed some sanity in her life. She just hoped sending the word to the press would help to protect her. "Send this to CNN also."

Carl gave her a thumbs up.

"How is it going with your associates?" Addie asked Carl. Bridget was overseeing what he was writing and sending.

"Good. Both of the reporters have dropped what they were working on to start sorting through this stuff. I think I might have had a job with one of the big boys if I hadn't been turned."

"Sorry about that," Addie said.

"Yeah, well, I always say things happen for a reason. Maybe my harassing you so much earlier meant this was destined to be. And now here I am, getting the word out to the world about what's gone down, and maybe I can do some good."

"As long as the FBI doesn't try to stop the press from releasing this information," Dan warned.

"So far, no mention of Alicia or Briggs, so I'm hoping that's a good sign," Addie said.

"Okay, sending the information to CNN," Carl said. "Maybe, if they feel this is accurate, they'll put it on the airways."

Addie looked up from the file she was reading and saw Chet still looking for more hiding places in the kitchen.

Dan and Hal had begun to read over the documents, looking for names too.

"The person I'm talking to at CNN says I'm no longer working for *The Denver Post*. I explained I've been working investigative pieces. Can I mention the sheriff's office in Yuma Town is coordinating this with me? I don't want to cause trouble for everyone."

"Yeah, let me talk to them," Dan said. "Everyone here can testify at a trial, except for you, Carl."

"What can we do about that?"

"Fake you're dying or something and get your testimony on tape." Dan joined Carl at the laptop and said to everyone, "I'm going live." He said to the news reporter on Skype, "I'm Sheriff Dan Steinacker of Yuma Town, Colorado, and with one of my deputies, one FBI agent, one agent who takes down wildlife traffickers, and a couple of other agents, we've located a cache of documents that supports what the investigative reporter, Carl Nelson, has told you already. We've had some real issues with assassins trying to take out the FBI agent, and us along with her, as we've fought to protect her. We need to get this on the air so that everyone who is involved in the graft and corruption, and trying to silence us, will back off."

Wendy Holcomb asked, "Can we air what you've just said, Sheriff Steinacker?"

Dan smiled. "You sure as hell can."

"We're still getting the documents in as we're speaking," Wendy said, "and we'll update you on all the latest information as we learn of it." The reporter signed off, and they realized what they were witnessing was her live broadcast while they were watching her on Skype.

"Thank you," Wendy said to Dan. "And to all of you who discovered this. We'll be posting more news on it as we go through the files." She paused and looked in someone else's direction. She nodded. "The FBI Director has already called our boss." She smiled. "He wouldn't if this wasn't real news. Keep the documents coming."

"Thanks," Dan said. "We figured we needed the word to get out to protect ourselves."

Then they ended the conversation, and Carl had to field calls from *The Washington Post* and *The New York Times*, the editors furious with him that he hadn't given them exclusive news stories.

"Hey, they're trying to kill us," Carl said. "I just got involved, but these hard-working law-enforcement officials' lives have been on the line since they tried to protect the FBI agent, whose mother, another FBI agent, first uncovered this."

That started another bout of questioning and Carl was in his glory, explaining all he knew. Addie knew then he was one of the team. He might still have to work on being well-liked, but he was one damned good reporter, worked well under pressure, and was in his heyday.

She began to go back over the documents and found some mentions of Alicia's job to watch over Addie's dad, to learn what he knew, if anything, about what Addie's mother had uncovered before she'd been murdered. It appeared Alicia had been telling the truth. She'd been there to protect both Addie's dad and Addie, but when he began seeing other women, Alicia had terminated the contract. Addie realized Alicia had fallen for her dad, and though it was supposed to be a marriage in name only, it appeared it had been more than that for her. She'd left and he'd been fine until Addie turned eighteen and her father was out with his girlfriend, also an FBI agent.

He'd mentioned her too.

Addie paused to look up newspaper accounts on the incident and learned they'd gone out drinking, had taken separate cars, and he'd died. She'd conveniently been following his car home when he drove off a bridge.

The girlfriend had stated no other cars had been involved, and the accident was attributed to him having had too much to drink and losing control of his car on the bridge. She was hysterical when she called the police and they came to investigate. She didn't call Addie, letting the police contact her instead.

Of course, Addie knew all about that from having lived it. Now she wondered if the woman was also part of this whole business. Like Alicia had said—the girlfriends had been in place to watch him, to listen, to learn if he knew anything about what Addie's mother had known.

"One of the field agents involved in stalking my mother before she died, according to my father, was Paris Pepion's father, Seth Pepion."

"What about any connection to Dirk Carter?" Dan asked.

"I haven't seen one yet." Addie was still looking for information about Briggs.

It was nearly eleven that night when she found a connection to Dirk. "He's the son of the woman who was dating my dad, the last one to see him alive the night he died. She'd divorced Dirk's father, and then used her maiden name. Dad says here she had a son who wants to join the FBI like me. Maybe we could be friends, though he was living with his father so I never met him. Dirk Carter."

"One mother, one father, both who could be directly related to your parents' deaths and who work on the same team as you. To protect their parents, they were to keep an eye on you?"

"We've only been working together for the last six months."

"Right before the attempt on your life," Dan said.

"You're still thinking it had to be either your boss, Briggs, or Alicia who had a hand in this," Bridget said.

"Yeah. How could we all be on the same team, I was sent on a mission, and then I am nearly killed, and it's all hushed up? Besides the team members, both Briggs and Alicia knew what we were doing."

They worked until midnight, sorting through everything. "Didn't find anything else," Chet said, sitting on the bed in the loft.

"I think we have enough files that will take investigators a couple of years to comb through, but I don't want the FBI to have it, not until we know they won't cover it up," Addie said.

"I've scanned the last of it," Chase said.

"Sending the last scanned documents to the newspapers and CNN," Carl said.

Addie looked at the send to addresses. "And *The Denver Post*?"

"Yeah," Carl said, looking up at Addie. "I wanted them to know that this time I had a real story. A noteworthy story. One that will hopefully do some good."

"You're all right, Carl," Addie said, giving him her seal of approval.

"Yeah," everyone else agreed.

"Are we about ready to leave?" Hal asked. "Should I lock up everything?"

"Do we take the files out of here? Or leave them here, now that we've scanned them and sent them to the news agencies?" Addie asked.

"Let's leave them here, secure for now. Just in case, I sent all the documents in the files to all the cougars in our area for safekeeping," Dan said.

"I love your town," Addie said, giving him a big hug.

"I love you." Dan hugged her back, and kissed her. "I'm sorry for all you've had to go through, and hope this is the last of it."

"What about the flash drives? Should we take those?" Bridget asked.

"No, let's hide everything back where we found them," Addie said, and began to put the files back in boxes.

Chase, Dan, and Hal returned the files in the hidden place in the vault's floor and moved the locker back in place. Addie returned the laptop to its secret place underneath the table. And the flash drives were all hidden in their respective hiding places. Once everything was secure, Addie locked everything up.

Carl swore under his breath. Afraid something bad had happened with regard to his contacts, like they'd all be arrested and the information they'd sent them confiscated, she realized it wasn't that at all. Not when he began stripping off his clothes.

"Do we wait for him to change back?" Bridget said.

"No, it could be hours. He can run as a cougar to the vehicles and get there even faster than us," Dan said.

"Yeah, much easier to trek like that," Chase agreed.

Bridget gathered up Carl's clothes and stuck them in her backpack. "Ready? Let's go."

Looking all growly, Carl was at the door, waiting for someone to open it as they all got their backpacks on. It was his own fault he got involved with them!

CHAPTER 16

Before they left the storage facility, Chet was watching the news on his phone and said, "Well, Fox News and the other stations are running with it now. Only problem now is they'll be all converging on Yuma Town for the story."

Dan shook his head. "We didn't have much choice. We had to stop this now." He got a call from his dispatcher and put it on speaker.

"Stryker's got a media firestorm here. Calvin's motel is booked, and so are Chase and Shannon's cabins and every other place far and wide with news media, looking to get the story. Uhm, Roger and Milly Haverton wanted to know why they didn't get the news first," Amy said.

Dan chuckled. "Don't tell them I said so but they're too small to deal with the fallout. In other words, I didn't want them getting hurt over this."

"Okay, that's what they thought, but I just wanted to warn you."

Hal agreed with Dan. "Mom and Dad don't know what we've been up against."

Amy said, "Right, well, they want to discuss this with you too."

Hal chuckled. "As soon as I get home."

"When are you returning, Dan? Stryker said he can't deal with the media. And he sure doesn't want Calvin talking to them. So far, Stryker's managed to tell them, 'no comment,' until you can get back here."

"We just finished up, and we'll be getting some sleep and heading out in the morning. We won't be arriving until the next morning. Stryker will just have to hold down the fort until then. No comment works for now."

"Mrs. Fitz has been having a ball, selling her pastries and such. She's been talking a lot to the reporters, which means everyone's over there getting whatever story they can from her."

Addie frowned. "She knows about all this business already?"

"No, just about what you've been through—the assassination attempts, etcetera. I think she believes if she tells the world how they're trying to silence you, that will keep them from trying to any further."

Addie got a call then and saw it was from her boss. Former boss. "Yes, sir?" She put it on speaker so everyone could listen in.

"Got to go," Dan said to Amy. "Give you a call later. Or call me if you have any further trouble."

"Yes, sir," Amy said, and ended the call.

"Hell, you could have given me a heads up about this,"

Briggs said to Addie.

"For what it's worth, your name wasn't mentioned in any of the documents, so as far as I can tell, you're clear of any wrongdoing."

"I could have told you that. In fact, I think I did."

"True. I didn't know we'd find anything when we had a hunch and looked into it. The other thing was no one's protecting me, or the rest of my team."

Several gave her a thumbs up. Dan hugged her.

"And, I didn't call you because I no longer work for you. I was fired. Remember?"

"My boss got a call from the Director, who wants to know what in the hell is going on. He wants you reinstated."

"I'm a whistleblower. It won't work out. I'm staying where I am." Or at least she was once she returned to Yuma Town. "Who put us all on the same team? Did you know that the man who was following my mother before she was killed was Paris Pepion's dad? Coincidence that she was on the team with me? Here's another: Dirk Carter's mother was the last one to see my dad alive. And then he's on the team with me. Who put the team together?"

"Alicia did. Damn it, Addie, why didn't you tell me about all this before?"

"Why did she hire Dan to work as my husband on some jobs?"

"As a safety precaution for you, in the event the agents on your team weren't watching your back?"

"Or as a ruse, to pretend she was trying to protect me. Except this time, she didn't think either of the last cases I was on warranted Dan's being there."

"What would her motivation have been? I don't see the tie-in."

"What if she was a woman scorned?"

Briggs didn't say anything for a moment, then said, "I don't see it."

"In my dad's documents, he said she was assigned to him right after Mom died, supposedly watching him, to see if he knew anything. But what if Alicia had a dual purpose in mind—she wanted to do the FBI's bidding, maybe believing it was for National Security, or maybe they had something on her and used it against her. And maybe she had a thing for my dad."

"You have proof?"

"Dad said she left him when he started seeing other women, all FBI agents who were also keeping an eye on him. How has she reacted to all the news?"

"She's furious with you and can't understand how I could have let this happen."

"Did you fire me, or was it her call?"

"I fired you. And if you have to know, I assumed the men and women protecting you seemed to be doing a hell of a lot better job at it than we could, so that's why I fired you. To get you out of here before someone took you out for good."

"Thanks."

"You're welcome."

"What are you going to do about Paris and Dirk?"

"Look into it. I can't fire them without finding evidence that supports your theories."

"Like they were there when I was nearly killed and they didn't even report it?"

"They've been good at covering their tracks. I'm sure they've had help. I've got to go. The media blitz is calling for my head." He hung up on her.

"Do you really think Alicia was in love with your father?" Chase asked.

"Yeah, I do." She opened the door and Carl ran out as a cougar and disappeared into the brush.

She hoped he didn't get lost. Everyone moved out of the building, and she locked the door. As soon as they began the trek in the dark, they heard a cat cry out in fury. Everyone hurried to spread out, guns out.

Carl might have run into another cougar, or something else out here and scared himself, or he'd run into real trouble. How could anyone have known they were here, if they were?

She didn't think they could have tracked her laptop in the storage facility. Their cell phones? Yeah, possibly.

They should have swept the vehicles and their clothes for bugs.

What about Carl? And the clothes he was wearing? What if they'd bugged them? Since he was working for them, but he didn't know about that.

Great.

With their cat's night vision, they spread far apart so they wouldn't all be shot in a barrage of rounds, crouching, trying to stay low to the ground. In that instant, she wanted to be a cougar, but she was such a good shot, she thought she would do better with her gun. Dan stuck too close to her, and she wanted him to move farther away from her. She knew he wouldn't though, afraid for her after the last few times.

She heard everyone moving forward, though she only heard them because she had a cougar's sensitive hearing. She prayed Carl was okay when she didn't hear anything more coming from the direction where she'd heard the cry. No shooting, nothing.

Her heart was pounding like crazy. She wished Carl would come bounding back to them so she knew he was all right.

She couldn't see the others now for the woods and the brush. Then she heard another cat off to the south crying out. Hal had moved in that direction. Though it might have been Chase. And then a cat cried out north of their location. She frowned, still moving forward, slowly.

Shots rang out.

Crap! Someone had to be out there shooting at the cats.

She and Dan rushed forward, trying to keep low when shots were fired in their direction. They both dove for the ground and the cover of the shrubs and tall grass, then rolled and moved again, so that whoever had fired on them wouldn't know where they were now.

She moved farther away from Dan, hoping he wouldn't follow her. Another cougar's cry sounded, only this time, someone had been wounded. She didn't know the cougars' voices so she didn't know who all was running as a cougar or who had been hit. No more rounds had been fired when the cat was wounded, so all she could think of was someone used a knife on him, or maybe a Taser. She heard someone moving in her direction, and she readied her gun.

When she saw Paris moving slowly toward her, Addie

couldn't believe the woman would finally come after Addie herself. Addie didn't hesitate, but shot her in the shoulder twice, forcing her to drop her weapon. Paris cried out, dropping to the ground for cover. As soon as Addie fired on Paris, shots were fired in Addie's direction, and she quickly moved out of the area.

"Can you move?" Dirk whispered to Paris.

Paris was groaning. "Just get her, damn it."

"Stay here. Can you shoot?"

"Just give me my rifle." Some rustling followed. "Go get her."

Dirk headed in the direction where Addie had been. These people knew Addie and her team didn't have night vision goggles and probably thought they couldn't see anything in the dark. They were so wrong.

Addie fired two shots at Dirk, but another couple rang out nearby, and she thought someone was shooting at her until she saw Dirk fall with a grunt. *Dan.*

Paris began shooting all over the place, not aiming at anything in particular. Her shots clipped the shrubs all around Addie, and she stayed low, praying she wouldn't get hit by a stray round. She hoped Dan was keeping just as low and out of harm's way.

She waited until the agent ran out of ammo. She was pulling out the magazine, and Addie dove in to take her down—alive.

Paris wasn't in shape to fight her much, though she tried to pull out her spare revolver, and Addie slugged her in the side of the head with her fist, hard enough to knock the woman out. She checked on Dirk, but he was dead. Then she put plastic ties on Paris's wrists and checked her for weapons. More gunfire rang out in the distance. Someone moved toward her, and she turned to see Dan holding his arm.

"No, Dan, are you going to be all right?" Addie whispered.

"Yeah, got to have one of these every once in a while, to prove to me I'm not infallible. Are you okay?"

"Yeah, the way she was shooting at everything I was afraid we'd both be killed in the barrage. Who cried out?" Addie pulled Dan's T-shirt off and tore it up, then wrapped his arm.

"Carl had to be the first cat."

"And the others?"

"The one south was Hal, Chase was north of us."

She worried that they hadn't heard anything more. No shooting, no cat cries. "Can you shoot?"

"Like Paris did."

"Okay, stay here with Paris and Dirk. I'll see if the others need our help."

"I'd rather we go together," Dan said. "Paris isn't going anywhere."

"You wanna bet? As much as bodies disappear around me?"

"All right, but don't get shot. I need someone to take care of me."

She gave him a hug and kissed him. "I'll do that. Keep your head low."

Then she took off to find the others, worried sick that some of her group had been injured or killed.

More rounds were fired north of her, and she heard someone moving in the brush. Then she saw a woman she hadn't seen in some years, and couldn't believe she was here, of all places. Alicia. Her ex-pretend mother for seven years. She was armed with an assault rifle just like Dirk and Paris had been.

She appeared to have been wounded, but when she heard Addie moving toward her, she frowned. "You've ruined everything. You and your mother."

"My dad never loved anyone else but my mother and me," Addie said, her voice hushed, not wanting to alert anyone else running around in the woods that she was here. It looked like a cougar had bitten her, but where was the cougar?

"I...tried to love you, at least to gain your father's affection, but he didn't buy it. I truly loved him."

"After you had my mother killed so you could be with my dad, you went after my dad because he was seeing other women when he was supposed to be married to you on paper only."

"Your mother could have put several of us in prison."

"Which is where you're going to now. Put the rifle down, now."

"I can't. You know it. I can't go to prison." Alicia raised her rifle to shoot Addie, but before Addie could react, shots rang out and Alicia collapsed.

Addie looked over to see Dan moving toward her. "I found Carl. He's been stabbed. Help me get him to the storage facility."

"Where's everyone else?"

"Here," Chase said, then pointed to Alicia. "Who's that?"

"My ex-pretend mother," Addie said. "Carl's been cut. We need to get him to the facility. Dan's been wounded and Dirk is dead. Paris is wounded and unconscious, for the moment."

Hal hurried to join them. "I took out another man. I checked, but couldn't find any others."

"Where's Bridget and Chet?"

"Here," Bridget said. "Chet and I were searching for any others and chased one man headed back toward our cars. We took him down."

Hal and Chase carried Carl back to the facility, while Addie made sure Dan didn't collapse on her. Bridget and Chet went to locate Paris, found her and carried her to the facility, though Addie hadn't wanted her to see the inside of it. "Can you bandage her outside of the facility?" she asked Bridget.

"Sure thing."

Chet went inside and got a lantern and a first aid kit and left again to help Bridget with Paris.

"Sit," she told Dan as he wanted to help with Carl.

"You might need me to help hold him down if he comes to and tries to bite us," Dan said.

"All right, but don't pass out on me."

Chase and Hal smiled at Dan.

Then Addie got another first aid kit out, and gave the cougar a shot to knock him out. Then she cleaned the wound and began to stitch it closed. She swore Dan looked like he was swaying on his feet a little. "Dan, we've got this. Go sit down."

"I think your mate's right," Chase said. "You look like you're ready to pass out and if you fall against this concrete floor, no telling what damage you'll do to yourself."

"Hell," Dan said, and collapsed on one of the chairs.

Addie paused to look at him, hoping they could get everyone to the vehicles and back to Chet's place safely. They had to gather up all the bodies too though.

Then again, the police would want to know why the bodies weren't left where they were so that investigators could learn the truth of the matter.

No matter what, that was going to be hard to figure.

"What do we do about everyone?" she asked Dan.

"We turn them over to the feds and let them deal with it," Dan said. "Including taking Paris into custody. We'll testify against them."

"And Carl?"

"He wasn't there."

She finished stitching Carl up. "You really want me to call the feds?"

"Yeah, I don't see any other way to handle this."

"Then they'll want to search the facility."

"It's not in your name. It's just an old metal building."

"So why were we here?"

"Someone said they were calling on Alicia's behalf to meet with you in the woods to discuss this business, but you took us with you to protect your back, not trusting whoever these people were. A gunfight ensued, and we came out the victors. We don't mention the storage facility."

"Everyone got that?" Addie asked. "We'll have to tell Carl the story when he wakes."

"Got it," Bridget said.

"Same here," Chet said.

"Then I guess we need to move this to the cars. Carl and you need to return to your house, and we won't let on that either of you were here, Chet," Dan said.

"All right, works for me. I'll just park in the garage and when you can return, you can help me carry him inside, unless he wakes enough to walk in himself."

Bridget patted her backpack. "Just take his clothes with you in case he turns into his human form in the meantime."

"I think we need to alert the press too," Addie said, "just in case."

After that, they helped Chet carry Carl to his car, Bridget tossed her backpack in the front seat, and Chet drove off.

"I wish you could have gone with them," Addie said to Dan as they returned a still unconscious Paris to the area where Addie had shot her.

"I was part of this. And I don't want to go to the hospital until you can come with me."

"Hang on then." She called the press first, then Briggs, telling him what had happened.

In the meantime, Chase called the hospital to send a couple of ambulances for two wounded people—one who needed to be taken into federal custody.

"We've got agents on the way," Briggs said. "I can't believe Alicia had taken part in all of this, but I understand why she had the three of you on the team then. We've located the courier's body, and he was killed like you said he was. We really do want to reinstate you."

"Thanks, but I like the change of scenery, and the people

here have my back."

"I understand. Warrants have gone out for the arrest of several key people. I'm one of the few who managed to keep my job. Take care. I'm sure I'll be seeing you when this goes to trial."

"Keep your nose clean, sir."

"I will."

The ambulances came for Paris and Dan about the time the agents arrived to get everyone's testimony. Addie quickly gave hers, and then left with Dan for the hospital. She hoped their stories all matched. It was hard telling what you did when you couldn't mention being a cougar part of the time.

She hadn't even learned what had happened with the others, but she hadn't wanted to discuss it in front of Paris, in case she was awake. And for her statement to the feds, she only needed to know her part in this. Chet would be sure to tell Carl what the story was and that he wasn't involved in the whole mess.

After about an hour at the hospital, waiting in the room with Dan after they removed two bullets from his arm, she kissed him and hugged him. He hugged her back with his good arm. "It will be so good to return home and take you to bed with me."

"I need to close out my apartment in Portland, Oregon," she said, just now realizing it. She wasn't ever going anywhere else, except on a job. To live? She was staying in Yuma Town. "I need to pick up my clothes and personal items. The apartment was furnished, so it all stays. My lease is up anyway."

"Would you mind too much if someone else

volunteered to pick up your things?"

"Personal items," she reminded him. "You don't have to go with me. The bad guys have all been taken down. Or at least when the rest of this documentation gets out there, they'll all be heading for cover."

"Or trying to take you out."

"For revenge? They'd be stupid to come after me. Not when they know what that will get them."

Dan shook his head. "I don't trust that it would never happen."

"You have to be busy with sheriff duties. I understand. I—"

He sighed. "I'll go with you."

"Only if you lie on the bed, watching me pack."

"By the time we get to your place—"

She gave him a stern look like she meant it, which she did. He was going to rest while she packed, no ifs, ands, or buts about it.

He smiled. "As you wish."

She knew he didn't mean it.

The sound of footfalls made her want to pull out her gun, but because of the investigation and her and Dan shooting Dirk and Paris, they had to hand them over.

Before the people reached the door, she readied Dan's tray to shove against the door. "Just us," Bridget said. "You probably feel as naked without your guns as we do."

"Yeah." Relieved, Addie moved the tray back toward the bed when everyone but Chet and Carl showed up.

"How's Carl doing, do you know?" Addie asked.

"We called Chet to see if we needed to go there first,

but he said Carl's still sleeping as a cat and seems to be okay. We'll be heading that way shortly," Bridget said. "We all need some sleep. Travis called, and I had to tell them what we were doing. He said he'd never leave me home alone again just to chill out."

"You were protecting me."

Bridget smiled. "Yeah, well, despite what you'd already been through, he had the mistaken notion nothing else would happen. Shows what he knows. Chase let Stryker know that Dan was wounded."

"I'm nearly ready to go home," Dan groused.

"The doctor said tomorrow," Addie said.

"We're delayed returning home," Bridget said.

"Not all of us," Addie said. "Hal, I know you need to get home to Tracey and the babies."

"I called Shannon and told her the situation. She's fine with me being here until we can get the two of you back home. We go together," Chase said.

Hal agreed. "It won't be but a few more hours. Tracey's family and mine are helping out and when I get home, that's all I'll do for a while."

"What about you, Bridget?" Addie asked.

"Leyton and Travis got their man, but they won't be returning until tomorrow night late. We should be there by then, or the next day, at the latest."

"I'm checking myself out of the hospital so we can get on the road," Dan said.

"No, you're not," Addie said.

He frowned at her. "You know how fast—"

"Not *that* fast."

"Did he ever tell you about the time he was wounded on the battlefield, and he refused to leave the rest of us during the heat of battle? Chase, Stryker and me?" Hal asked. "Our commander threatened to court martial him. He makes for a terrible patient."

Addie smiled. "How about if I play doctor and you're my patient, Dan?"

Dan smiled. "I'll go along with that."

CHAPTER 17

Dan couldn't believe all that they'd been through, and was glad Addie had decided to mate him and stay in Yuma Town, no matter what Briggs had offered her. She was right where she belonged—with him.

She stayed overnight with him at the hospital, despite that he wanted her to go to Chet's place to rest. She wasn't about to, and he knew it was because she still wanted to make sure he had protection. Though some of the time she had fallen asleep too.

They got an update from Chase about Carl when Dan was sharing his lunch with her. Carl was human again, and he was healing well. Which was good because they didn't want to have to make up some story of how he was cut, if he had to be brought into the hospital. The police would have to be notified then.

It was not until the next afternoon that Dan was released, against the doctor's objection, but Dan's wounds were healing too fast to be normal, and they needed to get on the road.

Chase picked them up and drove them to Chet's house.

"Are you all right to make the trip?" Dan asked Carl. "You could stay here and Chet could bring you later."

"No, I'm coming with you. If it hadn't been for all of you, I would be dead. And if I hadn't been a cougar when I was cut and had the faster healing genetics."

"All right. We're ready to go then. Thanks, Chet, for all your help with this," Dan said.

"I live for the danger and the excitement. Though I dodge better than you."

Dan laughed. "The woman wasn't aiming at anything. Just shooting indiscriminately. I couldn't have moved any faster to avoid getting hit."

"He's right. I was afraid she would hit both of us with lucky shots," Addie said, hugging on Dan.

He loved that she was his mate for real. He couldn't say it enough times or mean it any more than he did. "Let's go then."

They had a long drive ahead of them, and he suspected he and Carl were going to have to sleep more on the return trip than when they drove out to Cheyenne. He still wished Addie would let someone else pack up her things, but he understood how she felt. Now, with him, he wouldn't have cared if someone else had packed up his stuff and moved it.

"What happened to everyone during the shootouts? We heard three cats cry out," Dan said.

"The first one was me," Carl said. "Big mistake. I'm not used to being a cougar, and so when I came upon a woman,

I didn't know what to do. Especially when she smelled like a cougar."

"Alicia's pretend mother," Dan said.

"Yeah. She lunged forth with a long knife and sliced me. Damn near killed me. I collapsed. I guess she didn't want to shoot me and alert everyone they were out there. She didn't have a clue who I was either.

"Then she went back to lying in wait for everyone else. I just laid there feeling useless and like I was dying, praying one of you would come for me and save me, or that these faster healing abilities would kick in."

"Glad you made it," Dan said.

"Me too. And thanks, Addie. I learned you're the one who stitched me up."

"Yes. The scar will disappear completely in a few days. You'll need to take it easy for a while," Addie said.

"Who was the second cat that let out a yowl?" Carl asked.

"Hal. He was warning us he'd found one of the guys, right before he killed him," Bridget said. "And Chase was the other cat who called out. He killed the guy too."

"Hell, two men dead from cougar bites," Dan said.

"No problem. Chase and Hal corroborated that a cougar had attacked the men, and Chase said Alicia killed it. They'll find the cougar's DNA on the knife that Alicia had dropped when she went to shoot Addie," Bridget said.

"Who fired the other shots?"

"I did. I took out two other men while Chase and Hal were cougars. They hadn't had a choice about killing them as cougars. They were trying to locate them, but they were afraid the rest of us would walk into their ambush," Bridget said.

"How in the hell did they learn where we were?" Dan wondered if they'd followed their cell signals, or something.

"Okay, now that's the bad part," Carl said. "And I can't apologize more for it, except we took out the rotten asses."

"What did you do, Carl?" Addie asked, sounding highly annoyed.

"The woman who hired me—Paris—grabbed my wrist at one point, as if I had intended to leave before she was through talking to me. I wasn't. It didn't occur to me that something else was going on," Carl said.

"Chet ran a bug detector over Carl's clothes and it came up with nothing. He suspected if anyone was wearing a bug, it would be the man who was working for the bad guys. Then Carl remembered he had left his watch on the floor of the car when he was in a hurry to shift the one time. Chet checked it out, and sure enough, it had a bug on it," Bridget said.

"I didn't know it. I swear to God, I didn't."

"We believe you," Dan said, though he looked at Bridget for confirmation. She nodded. "Addie wouldn't let me watch the news while I was supposed to be sleeping. What's the latest on that?"

"Addie's boss is stating left and right he's taking down the corrupt agents in the Bureau, and he's been promoted to take Alicia's place," Bridget said.

"If you all don't need me for anything, I think I'll go to sleep," Carl said.

"Why don't you get some sleep too," Addie told Dan. "You know I can drive on the way home."

Addie didn't answer him.

Bridget smiled over the passenger seat at him. "I think her silence means no way in hell."

He chuckled. "I kind of got that impression. All right. Your loss." He settled back on the seat, hoping they wouldn't encounter any problems, and fell asleep.

***

A week later, Addie wanted to go home and take care of the apartment. She'd lose her deposit for not giving two months' notice, but she and Dan were willing to pay any price to be over and done with it. He'd still tried to talk her out of going, but she was dead set on doing this herself, reminding him he didn't need to go with her. No way was he going to let her go without accompanying her.

Several agents were being held on bond, and an internal investigation was ongoing. He really didn't feel she was in danger from any more attempts on her life. He'd still feel better once she was home again with the cougars in Yuma Town.

Ricky was all healed up, and so was Carl. She wondered if the two of them would ever forgive each other for injuring one another. The same with Kolby, but some had faith they would.

They'd learned from the fingerprints they'd taken of the two "FBI agents" they'd killed in the morgue, they'd been FBI interns during their undergraduate schooling, and had been assigned to the same office as Alicia had worked. Currently, they'd been guns for hire, so they assumed Alicia had hired them for the body removal at their morgue.

***

Two days later, Dan and Addie arrived at her apartment with several packing boxes to find her manager was already showing her place, annoyed she'd left it in such a mess. She hadn't wanted Dan to see her place when she hadn't picked it up, though she said she thought it was never that much of a mess.

The place had been trashed! Hell, Dan was glad he was there for Addie. "Go ahead and start packing, and I'm going to talk to your manager."

"I can't believe she's such an idiot that she can't recognize a messy place from one that has been broken into and ransacked!" Addie just stood in the middle of the mess and Dan took her in his arms.

"Why don't you tell her that, I'll call the police, and—"

"I'm liable to say or do something I'll regret. I'll be fine. I'll call the police."

Dan waited a minute more, rubbing her back, comforting her. "All right. I'll be right back." He was liable to say or do something *he'd* regret. He stalked into the apartment manager's office, and she folded her arms and looked cross at him.

"I want to know how someone broke into Addie's apartment and you were too blind to realize her place has been ransacked. For the record, I'm Sheriff Dan Steinacker of Yuma Town, and anyone with an ounce of sense can see the place has been rifled through. She keeps her place neat as a pin, but after she was nearly killed by assassins, they must have come in search of something at her apartment. You're lucky they didn't kill you."

The woman's jaw hung agape, her brown eyes wide.

"She's moving, not because she wants to, but because she's identified several FBI agents who were involved in the murder of her parents, both FBI agents. And she is one also. Or was. She's a deputy sheriff for Yuma Town now, but also under my jurisdiction in case she has any more hits ordered on her. You can see why she couldn't give two months' notice."

"Of course. Yes. She has to move. Once the place is tidied up, I'll give her deposit back."

"The police have been alerted."

Her jaw dropped again.

"She'll appreciate your goodwill gesture of returning her deposit. Thanks for supporting your law enforcement officials." Then Dan stalked out of the manager's office and returned to Addie's apartment and found her staring at the mess. "Hey, honey, I'm so sorry about this. What can I do?"

"The police are on their way. They know about the case and they've called the FBI."

"Your manager has graciously offered to refund your deposit."

That earned Dan a smile and he loved when Addie was all smiles. He drew her into his arms and kissed her.

She wrapped her arms around him and hugged him tight. "How in the world did you manage that?"

"I told her that she'd be safer if you were out of here."

Addie laughed. "Thank you."

He kissed her soundly, wanting to take this to her bedroom, but afraid of what they'd find in there.

She pulled away and sighed. "Let's start packing. Unless the police find a dead body, they're not going to check for fingerprints. I need to see if anything's missing, but I imagine they did this when I was hospitalized."

"I'll get the boxes." Dan carried the boxes in and then began taping them up so she could fill them.

She was folding her clothes into one while he wanted in the worst way to straighten up the place so she wouldn't feel so bad about it, not to mention they could move about more easily. They needed to leave things the way they were, except her clothes were fine to pack away. The bastards had torn up her couch cushions even. He suspected the same with her mattress. He headed in there to see what a disaster it was. Just as he figured. The mattress was ripped apart and the thugs had searched through it.

"Police are here. And I guess FBI agents." Addie asked, "Did you bring a spare gun?"

"Yeah, what's the problem." He stalked back into the living room to see what was going on.

"They're arguing with the police, telling them this is their jurisdiction and to get lost. The police are holding their own, and now they're both on phones, probably calling their bosses to sort it out. I really don't like the looks of it."

"Why don't we go outside and talk to both of them, so that we're not a target if the police are there, witnessing this whole thing?"

"I've got another idea too." She called the local paper and told them who she was and if they wanted a news story, come right over. "Hurry. The police are here, but the FBI agents are trying to make them leave... Thanks. See you in a few minutes." She gave them the address.

Then the two of them went out to meet with the agents

and the police.

"Forgive us if we feel a bit paranoid after all that's happened, but we'd appreciate if the police hung around too," Addie said.

"This is our jurisdiction. The police aren't authorized to be here."

"Can we see your credentials?" Dan asked. He examined them, then gave them to Addie to check out.

A news crew showed up and Addie said, "These nice officers and agents are here to see the break-in I had." She gave them an impromptu interview.

"I'll just give my former boss a call and see what he has to say." Addie called Briggs. "I have two agents here at my apartment that was ransacked, probably at the time that I was hospitalized. I need to move my clothes and personal items to my new home. I wanted someone to verify that my place was torn up during a burglary. I want the local police here because, as I'm sure you can well understand, I'm wary of anyone posing as federal agents." She nodded and handed her phone to one of the agents.

He continued to look at her and said, "Yes, sir. I understand."

Then he handed the phone back to her and said to the police, "After you."

They went back inside and the police took her statement. She'd have to call her renter's insurance to help pay for the damages. She continued to pack while the agents looked around, but Dan followed them everywhere. He wouldn't let the men out of his sight. He didn't trust them.

The film crew came inside to take pictures.

The police looked around too, asking Addie if she knew if anything had been stolen. "I had my gun with me, and that was stolen, along with my badge when I was hospitalized. That's all I had that would have been too important to lose."

"We'll file a report," the agents said, acting annoyed that Dan had been following them all over the place. The police said the same and the news crew thanked them and they all left.

"Okay, good, I can file with my insurance. Let's pack everything up. I thought we'd stay the night, but I just want to pack up your SUV and head out of here."

"Sounds good to me." He began to straighten up what he could. And taped up the rest of the boxes. When she was done with a box, he'd carry it out to the car and pack it in. "Nothing but clothes and...?"

"Toiletries in the bathroom. If you don't mind getting them."

"Will do." He grabbed a box and packed her makeup, shampoo, toothbrush and toothpaste. "Towels?"

"Yes, mine. Toilet paper, box of tissues, bath rug. Anything not nailed down."

He finished with that and went into the bedroom. She'd already pulled all her clothes out of the dresser drawers that were lying in a jumble on the floor. He put the drawers back into the dresser. Luckily, they hadn't been damaged. "Pillows? Sheets? Pictures?"

"Pillows, sheets, comforter. No pictures. They belong to the apartment. Same with dishes and silverware. Food is mine. Oh, antique clock is mine."

He had packed her sheets in with the bathroom items,

but the comforter and pillows could just lie on top of the boxes. They would take up too much room.

"On the wall over my dresser."

The pictures were all on the floor. He looked under the bed and found the chiming clock kicked underneath the box springs. He was glad it hadn't been damaged. At least he hoped not. It looked okay, no damaged or missing pieces. He carefully wrapped it in a bath towel and put it in with the other bedding. Then he labeled the box, taped it up, and carried it out to the car.

They packed up her food that they could take. And she told her manager she could keep the food in the fridge and freezer and the cleaning supplies. She turned in her keys, thanked the manager, and accepted the check for her deposit. "Insurance should cover any costs related to the break-in." She gave a copy of the police report to the manager.

Then Dan drove, while Addie deposited the check in her bank account before the manager changed her mind.

They hadn't driven very far when she asked, "Did you get my clock?"

"Yeah. I packed it in the box with your bedding. It looked good, no damage that I could see."

"Good. It was my dad's father's. And I always loved that clock."

"Does it chime?" Dan asked, hoping it wouldn't keep him awake at night, but truly he'd do anything for Addie, even listen to a chiming clock.

She smiled. "We don't have to wind it up if it bothers you. It took me a while to get used to it chiming in the middle of the night. It has sentimental value, so I don't mind if it doesn't really tell time."

"We can see if I can get used to it. I'm a light sleeper. I thought we'd drive as far as we could tonight, and stop somewhere for the night."

"All right. I'm serving as lookout."

"Think someone will still come after us?"

"I sure hope not. I'm still watching, just in case."

They drove for six hours, Dan three and Addie the next three, and then they stopped at a hotel. "Too bad the pool is closed at this hour."

"That would have been a nice way to unwind, but I have another way."

They got their room key, and with bags in hand, went to their room. Dan called Stryker to let him know they were stopping for the night and should get in at midnight the next evening if everything went well, allowing for meals, bathroom breaks, and gas fill-ups.

"Any trouble along the way?" Stryker asked.

Dan explained about her place being all torn up.

"Did they get anything?"

"Nothing that she could see. We'll call sometime tomorrow to let you know we're still fine."

"All right. Nothing going on much here."

"Good. We'll be home soon." Dan smiled as he ended the call and saw his already naked mate stretched out under the sheets.

"Done with business?" She ran her hand over her breasts, her nipples peaking under the sheets.

"Hell, yes."

"You sure your arm's all right?"

"Been all right since yesterday." He couldn't believe she'd been postponing his making love to her until she was assured he was healed all the way and that he'd gone along with it to appease her.

He stripped off all his clothes. "You saw me lifting all those boxes. No grunts. No grimaces. No crying out in pain."

She smiled.

He yanked aside the sheet and settled on top of her. "When are we going to get married? The whole town is waiting to hear when we're going to set the big day."

"I guess this business is taken care of as much as it can be until everyone indicted goes to trial."

"Yeah. No more stalling."

"Let's set it for a month from now so everyone who wants to participate can."

Dan yanked his phone off the bedside table. She groaned. "I thought we were done with business." She raked her nails down his sides to his buttocks and smiled wickedly.

He quickly called Stryker back. "Tell everyone the wedding's a month from today."

"What day of the month is that?" Stryker asked.

"Hell, I don't know what day that falls on. Just do it."

Stryker laughed out loud. "Will do."

Then they ended the call and Dan began kissing Addie's lips, his hands on hers, resting against the pillow, rubbing his body against hers. "I want to make love to you all night long."

"What"—she licked his nose—"are you waiting for?"

He rubbed his whiskery chin against her breast, then licked and suckled one. She ran her nails through his hair, lightly scratching his scalp. He was in heaven with the she-cat. She was beautiful and just perfect for him.

She groaned and held onto his hair as her pheromones kicked into play.

"You're beautiful," he breathed out against her other nipple, and licked and suckled.

"You are too...uhh..."

He moved off her and slid his hand down her silky stomach and lower until he brushed her curly hairs and reached her feminine folds. He wanted to make love to her all night long, but they needed to sleep and be well-rested for the long drive ahead of them tomorrow. Still, he tried to draw this out, to help her come before he entered her. As soon as he slid his finger into her creamy center, he knew she was already ready for him. He began to stroke her, to make her come. She grabbed his shoulders and hung on.

He kept working her, kissing her belly, licking her naval, and her hands tightened on his shoulders and suddenly she cried out. "Oh, Dan, yes!"

Then he was joining her, sliding in and out, thrusting deeply. He wrapped his arms around her knees pressing them higher so that he could thrust deeper. He was consumed by her, surrounded by her wet heat, the sexy she-cat smell of her, the musky smell of her sex, and the headiness of their pheromones dancing around each other.

"Hurry," she said, as if she'd die if he didn't press harder, if he didn't rub her into oblivion again.

He was only too eager to oblige and continued to rub against her, and thrust, finally finding release deep inside her. And she growled out a satisfied, "I love you."

"God, I love you too, Addie. With all my heart."

And then they were kissing and snuggling and continued to cuddle, until around three in the morning when his car alarm went off, waking them at once.

CHAPTER 18

Hearing his car alarm go off, Dan jumped out of bed and dressed in jeans, and grabbed his gun. "You stay here. You don't have your gun with you to protect you."

"All right." She got on the hotel phone and called hotel security. "Someone is trying to break into our SUV."

Dan hurried out of the room and raced for the elevator. He was glad she didn't come with him.

Standing near his vehicle, a man dressed in a security uniform greeted Dan. "Is this your car?"

"Yeah, I'm Sheriff Dan Steinacker." He offered his hand to the man and the guard shook it.

"I saw a man approach your car and try to unlock it when I was making rounds outside. Since he was wearing all black, I was suspicious. As soon as the alarm went off, I headed in the direction of the vehicle and then got a call from your missus."

"Thanks," Dan said. "Can I give you something for your

trouble?"

"That's what I'm paid for. I see you have a lot of boxes in there."

"Yeah, my new wife is moving with me to Yuma Town. It's just clothes and stuff like that. Nothing valuable, but no one knows that."

"I'll keep an eye on it for you until you leave."

"Thanks, appreciate it." Dan headed back up the elevator to their room. He entered the room and saw Addie watching out the window.

"Our personal security officer is going to watch it because of all the boxes we have out there. He said the guy was dressed all in black."

"And he only targeted our car."

"Because of all the boxes. Nothing to worry about." Because Dan would do all the worrying. "Let's go back to bed. We can get up in a couple of hours and take off."

Neither of them could sleep though, so at four-thirty, they got up, took showers, had a complimentary breakfast, and thanked the security officer.

"Congratulations to the both of you."

"I mentioned we were newlyweds," Dan said to Addie.

"Oh." She smiled. "Thanks. And thanks for earlier this morning. We might not have anything that valuable in the car, but it's all I've got right now."

"I understand completely," the guard said.

Then Dan said good-bye again and they drove off.

"Another eight hours and we should be in Yuma Town."

"I'll be glad for it," Addie said. "And I really am glad to have my clothes too. Otherwise it's like living out of a suitcase on a permanent basis. I never thought my life would change so much that I'd actually move in with you."

"And be my mate."

She smiled. "Best thing I ever did." They drove for a while longer and she said, "I keep thinking about that man dressed in black who tried to break into the car early this morning."

"I keep thinking about our bed at our home and how I can't wait to make love to you there. When I go to the office, everyone will know why I'm wearing the biggest smile no matter what business comes up during the day."

Addie laughed. "Glad to know you have your priorities straight—me. You don't mind if I take off a couple of weeks before I begin working for you, do you?"

He pumped his fist. "Yes! You're working for me and not with the others. Unless we do some joint missions, which often happens."

She smiled. "Did you think otherwise?"

"The way Bridget was pushing you to join them, yes."

"We've functioned well together so far, so I'm willing to try it. I can always take another job if it doesn't pan out for us."

"It will work for us."

She smiled. "About the two weeks?"

"You don't have to work at all, if you don't want."

"That would drive me crazy. At least until we have kids. I just want to take off some time, to...decompress after all that's happened and settle in a bit. And make the wedding plans too, with the help of all the ladies who want to pitch in."

"That will be a ton of them."

"Good."

"Sure thing, honey. Whatever you want."

She smiled. "I like this arrangement." Then she frowned. "Are you really glad that Dottie found Jack again?"

"Yeah, I am. They were meant to be together. I just worried the guy might be like the other man she'd married, so I might have given Jack a hard time over it until I was sure he was good for her. I offered him a job too. I wouldn't have done that if I didn't like him. He's a decent mate and father to their kids. It worked out perfectly for them."

"Okay, I thought so, but was just making sure."

Dan drove for about an hour, thinking on the business with the break-in at her apartment again. "About the break-in, they had to have been looking for all that stuff at your apartment when it was actually at the storage facility, but they didn't know that."

"I agree. When you were packing boxes, did you find any paperwork? I had some files of receipts, insurance paperwork, utility bills, stuff like that, in one of those manila expandable files. I didn't pack it and just wondered if you had."

"No, I didn't see anything like that."

She didn't say anything for a moment. "Well, damn. Okay, so they stole the set of old keys that didn't belong to anything any longer and all my paperwork—"

"Looking for what the keys might go to, maybe to see if you were paying for a storage facility."

"That was under our dummy corporation's name. And it was owned outright, so no monthly payments."

"Except you'd have to pay the taxes."

"Right, and I paid that and never kept any evidence of it around the apartment."

"I would think with the tons of information we found and shared, they'd know their gooses were already cooked."

"I agree." Addie sat in silence for another hour while Dan tried to think of another reason they might still be targeting Addie's possessions.

"Unless someone is still worried we'll find more information that would blame someone else," Dan said.

"Like my boss? He was promoted when Alicia died. Briggs has been the only other person who has been in the know all this time. Besides the other team members, but they were never where I was when I had all the trouble."

"Yeah. Like him."

"I didn't find him mentioned in any of the documents. I looked through every one of them."

"We don't wear jewelry very often because of the problem with shifting and worrying about losing it. You don't have any jewelry keepsakes, do you? Your clothes are probably fairly new and not what you would have had before your dad died. What else did you have from when your dad was still alive?"

"The antique clock. It's something I'd never get rid of. I always loved it. It was my dad's father's clock. Unlike clothes or anything else I might own, he knew that was the one thing I'd keep forever."

"Let's check it out then." Dan pulled into the next travel center a mile up the road and parked in front of a pump.

"If you know where the clock is packed, you can get it

out while I pump some gas."

"Okay." Dan moved several boxes before he found the one with the linens and clock in it. He ripped off the tape and carefully unwrapped the clock.

Addie finished pumping the gas and put the nozzle back and closed the cap on the gas tank.

"It looks all right." Dan turned the clock over and opened the back. "If I'm not mistaken, this looks like it could have a secret compartment at the bottom inside." He pushed and poked and prodded, but nothing happened.

She pulled a fingernail file from her backpack and used it as leverage. A little lid snapped off and inside the hidden nook was another flash drive. She dug around in her bag and pulled out the cord to attach the flash drive to her phone. "Do you mind driving some more? I'll read what's on the flash drive and see if there's anything new on there."

"Good idea. I'll drive for however long it takes you to get through it. With being a speed reader and having a photographic memory, you'll get through it faster than I will."

"Okay."

After they'd been driving for a while, Addie suddenly said, "Holy crap. We were right. Briggs was involved in this all along. I'm sending these files to Stryker and Carl, as insurance, in case anyone tries to stop us and search for this evidence."

"That's why they were still looking for any other evidence. Briggs is up to his eyebrows in it, and he might assume you did know it too."

"Why didn't my dad ever tell anyone about it?"

"Both your dad and mom did and you see where they

ended up. With you, you were lucky and had me."

"Boy, was I ever." Addie sighed. "Stryker's sharing it with everyone. Carl's contacting the news media about the latest development. I can't believe he's working for Hal's parents' paper now and loving it. And having to bake on the side under Mrs. Fitz's tutelage."

"I think she was just lonely."

"I think Carl needed some real friends too. I'm glad she wasn't too upset about what happened to Alicia since they'd been friends."

"She was furious to learn of Alicia's involvement in the murder of your parents and the attempts on your life. She said it served Alicia right to have contracted me to protect you. That was the only good thing she'd done, but it backfired on her."

CHAPTER 19

It was midnight when they arrived at Dan's house, though it was Addie's now too, after the long drive from Portland, Oregon, and she couldn't wait to climb into bed with Dan, make love, and sleep for hours the next day. Though she was certain, Dan would want to run into work so everyone remembered he was still the sheriff.

What they hadn't expected was to see a line of vehicles parked in front of the house, curbside, with only the driveway clear for them to drive in. She hoped they hadn't had a break-in here.

As soon as they hesitated to pull into the driveway, Stryker called Dan. "Hey, come on in. We're all here to help you unload your car so you can hit the sack faster."

"Hell, Stryker, can I say you guys are the greatest? Though we hadn't planned to unpack tonight."

"Yeah, but we need you at work tomorrow. A slew of reporters are still hanging around for the latest news."

Dan laughed and drove the SUV into the garage. Everyone poured out of the house, gave them hugs, and started hauling in boxes—Leyton and Travis, Jack and Carl, even. Calvin and his wife were there. Dan's dispatcher, Amy, was there too.

Dan hoped Addie wouldn't mind all the help from the cougars, without okaying it with them first. She was smiling, like this had been the best welcome home ever.

Dottie, Shannon, Bridget, Kate, and Tracey wouldn't let her carry one box, but started to ask her what she wanted to do for the wedding. Even Yvonne was there, ready to make a list for invitations. Dan had to smile at his mate when she cast him a "help me out here" look, but he was helping the guys put the boxes in the right places, and he had already warned her that a ton of the ladies would want to help with the wedding.

Mrs. Fitz showed her a book of pictures of various cakes Addie might like to have for the wedding.

Chase and Hal were out back grilling steaks for everyone.

"Where are the kids?" Addie asked.

"We had sitters come over to stay with them, in anticipation of your arrival home," Shannon said, all smiles. "It was much too late to drag them all over here this time of night."

Coming home to Yuma Town, at any hour, was a celebration like no other. Dan was glad Addie seemed to appreciate it as much as he did.

"Of course, we wanted to welcome you home right," Stryker said, grabbing another box, "and I did want you to take care of the reporters, but we wanted to share the good news, if you didn't hear it on your way here. Clinton Briggs has resigned his position, and has lawyered up. We got him."

Dan smiled. "Hell, that's great news."

"I know how you really want to get back to work, but I can handle everything for a few days longer, including the reporters, so you and Addie have a chance to spend some real quality time together."

Dan glanced back at Addie and she said, "Let's go to the cliffs, camping."

"First thing in the morning? You don't want to rest up a bit?"

"No. I want to see what you said you had to offer me. In the surrounding area," she quickly added.

"North Peak Cave and Carver Falls."

After the steak dinner and the cake Mrs. Fitz made saying, Welcome Home & Congratulations!, everyone said their goodnights.

"One thing I don't understand," Dan said. "The name Alicia that was written on that one piece of paper and left behind at my house when the assassins tried to take us out."

Rick raised his bottle of beer. "Forensics came back on that piece of paper today. One thumb print belonging to Briggs."

"He intended to implicate her and take her position once she went down for her part in this," Dan said. "His goose is cooked."

***

The next morning, early, Dan and Addie packed the vehicle with everything they needed for a fun camping trip.

They drove by the sheriff's office and saw Stryker with hands on hips speaking to a bunch of reporters. When he saw Dan and Addie driving by, he smiled and tipped his Stetson to them.

"I love your town and everyone in it," Addie said, settling back against the seat and closing her eyes. She needed more sleep. After making love to Dan last night, she couldn't believe how tired she was, like she'd been on an all-night stakeout. Except that being with Dan was lots more rewarding.

She woke when he parked the vehicle.

"Here's where we start our hike."

They carried all their gear toward the cliffs in the distance and she loved this, loved being with her sheriff cougar. "Do...do you smell a lot of cougars' scents that have been here recently?"

"I wouldn't be surprised if some of the folks who came over to welcome us home last night, didn't leave a little something in the cave we'll be camping in."

Now she couldn't wait to see what they might have done. "Why do you think so?"

"Not only because we smell their recent scents, but because we did something special like that for Kate and Leyton when they were camping, and because the cougars want you to feel at home here."

Addie walked even faster.

Dan laughed. "Are you rushing us?"

"Yeah, aren't you curious?"

"Yeah, but what if I'm mistaken?"

She sighed. "Then I'll be disappointed." She frowned.

"You said this path leads to the cave up in the cliffs straight ahead, but their scents go off in that direction."

"We have a choice, follow their scents, or go up to the cave and drop off our stuff first. I suggest we go up to the cave first."

"I was going to say to follow their scents, but you're right. Dumping our gear would be a better idea, and then we can explore."

Dan and Addie climbed up the cliffs with their climbing gear, backpacks, sleeping bags, and cooking equipment and set up camp in the cave overlooking Carver Falls. "It's beautiful," Addie said, practically forgetting the mystery of the cougars' scents. "Just beautiful. I could listen to the sound of water falling over rocks all day and night."

"I could too. Ready to check out the scents?"

She started stripping off her clothes. "As a cougar, yes!" In no time, she'd turned into her cougar and was bounding down the cliffs, wanting to check out the waterfall and the pond below it first.

Dan was chasing after her, springing onto the next shelf beside her, until they were at the base, but next to the waterfall. She realized they couldn't reach the waterfall from the path as humans.

She ran beneath the rock face and the waterfall, sticking her tongue out to gather the water on it and drink. Then she saw through the screen of water, a canopied café sat on the flat rocks nearby, the green canopy trimmed in flowers and sparkling lights. A couple of beach balls were bobbing in the waterfall pool, and two ice chests were sitting next to the table.

She leapt into the pool and swam to the slab of rock and climbed out. Dan was right behind her. She shifted and peeked into the ice chests. Cooked shrimp on ice, champagne, vichyssoise for lunch, and the other ice chest had salmon steaks to grill for tonight.

Dan shifted, rubbed her arms, and kissed her cheek. "Aren't you glad you stayed?"

She wrapped her arms around him. "Yeah. Now the only question is, do we make love after lunch, or before?"

He leaned down and closed the lids to the ice chests. "You have to ask that question? The question should be: where?"

She pulled him into the pool. "I would think the answer to that would be obvious." And then she wrapped her body around him while he paddled to keep them afloat and began kissing her.

She had found heaven in her faux agent husband, and would never let him go.

Dan couldn't have been happier, that from all the men on her list, she had chosen him to protect her that day at the Hamburger Stop. And she was damn good at protecting him too. He loved her with all his heart as he held onto his naked mate, the water splashing about them, and made love to her.

He would never look at the waterfall, the pool, and North Peak Cave the same way. "I love you."

She smiled up at him. "You make every day special, Dan. I love you."

They might be out of the Bureau business, but they'd have all kinds of wild adventures on their own. And with work too.

EPILOGUE

Dan decided he'd put Stryker in charge of all media announcements when he returned to work, though Stryker was hoping he was kidding. The ladies had all figured out how the wedding would go, and the event was even wilder than Kate and Leyton's wedding. Mainly because Kate's water broke in the middle of it.

With a rush to the hospital, they were one unified cougar pack. Who says only wolves have packs?

The new doctor, Dr. William Rugel, had been on board only a week at the clinic, but he was ready to deliver his first cougar shifter babies. Would they be two boys, two girls, or a boy and a girl?

That was the mystery.

The mystery woman in Dan's life? She was for real, and loved being a deputy sheriff, though Dan had to counsel her on writing too many speeding tickets for out-of-towners. When she gave him one, he knew she was the right cat for him.

Addie was having a blast living in Yuma Town with her sheriff husband and being part of the cougar community. She was glad he had a great sense of humor, but even so, she was serious about him paying his speeding fine. She smiled, loving the alpha male cat.

Stryker swore the next mystery woman was his. Guaranteed.

ABOUT THE AUTHOR

Bestselling and award-winning author **Terry Spear** has written over sixty paranormal romance novels and seven medieval Highland historical romances. Her first werewolf romance, *Heart of the Wolf,* was named a 2008 *Publishers Weekly*'s Best Book of the Year, and her subsequent titles have garnered high praise and hit the *USA Today* bestseller list. A retired officer of the U.S. Army Reserves, Terry lives in Spring, Texas, where she is working on her next werewolf romance, continuing her new series about shapeshifting jaguars, writing Highland medieval romance, and having fun with her young adult novels. When she's not writing, she's photographing everything that catches her eye, making teddy bears, and playing with her Havanese puppies. For more information, please visit www.terryspear.com, or follow her on Twitter, @TerrySpear. She is also on Facebook at http://www.facebook.com/terry.spear. And on Wordpress at:
Terry Spear's Shifters

http://terryspear.wordpress.com/

ALSO BY TERRY SPEAR

Heart of the Cougar Series: Cougar's Mate, Book
Call of the Cougar, Book 2
Taming the Wild Cougar, Book 3
Covert Cougar Christmas (Novella)
Double Cougar Trouble, Book 4
Cougar Undercover, Book 5

* * *

Heart of the Bear Series
Loving the White Bear, Book 1

* * *

The Highlanders Series: Winning the Highlander's Heart, The Accidental Highland Hero, Highland Rake, Taming the Wild Highlander, The Highlander, Her Highland Hero, The Viking's Highland Lass, His Wild Highland Lass (Novella), Vexing the Highlander (Novella)
Other historical romances: Lady Caroline & the Egotistical Earl, A Ghost of a Chance at Love

* * *

Heart of the Wolf Series: Heart of the Wolf, Destiny of the Wolf, To Tempt the Wolf, Legend of the White Wolf, Seduced by the Wolf, Wolf Fever, Heart of the Highland Wolf, Dreaming of the Wolf, A SEAL in Wolf's Clothing, A Howl for a Highlander, A Highland Werewolf Wedding, A SEAL Wolf Christmas, Silence of the Wolf, Hero of a Highland Wolf, A Highland Wolf Christmas, A SEAL Wolf Hunting; A Silver Wolf Christmas, A SEAL Wolf in Too Deep, Alpha Wolf Need Not Apply, Billionaire in

Wolf's Clothing, Between a Rock and a Hard Place, Dreaming of a White Wolf Christmas, SEAL Wolf Undercover, Flight of the White Wolf, Billionaire Wolf Christmas

SEAL Wolves: To Tempt the Wolf, A SEAL in Wolf's Clothing, A SEAL Wolf Christmas, A SEAL Wolf Hunting, A SEAL Wolf in Too Deep, SEAL Wolf Undercover (2017)
Silver Bros Wolves: Destiny of the Wolf, Wolf Fever, Dreaming of the Wolf, Silence of the Wolf, A Silver Wolf Christmas, Alpha Wolf Need Not Apply, Between a Rock and a Hard Place

White Wolves: Legend of the White Wolf, Dreaming of a White Wolf Christmas, Flight of the White Wolf (2018)

Billionaire Wolves: Billionaire in Wolf's Clothing, Billionaire Wolf Christmas (2018)

Highland Wolves: Heart of the Highland Wolf, A Howl for a Highlander, A Highland Werewolf Wedding, Hero of a Highland Wolf, A Highland Wolf Christmas

* * *

Heart of the Jaguar Series: Savage Hunger, Jaguar Fever, Jaguar Hunt, Jaguar Pride, A Very Jaguar Christmas

* * *

Romantic Suspense: Deadly Fortunes, In the Dead of the Night, Relative Danger, Bound by Danger

* * *

Vampire romances: Killing the Bloodlust, Deadly Liaisons, Huntress for Hire, Forbidden Love

Vampire Novellas: Vampiric Calling, Siren's Lure, Seducing the Huntress

* * *

Futuristic/Science Fiction Romance: Galaxy Warrior

Other Romance: Exchanging Grooms, Marriage, Las Vegas Style

* * *

Teen/Young Adult/Fantasy Books

The World of Fae:

The Dark Fae, Book 1

The Deadly Fae, Book 2

The Winged Fae, Book 3

The Ancient Fae, Book 4

Dragon Fae, Book 5

Hawk Fae, Book 6

Phantom Fae, Book 7

Golden Fae, Book 8

Phantom Fae, Book 9

Falcon Fae (TBA)

The World of Elf:

The Shadow Elf

The Darkland Elf (TBA)

Blood Moon Series:

Kiss of the Vampire

The Vampire...In My Dreams

Demon Guardian Series:

The Trouble with Demons

Demon Trouble, Too

Demon Hunter (TBA)

Non-Series for Now:
Ghostly Liaisons
The Beast Within
Courtly Masquerade
Deidre's Secret

The Magic of Inherian:
The Scepter of Salvation
The Mage of Monrovia
Emerald Isle of Mists (TBA)

CPSIA information can be obtained
at www.ICGtesting.com
Printed in the USA
FSHW02n0627280918
52602FS

9 781633 110250